J.H. MONCRIEFF

THOSE WHO CAME BEFORE

This is a **FLAME TREE PRESS** book

Text copyright © 2019 J.H. Moncrieff

FLAME TREE PRESS
6 Melbray Mews, London, SW6 3NS, UK
flametreepress.com

Distribution and warehouse:
Baker & Taylor Publisher Services (BTPS)
30 Amberwood Parkway, Ashland, OH 44805
btpubservices.com

Publisher's Note: This is a work of fiction. Names, characters, places, and
incidents are a product of the author's imagination. Locales and public names
are sometimes used for atmospheric purposes. Any resemblance to actual
people, living or dead, or to businesses, companies, events, institutions, or
locales is completely coincidental.

Thanks to the Flame Tree Press team, including:
Taylor Bentley, Frances Bodiam, Federica Ciaravella, Don D'Auria,
Chris Herbert, Josie Karani, Molly Rosevear, Will Rough, Mike Spender,
Cat Taylor, Maria Tissot, Nick Wells, Gillian Whitaker.

The cover is created by Flame Tree Studio with
thanks to Nik Keevil and Shutterstock.com.
The font families used are Avenir and Bembo.

Flame Tree Press is an imprint of Flame Tree Publishing Ltd
flametreepublishing.com

A copy of the CIP data for this book is available from the British Library
and the Library of Congress.

HB ISBN: 978-1-78758-299-6
PB ISBN: 978-1-78758-297-2
ebook ISBN: 978-1-78758-300-9
Also available in FLAME TREE AUDIO

Printed and bound in Great Britain by Clays Ltd, Elcograf S.p.A.

J.H. MONCRIEFF

THOSE WHO CAME BEFORE

F
MON
cel

FLAME TREE PRESS
London & New York

Dedicated to Tina Fontaine and all the missing
and murdered indigenous women and girls.

Never forgotten, always remembered.

CHAPTER ONE

The fighting began before we were a half mile down the road.

It was easy to tell Jess was pissed, not that she attempted to hide it. Her arms were folded across her chest, and when her head wasn't turned away, I saw her jaw was clenched so tightly it was a wonder she didn't crack her teeth.

I considered asking her what was wrong, but why poke a tiger with a stick? It was obvious what the problem was, and knowing Jess, the silent treatment wouldn't last long.

It lasted about five minutes.

"If you knew you were going to be late, why didn't you text?" Each word was forced from between bloodless lips, as if it were an effort to speak.

"Jess, it was only twenty minutes. Do you have to make a big deal out of this?" Of course she did. Jessica turned everything into a catastrophe of epic proportions lately. I had to have been insane to agree to this camping trip.

"Only? *Only* twenty minutes? I've been waiting for you since five o'clock. Do you get how long twenty minutes seems when you're standing around waiting for someone?"

Since I was always the one running to catch up, I couldn't empathize, but I knew how long five minutes with Jessica felt whenever she got angry. "I get it," I said, unable to keep the edge out of my voice. "I'm an ass. I'm sorry."

"I'm an ass. I'm sorry," she mimicked, making me sound as dumb as Moose from the Archie comics. "Is that all you can say, Reese? It's getting old. Correction: it got old a long time ago. Do you have any idea how many times Kira texted me, asking when we planned on getting there?"

A lot, if I had to guess. Kira's boyfriend Dan was okay, but Kira herself was a bit of a control freak. Yep, no doubt about it – this was going to be the camping trip from hell. At least it would be the last one I'd have to endure. After the weekend, I would end things with Jess. The sex had kept me going for a while, but even that wasn't so hot these days. I didn't find her attractive anymore, probably because she was always scowling at me.

Sure enough, when we arrived at Kira's apartment, both Kira and Dan were waiting outside, camping paraphernalia littering the ground. Dan gave me a sympathetic smile, while Kira barely looked up from her phone.

"Sorry I'm late." I tried to ignore my girlfriend, who was rolling her eyes so hard I half expected them to fall out of her skull. "The packing took longer than I thought."

"It always does, doesn't it? You'd think we were going for weeks instead of a couple days." Dan grabbed a cooler and headed to the back of my truck. "No worries, buddy. Thanks for driving."

Some of the tightness in my chest eased. Thank God for Dan. He was the one person who would make this trip bearable.

Jess was already engaged in an intense, whispered conversation with her girlfriend. I was pretty certain I could accurately guess the topic du jour. Their chatting came to an abrupt halt when Dan began to slide the cooler into the space I'd left for him.

"Wait," Kira called, checking her phone again before slipping it into her back pocket. Her shampoo-commercial hair caught the light and gleamed as she hurried toward us. Once upon a time, I'd thought she was pretty. Then I'd gotten to know her.

"You can't put that there." She pointed at the cooler.

"Why not?" Dan asked, sounding confused but not irritated. Where did he get his patience?

"You'll box it in. What if we get thirsty on the road and want a drink? What if we decide we want to cook dinner as soon as we get there? It should be easy to get at, don't you think? We should put it in last."

Dan shrugged. "Doesn't matter to me. Hand me something else, then."

As Kira leapt into action, organizing the supplies and handing them to Dan one by one, I moved out of the way. Anything I did to help would be wrong, and I couldn't handle Kira's criticism today.

I wandered over to Jessica, who glared at me.

"Can we get past this, please?" Offering an olive branch was better than spending the weekend in stony silence. "I misjudged my time. It won't happen again."

It would, but not with her. All I had to do was survive the weekend, and I'd never have to see her again.

"I just wish you would have texted me. I have better things to do with my time than stand around waiting for you."

The words may have been angry, but her tone was softening, as I'd hoped it would. Kira's bragging about her 'perfect' relationship with Dan drove my girlfriend mad. There was no way she'd want to fight in front of them for the whole weekend.

"You're right, I should have let you know I was running behind. I'm sorry."

She nodded. "All right," she said before drifting over to help her friend. It wasn't the most enthusiastic apology acceptance in the world, but I figured I'd gotten off easy. Jess could hold a grudge until the end of time.

★   ★   ★

With country-western tunes blaring over the speakers and the city streets giving way to the green comfort of fir trees, I relaxed. I even felt a tiny bit of optimism. Maybe it would be an enjoyable weekend after all. I loved the campsites at Strong Lake; they were so peaceful and private. This late in the season, we'd probably have the place to ourselves.

"Can you turn that shit off, please? I have no idea why he listens to this crap," Jess apologized to her friends, but for once, I didn't care what she thought. The opening strains of John Denver's 'Country Roads' flooded the cab as I cranked the volume.

"It's tradition," I yelled over Denver's warble. "This music was made for road trips."

Jessica looked like she'd eaten something sour, but from my glimpses in the rearview mirror, Dan and Kira appeared to be enjoying themselves. Kira sang along during the chorus in a low, sweet voice that surprised me, as Dan leaned over the seat to pat Jess on the shoulder.

"Whoever drives picks the music. It's the rule."

The camaraderie came to an end when we arrived at the campground entrance. Dusk had fallen, but in the glow of the truck's headlights, the sign was still legible.

Closed for the season.

Thwap! Jessica struck my shoulder hard enough to make me wince. "Didn't you call? You were supposed to call them."

"Hey, now. There's no need to resort to violence," Dan said.

"Well, what exactly are we supposed to do? We drove for two hours to get here and it's *closed?*"

"Take it easy. At least no one will bother us." A smile came over my face in spite of my stinging shoulder.

"What are you talking about? The camp is closed. We can't stay here."

"And who's going to stop us? I don't see anyone, do you?"

Kira and Dan were quiet in the backseat, and as far as I was concerned, silence was consent. I revved the Chevy's engine.

"Don't be crazy, Reese. What are you going to do, drive through the gate?"

I'd considered it. The flimsy particleboard wouldn't put up much of a fight, but it might scratch the paint. "Nope, I'm going around. Sit tight, boys and girls."

Shifting into four-wheel drive, I plunged the truck into the ditch that flanked the ticket kiosk. Kira squealed as she was tossed back and forth. I was beginning to like this chick.

Before Jessica could protest, we were out of the ditch and on the other side of the gate.

"Woo-hoo!" Dan cried. "That was awesome."

I grinned. It *had* been awesome. This was going to be perfect. Not only would we have our pick of any campsite we wanted, it would be free. No one would hassle us.

"That's great, Reese, but we won't be able to get any wood. The campsite is closed. Unless you plan to drive through that too?" Jessica gestured at the metal box that held the firewood. It was rusty but solid. Unless someone in our group was a master lock picker, there was no way we were getting into that thing.

"We don't need it. These woods are full of old sticks and dead trees that are begging to be burned," Dan said. "Plus, if worse comes to worst, I brought my axe."

"I like the way you think, my man." Putting more weight on the gas pedal, I let the truck lunge forward, echoing my own eagerness. I could hardly wait to pick a site. Besides, I had to piss. It had been a long drive, especially after the argument with Jess.

"Well, I don't. You can't cut down the trees. It's illegal." The pout was audible in Jessica's voice. She wasn't used to people disagreeing with her.

"We won't cut anything that's living. Just the stuff that's already dead," Dan promised.

"And what if the conservation officers do a patrol? We'll be in huge shit. We can't plead ignorance – it's obvious the campground is closed."

"Oh, lighten up, Jess. Live a little. It'll be an adventure." Kira jostled Jessica's shoulder. As she did, her arm grazed mine. An electric current passed between us, and the skin on my upper arm broke out in gooseflesh.

This weekend was going to be more interesting than I'd thought.

"Okay, fine. Obviously I'm outnumbered. But don't come bitching to me when we get fined." Jessica folded her arms across her chest again and stared out the window at the darkening sky.

Shit. After the work I'd done to defuse her. However, for some reason, I found I didn't care as much this time.

Selecting a campsite resulted in the expected amount of bickering. Kira wanted to be close to the lake and the hiking trails, while Jessica preferred to stay near the showers and toilets. Dan kept quiet, willing to go along with whoever had the most persuasive argument, but I was sick of being outvoted and outnumbered. I sped past the sites the girls indicated, ignoring their cries of protest. Backing into the far corner lot, I couldn't help but be pleased with myself. My truck was now tucked into the trees, out of sight if any conservation officer decided to do a quick check.

"What the fuck is this?" A sneer twisted Jessica's features. How had I ever found her attractive? "This is a joke, right?"

"I get that you'd rather post a sign saying 'Arrest us' by camping over by the showers, but I'm not interested in getting caught." I refused to allow her to ruin my good mood. Glancing into the backseat, I saw Dan sported his usual happy-go-lucky expression. Kira shrugged as she opened the door. Although I hated to admit it, I was gratified to notice they'd been sitting far apart.

A sharp smack on my shoulder jolted me from thoughts of Kira. It was the same place where Jessica had clouted me before. A wave of fury crashed over me, and it was all I could do not to shake some sense into her.

"Do that again and I'll return the favor."

"Hey, hey, hey, let's break it up." Dan tried to sound lighthearted, but I could hear the concern in his voice. "This is supposed to be fun, remember?"

"I'll have a tough time thinking this is fun when I'm struggling to find the bathroom in the middle of the night," Jessica snapped. If I'd thought *I* was angry, my rage paled in comparison to hers. She was so furious she practically spit sparks. "I'm afraid of the dark, remember?"

I instantly felt guilty. Jess could be a witch, but maybe I was to blame for some of her attitude this time around. I hadn't been thinking of my girlfriend when I'd chosen the campsite. The only woman who'd entered my mind had been the wrong one.

Still, who goes camping if they're afraid of the dark?

"We're not that far away." It was an attempt to soothe her, but I realized it probably sounded patronizing. "And you can have the Maglite. Or, if you're desperate, you can pee in the bush."

"I am *not* squatting in the dirt. That's disgusting."

Kira linked her arm through Jessica's. "There's a trail over here. It's a good shortcut. Let's go now, while there's still light."

I handed her the flashlight. "Thanks."

"No worries. We'll be right back."

Why had I thought Kira was a control freak? She was awesome.

"Houston, we have a problem." Dan surveyed the woods surrounding our site.

Squaring my shoulders, I went to join him. It was time to get to work. The light was almost gone, and we had tents to set up. "What's wrong?"

"I'm not seeing a lot of deadfall. Everything looks pretty green."

I swore under my breath. Green wood would smoke rather than burn, which meant no fire and no hot meal. My stomach grumbled in sympathy. I'd already been fantasizing about the chili and biscuits packed in the cooler.

"There has to be something. Maybe farther back?"

"Kindling, maybe, but nothing that's going to give us a decent flame."

Treading on the carpet of pine needles, I peered into the forest, my heart sinking as I saw Dan was right. In spite of the lush overgrowth, these were young trees. I could smell the sap. Maybe Jessica'd had a point. This had been a stupid idea. The thought of admitting it to her made me cringe.

Then I spotted something in the clearing, where no other trees grew.

"Dan, you got a light?"

He flicked on the LED flashlight he kept on his keychain. It wasn't my Maglite, but it was better than nothing.

"What about this one?"

He followed my gesture with the light. "I don't know. It looks burned already."

Taking his keychain, I pushed through the trees, sticks snapping under my hiking boots like bones breaking. A bramble bush scratched my arm, drawing blood, but I was too focused on the tree to notice the pain. Once I was close enough to touch it, I got what Dan had meant. The tree's bark was pitch black. I ran my hand over its gnarled surface and fire flared through my fingers. Jerking away, I shook my fingers to cool them, but there was no need. The sensation had dissipated as suddenly as it had occurred.

"Are you okay?" Dan called.

"Yeah, just got a shock for some reason. It seems solid, though. I don't think it's charred."

He crunched through the underbrush toward me. "A shock? From a tree?"

"Maybe it's a stinging nettle tree." Using Dan's flashlight to examine my palm, I couldn't see anything wrong. It was as pale as before.

"Never heard of it. Is that a thing?"

"Poison oak tree?" As I said the words, I hoped not. I'd had a nasty case (was there any other kind?) of poison oak once and didn't care to repeat the experience.

Dan whistled under his breath. "It's a big bastard." He pounded on it with his fist, and aside from a whisper of loose bark drifting to the ground, it didn't budge. "You're right. I think it's dead, but it hasn't been burned. Have you seen anything like it?"

I hadn't, but that didn't mean anything. I wasn't a tree expert. Perhaps black trees were common at Strong Lake. I didn't know, and to be honest, I didn't give a fuck. "Can your axe handle it?"

"I'm not sure. This is a lot of wood. I could maybe get some of the smaller branches off. That should be enough for tonight." Grasping a branch, Dan hoisted himself onto one of the lower limbs, testing its strength. He was clearly impervious to the stinging-nettle effect. Maybe it had been my imagination, but I had no desire to touch the tree again.

The 'smaller' branches were as thick as our thighs. "Sure, man. That'll do. Go for broke, and let me know when you want me to spell you."

"You can't be serious." Jessica stood outside the clearing, glaring at us in the waning light.

"You want to have a fire, don't you? Or would you prefer to eat your dinner cold?"

"Yes, I *do* want a fire. That's why I wanted to go to a campsite that was open, not watch while you guys destroy a forest."

Normally her tendency to exaggerate rolled off my back, but every word out of her mouth irritated me today. "We're not destroying anything. We're chopping down a few branches. That's it. No one will miss them."

"Yeah, no one except the birds and the squirrels who live there."

"There's no birds or squirrels living in this tree, Jess. Trust me." Not even grass grew around that sucker. You didn't have to be a horticulturalist to see it was an ugly-ass tree. Hell, cutting it down would improve the place.

"Why should I trust someone who can't read?" She pointed at a sign I hadn't noticed. The sun had set enough that I needed Dan's tiny flashlight to read it.

> ### DO NOT USE TREES FOR FIREWOOD.
> ### FIREWOOD IS FOR SALE AT THE CONSERVATION
> ### OFFICE FOR $5 PER BUNDLE.

Well, that was helpful.

"Are you two fighting again?" Kira shined the Maglite in my face. I squinted, raising my arm to block the beam. "This is getting old. Seriously, knock it off."

"Hey, hon, do you remember if I packed the saw?"

Kira swung the light around to blind Dan as he jumped down from the tree with a thud. "*That's* the tree you guys want to cut down? I'm with Jessica – this is a stupid idea."

"Not the whole tree, just a few branches." Dan brushed past her, plucking the Maglite from her as he went. I was grateful. In her hands, it was a deadly weapon.

"I don't think that's a good plan. It looks diseased."

"We're not going to eat it," I said. "Just burn it."

"But won't the smoke hurt us if there's something wrong with it? We'll breathe it in."

"It's fine. It's an ordinary tree, a tree that will keep us warm and help cook our dinner. Let's get those tents set up."

I was keen to change the subject, and not simply because I wanted firewood. There was something about the tree that bothered me too, but that was silly. As I dragged the nylon tent sacks out of my truck and handed them to the women, I couldn't stop thinking about the pain that had spread through my fingers like flames.

The thought of going near that tree again gave me the creeps, but I knew I was being ridiculous.

It was only a tree.

Still, I hoped Dan wouldn't need my help.

CHAPTER TWO

Not even a bonfire could thaw the ice surrounding my girlfriend.

We had the accouterments of an awesome evening: great food, a roaring campfire, cold beer, but none of it was working. We ate in stony silence. Somehow, the bitterness between Jessica and me had infected Kira and Dan.

The four of us stared into the flames, unable to think of anything safe to talk about. Thankfully, the hotly contested tree burned like any other. I'd kicked things off with the *DO NOT BURN TREES FOR FIREWOOD* sign, but only Dan appeared to appreciate my sense of humor.

"I think I'm going to bed." Kira stood up and stretched. "I'd like to say it's been fun, but it really hasn't been."

Jessica leapt to her feet as if she'd been waiting for her cue. "Me too."

"I'll be right in, babe. Just going to finish my beer." Jess and I may have had our differences, but if there's one thing we did well, it was makeup sex. That and the beer would go a long way toward making this trip tolerable.

"Get in whenever you want. I'm staying with Kira tonight."

"What?" I'd known she was pissed, but she'd never been *that* mad before.

"Yeah, what?" Dan sounded as happy about the situation as I was.

"My girl needs some space and I told her it would be okay. The two of you can bunk together. It'll give you some time to bond."

I heard the snicker in Kira's voice and didn't appreciate it. This wasn't what I'd had in mind. *Fuck.*

With a slither of nylon and the finality of the tent zipper closing, they were gone. From time to time, we could hear giggling. Their foul mood had disappeared as soon as they'd ditched us.

There went my fleeting attraction to Kira. *Bitches*, I thought, sipping my lukewarm beer. *Who needs them?*

After a few minutes, Dan broke the silence.

"Well, this sucks."

I burst out laughing. "Yeah, it does. Why did we come here again?"

"Beats me. I certainly wasn't planning on curling up in a tent with you. Not that you're not cute. You're just not my type."

"I understand. I'm not looking for any *Brokeback* moments myself."

Dan tipped his bottle at me. "That's a relief."

"You did a great job with that tree. A little appreciation would have been nice." To my surprise and relief, Dan hadn't needed my help a bit. The man was a machine.

"And you did a great job with the fire." He nudged a charred log into the flames with his foot, setting off an explosion of sparks.

"Thanks." I hadn't expected Jessica and Kira to rave over my Boy Scout skills, but they hadn't even acknowledged our hard work. If it hadn't been for us, they would have been reduced to eating cold SpaghettiOs out of a can. There was still plenty of tree left over for the elusive birds and squirrels, assuming they wanted any.

"I know it's a pain, but what would you think of leaving early?" Dan asked.

"Like the second we get up? I think that's a grand idea." There were lots of things I could do with a long weekend that would be more enjoyable than this camping trip. Grout my tile, for instance.

After draining the rest of his beer, Dan tossed the bottle into the fire. "I'm going to brush my teeth and turn in. The faster I go to sleep, the faster it'll be morning and we can get the hell out of here."

I'd been tempted to forego the teeth brushing in favor of crawling into the tent and crashing. The smoke from the campfire made my head spin, or maybe that was the beer. All I wanted was to go to bed, but I didn't want to gross out my new roommate. Sleeping side by side in a two-man tent was already going to test our friendship.

"I'll go with you."

"Nah, someone should stay with the girls. I'll be back in ten."

As soon as Dan left, the air felt colder. I shivered, zipping my fleece closed. Usually I could stare at a fire for hours, but even that had lost its appeal. Banking it so it wouldn't become a blazing inferno while we slept, I was careful not to touch the logs with anything other than the sole of my boot.

Reese.

I spun around, startled, as someone breathed my name against my neck. Goose bumps sprouted along my spine. When I saw no one was there, I rolled my eyes.

"Very funny, ladies."

There was no answer, not that I'd expected one.

A chill crept into my feet, traveling up my legs and making me feel like it was winter instead of fall. As I stamped my feet to warm them, I wondered what was taking Dan so damn long. Surely it had been more than ten minutes?

You're not welcome here.

This time I looked over my shoulder as fast as I could, but I was too slow. Nothing greeted me but darkness.

"Okay, knock it off. I'm not in the mood to play games."

"Then tell Dan to stop playing with you," Kira called from the tent, inciting new giggles from Jessica.

Shit. Both women were in the tent? Then maybe Dan – nah, if Dan were trying to freak me out, he wouldn't breathe against my neck. That was a little too…*Brokeback.*

At that moment, the man himself came crashing through the bush, making me jump.

"Sorry, did I scare you?"

"No more than usual."

"The womenfolk are okay?"

"Unfortunately."

He grinned and handed me the Maglite. "Better than the alternative. Can't live with 'em, but can't live without 'em, right? I'm going to bed. It's all yours."

I was tempted to ask him to go with me, even though he'd think I was crazy. What the hell was I worried about, and why was I jumping at shadows?

For Christ's sake, Reese, get a hold of yourself. You're too old to be afraid of the dark.

Even so, I tucked Dan's flashlight into my back pocket. Better safe than sorry.

★　　★　　★

I woke up gasping, unable to catch my breath.

Drip...drip...drip.

The tent was an oven. *How long had the sun been up?* I was suffocating in a nylon prison, my sleeping bag having acquired a stranglehold on my neck during the night.

Drip...drip...drip.

Great. The tent was leaking. It must have rained. The campsite was eerily quiet. *Why didn't anyone wake me?*

Drip...drip...drip.

Wiping the sleep from my eyes, I studied the nylon ceiling. Dan had committed the ultimate sin of camping. His tent was dark blue, almost black. No wonder it felt like I'd been cooked alive.

It was stained too. Great patches of something dark dotted the ceiling and the walls. Some of them were still moist, and that was where the dripping sound was coming from.

Drip...drip...drip.

Liquid spattered on my nose, and I shot upright, wrestling with the sleeping bag. Panic squeezed my chest when the zipper stuck, but in a few seconds I was able to work it free.

As I wiped the water off my face, I caught a glimpse of my hand. It was red. Bright red.

That isn't water.

I patted my head and face, searching for a wound. Sometime during the night, something must have cut me. It was too much blood for a mosquito bite.

Shaken, I crawled out of my sleeping bag, desperate to join the others. I couldn't find anything wrong, and I wasn't in pain, but they would see the injury, whatever it was. Maybe they knew what had happened, but why had they left me alone?

My nose was always stuffy in the morning, but by now it had cleared enough that I could smell my own blood. Thick and heavy, with the sour tang of old pennies. Inexplicably, my mouth watered. My stomach churned.

It was then I noticed the other sleeping bag. Dan must have had an uneasy night too – his mummy bag was wrapped around him. Only a tuft of dark hair peeked out the top. At least he hadn't abandoned me. I was grateful I'd kept the keys to the truck in my pocket. I wouldn't have put it past the girls to drive back to the city and leave us stranded.

"Dan," I whispered. "Dan, something's wrong with me. I think I'm hurt."

He didn't move. Odd. Hadn't he joked the night before about being a light sleeper?

I stared at him, watching for the slightest movement, but he was completely still. The silence grew more ominous.

"Dan?"

Reaching out to touch his arm, I stopped. What if he wanted to sleep in? What if he got pissed at me for waking him?

As I continued to study my roommate, a chill came over me in spite of the heat.

I can't see him breathe.

"Dan!" Grabbing him by the shoulder, I shook him. To my shock, he tumbled out of his sleeping bag.

Or at least, what was left of him did.

As I knelt there in horror, too stunned to move or call for help, the severed head of Dan McGraw rolled over to rest against my knee. His eyes were huge and terrified. Vocal cords trailed out of his neck like the tentacles of a jellyfish.

A spot of blood bloomed on the leg of my jeans where Dan's head touched me, as if what had happened to him was contagious. Trembling, I kicked him away. His head wobbled across the tent and came to a rest against the far wall. His dark eyes stared at me, accusing.

You're not welcome here.

I screamed.

Drip...drip...drip.

CHAPTER THREE

Maria Greyeyes sized up the young man sitting across from her. Even though she'd turned the heat up twice, he was still shaking. He pulled the foil blanket tighter around him before clutching the cup of steaming coffee she'd given him. They'd been in her office for an hour, and he'd yet to drink a drop. She just kept bringing him a fresh cup whenever the one he was holding cooled off.

"What was your relationship with Ms. McCaffrey?"

He flinched, and Maria suspected he was visualizing the last time he'd seen his girlfriend.

"I told you – I was dating her."

"For how long?" She kept her tone casual. She didn't think this kid had it in him to tear his girlfriend and her friends apart, but no one had suspected Ted Bundy was slaughtering women on his days off from the crisis hotline, either. You never knew. Maria would never forget the face of an angelic ten-year-old boy who'd sobbed uncontrollably after his mother committed suicide. No matter what the evidence had indicated, she'd believed him, right until the moment he'd confessed to shooting his mother. She'd vowed that day to never again be fooled by appearances.

"About three months."

"You seem very upset for three months."

The young man gaped at her, his eyes widening as if she'd hit him. Shadows stood out on his pale face. He could play the wounded victim with her, but he couldn't fake the pallor of his skin. Still, maybe he was human enough to be horrified by what he'd done.

"You were out there – you saw...what they...what they *did* to her. Even if I'd never seen her before in my life I'd be devastated."

Maria leaned forward in her chair. Her mind, trained for years to catch subtleties most people never noticed, had sounded an alarm. "Who are *they*, Reese?"

He lowered his gaze to the table, bringing a hand up to shield his forehead, as if the weak glow of the fluorescents hurt his eyes. "I don't know."

"But you said 'they'. You must know something. There's no evidence of two assailants at the scene."

There wasn't evidence of anyone at the scene except Reese and his friends, but she wasn't about to tell him that. Not yet, in any case. However, to commit such a crime on one's own would require superhuman strength. Had Reese gotten his friend Dan to help, and then killed the young man to keep him silent?

She didn't believe it. Maria had witnessed a lot of terrible things in her twelve years as an investigator, but she'd never experienced a crime scene that rivaled this one in terms of sheer violence. Even with keeping the Ted Bundy factor in mind, she couldn't picture this man being capable of the level of bloodthirsty frenzy these murders had required.

"Did you have a good relationship?"

Reese looked at her in surprise, but glanced away as quickly. "It was all right."

She'd talked to him for an hour now, and this was the one time Maria had seen him appear guilty. "This will go better for you if you tell me the truth."

"If I tell you the truth, you'll think I did it."

"Not necessarily, but if you lie to me about this, I'll wonder what else you're hiding."

He chewed on the skin of one of his fingers for a moment. *Nervous habit.* It obviously wasn't a new one, because the skin around each of his nails was ragged. "Okay, maybe we weren't getting along so well."

"You're going to have to give me more than that, Reese." She kept her voice soft, hoping she could get the information she needed without lawyers getting involved. As soon as a lawyer was in the mix, he'd never talk to her so directly again.

"She – she wasn't always an easy person to like. I mean, I'm not blaming her for everything. I did some stuff that pushed her buttons too. But she's a hard woman sometimes."

Not anymore. Maria forced herself not to think of the torture the young woman must have gone through. She had to focus on the task at hand. Later that evening, when she was home and the smell of the blood had been washed from her hair, then she could mourn the victims. Right now, the best thing she could do was find the person who'd killed her.

"Why did you stay with her if you weren't getting along?"

He shrugged, and she saw the briefest hint of color come into his cheeks. "You know."

"I'm afraid I don't."

"We were—" Reese blew out a frustrated breath. "Geez, do I have to say it? We were pretty compatible in the sack."

Maria had to concentrate on taking deep breaths of her own. Her fingers tightened, but she forced them to relax. It was all she could do not to smack him. That poor young woman had been savaged, and it turned out she'd spent her last hours with someone who only valued her for what she could do for him in bed.

"I realize that sounds bad," he said, making her wonder if her disgust had been obvious. "But I'm not a total creep. I was going to break up with her after the camping trip."

"Why wait? Why not do it before?"

"I'd thought about it. But she was so excited about the trip. It was supposed to be our last bit of fun before we had to grow up and get real." His voice trailed off, and she knew the reality of the situation had begun to sink in. "Shit."

"You recently graduated?"

"Yeah, in June. We met at college – or, rather, I met Jessica and she introduced me to Dan and Kira. They were her friends." The color drained from his face again. "Kira – did you find her? Is she—?"

"I'm sorry," Maria said, softened by his obvious distress. "She didn't make it."

She didn't make it. That was one way of putting it. Once she got over the shock of seeing Jessica McCaffrey's body, Maria had thought it was the worst thing she'd ever witness in her career.

She'd been wrong.

"Shit," Reese said again, his voice breaking. He curled his upper body into a fetal position, fingers tearing at his hair, clawing at his scalp. "This is so fucked up." His body shook with sobs.

"I'm sorry." This time she meant it. She was pretty sure by now that this kid wasn't her killer. His despair and shock were too real.

Maria couldn't help but notice the news of the other girl's death had affected him much more than what had happened to his girlfriend.

Once again her heart went out to Jessica. Men were such shits sometimes. Especially young men.

As she waited for him to calm down, Maria refilled Reese's coffee cup and got some water for herself. She could barely choke it down, but her mouth felt coated with ash. She needed something.

"Can I call my parents?" Reese lifted his tear-streaked face. "I need to talk to my parents."

"We already called them. They're on their way. I have a few more questions."

He nodded, but she noticed how he slumped in his chair, resigned. She didn't blame him. She was the investigator and she didn't want to talk about it, either.

"What was going on with Kira, Reese?"

His head shot up. Now she had his attention. "What do you mean? Nothing was going on. She was with Dan."

"I find it interesting that your biggest outpouring of emotion was when you found out *she* was dead. Not when we discussed your own girlfriend, but when you heard about Kira."

"I'm messed up about all of them."

A muscle in his jaw twitched, and Maria knew she'd hit a nerve.

"Put yourself in my place. How would you feel if you went camping with your friends, and the next morning everyone was dead? And not just dead, but—" He shook his head. "They were my friends, and someone ripped them apart. Fucking ripped them apart. How do you think I feel?"

"That brings up another question. How did you not hear anything? There must have been a lot of noise. There would have been screaming...."

"I told you, I don't know. Don't you think I've asked myself that a hundred times already?" His eyes were wild with pain and fury, but Maria was willing to bet his anger was the rage of an innocent man. "All I know is that when I went to sleep, everyone was fine. And then I woke up and found Dan—"

"Calm down. No one is accusing you of anything."

There was a light tap at the door, and one of the deputies poked his head in. "The parents are here, Detective. They're demanding to see him."

She heard the question in his voice, and took it as her cue. "Send them in. They can take him home."

Before leaving the interrogation room, Maria touched Reese's shoulder. It trembled under her hand.

"I want to talk to you again once you've had some rest. And next time, I want you to be honest with me."

CHAPTER FOUR

A hawk screamed, startling her enough that she went for her gun.

Her partner laughed. "I don't think we'll be able to bring him in, Detective. He's in the wind."

Maria did her best to smile, but it was a weak attempt. Even this far away, she could smell the blood. It made her stomach flip.

Jorge fell quiet as they plodded down the gravel path toward the last campsite. They walked carefully, slowly, absorbing the scene, searching for anything out of place. But as before, there was nothing. Just the eerie feeling they were being watched.

"You feel that?" Maria asked, keeping her voice low. The hairs rose on the back of her neck. She kept her hand on her gun, unsnapping the holster.

"Yeah, something's hinky." Her partner scanned the trees, but if anything was out of the ordinary, he couldn't see it. This scene was getting to them both, but Maria was convinced it was more than that. This place was wrong. It was *damaged*, somehow, in a way that had nothing to do with the horrific crime that had taken place.

Some places had a darkness about them. She'd experienced it before, when she'd visited Auschwitz with her sister, and she felt it now. Why those kids had decided to spend the night here, instead of running away screaming, she'd never understand. But then again, most people tended to ignore their instincts. She'd spent years learning to listen.

"You don't need to do this, Maria," Jorge said, taking her nerves as a sign of reluctance. "The coroner's here. Forensics is here. Ball's in their court now."

"Yes, I do." As the metallic odor of blood grew stronger, it strengthened her resolve. She would not balk from what had happened to them. She would look them in the eyes and she would find their killer. "I need to see."

The campsite was bathed in red and blue from the cruisers' roof lights, giving the trees an otherworldly glow. Maria ducked under the yellow tape cordoning off the area. In this case, it was an unnecessary barrier. It was the world's most secluded crime scene. The conservation officers they'd met that morning were long gone.

She couldn't blame them.

The coroner walked to meet her. He reached out his hand and Maria took it in her own, briefly squeezing his cold fingers. She'd often thought Roger Layton held the sadness of the universe in his faded blue eyes. That sadness was even more apparent today.

"Maria," he said, looking as frail as ever, but she'd worked with him long enough to understand this weakness was an illusion. With his gaunt, caved-in cheekbones and wispy gray hair, he looked like he was in his eighties. But he'd looked the same when she'd met him twenty years ago. He hadn't aged a day. She suspected the man had been born old.

"Roger."

"We're ready to take her down now. Whenever you give the word."

His normally ramrod-straight spine was stooped, his eyes red behind wire-rimmed glasses. He'd waited for her, she realized. Roger had known she'd want to see the girl again.

Pulling plastic booties out of her pocket, Maria slipped them over her shoes before approaching the scene. Knowing what to expect hadn't lessened the impact of seeing her. If anything, it only made it worse.

The smell of her had gotten stronger. It coated Maria's nostrils and made her eyes burn. Brushing away the thickening clouds of flies, she tilted her head back. What had been done to Jessica McCaffrey she'd only seen in drawings dating from the Middle Ages.

A tree had been sharpened into a stake, and it was on this stake the young woman was impaled, the deadly spear thrust deep inside her. It had traveled through her birth canal and onward, likely destroying her internal organs. The surface of the tree was slick with blood and other fluids.

Jessica's bare, crimson-streaked feet had turned purple. Her body was naked and there were what appeared to be claw marks on her breasts and abdomen. Her expression was frozen in a rictus of horror, her colorless lips open in a silent scream. Her hair was so soaked with blood it was impossible to tell what color it had been, but Maria knew from the woman's driver's license it had been blonde.

The men surrounding her kept respectfully quiet. No off-color jokes or black humor disturbed McCaffrey's resting place. Her death had shattered their defenses.

Seeing her again, Maria was convinced Reese hadn't killed her. The strength it would have taken to drive the tree so deep into the ground was immense, not to mention the power required to impale a healthy young woman who had no doubt fought for her life. Reese may have been wiry, but he wasn't strong enough to have done this. At least, not on his own.

"Do you want to see the other one?" Roger asked when she finally looked away. Maria shook her head, not trusting herself to speak. As terrible as Jessica's death had been, at least she appeared human. Kira, on the other hand, looked like she'd been put through a meat grinder. Roger would have to use a shovel to get her into a body bag. It wasn't a scene that inspired gratitude, but Maria was grateful Reese hadn't checked the girls' tent. He never would have recovered.

You're not welcome here.

Whoever spoke was close enough that she could feel their breath against her neck. Maria whirled, expecting Jorge.

"What did you say?"

Roger's eyes widened. He stared at her hand, which had gone to her gun again, and then at her face. "I didn't say a word. Maria, what's wrong?"

"Someone just said something to me. Did you hear it?"

"No, I didn't hear a thing. Are you all right?"

"I'd feel a lot better if I knew who'd said that." Her voice cut across the campsite. Jorge and the other men gawked at her. Maria saw her partner's hand move to his own gun. They were too on edge. None of them would have played a prank on her. Behind her, there was only the gravel road. She turned, but it was empty. Still, the feeling that someone was watching her grew stronger than ever.

Ignoring the powerful urge she felt to get the hell out of there, Maria faced the trees and yelled, "This is the Clear Springs Police. You are trespassing on a crime scene. Come out of there with your hands up."

Her colleagues were startled, but everyone studied the trees and waited, hands on pistols. Roger retreated until he was almost hiding behind her.

They waited for an ungodly minute while the tension in her chest grew. Someone was here with them. Maria knew it. She could *feel* it. Sweat trickled down her spine.

"This is your last warning. Show yourself now!"

Nothing but her own voice echoed back. The day was unusually calm. There was no wind to rattle the branches, nothing to send a draft of cold breath along her neck.

She nodded at her partner, and they unholstered their weapons, rushing toward the trees in a crouch, guns at the ready. They plunged into the woods, twisting their heads this way and that as they scanned the forest for any movement. Adrenaline surged through her body, chasing away the last of her fear.

Crashing through the bush, they ignored the branches that slapped and scratched them as they searched for their unwanted guest. *Could the killer still be here?* The thought triggered a flood of anticipation and fear. Maria's fingers tightened on her weapon.

She could hear twigs behind her snap as her guys fell in behind. She was glad they were there. Whoever had killed those girls was stronger than a meth head and infinitely more insane.

"Jesus Christ."

Maria's partner had reached the clearing before her, and stopped so quickly she almost ran into his back.

At six feet, she was considered tall, but Jorge was six foot five. She had to step around him to see why he had stopped, but as she did, she was filled with dread. Was it another body? Had another camper been murdered?

When she saw what Jorge was staring at, Maria froze.

It was a tree.

The trunk had been folded back like a banana peel, as if something had erupted inside it.

"What on earth would do something like that?" her partner asked.

"I don't know." Maria saw something wink at her in the grass and picked her way over to it, careful not to step too close to the tree. She wasn't taking any chances.

Snapping on a pair of latex gloves, Maria knelt to check out her find, brushing some of the weeds away.

It was an axe, its worn blade pockmarked and chipped.

"You think this was used on the vics?" Jorge asked.

The axe was too small and dull to be responsible for the level of carnage they'd found at the site. "No. My guess is they used this to cut firewood."

One by one, the men crowded into the enclosed space. Johnson, who was still young enough to feel immortal, did what no one else dared. He strode over to the tree and peered inside.

"It looks like it exploded from the inside out."

The officers crowded closer, taking turns staring into the tree. Johnson was right – it was as if a giant had reached in and taken the core, leaving only the shell of a tree behind.

"Have you ever seen anything like this?" Jorge asked Maria.

"No, but this isn't my area of expertise."

Johnson turned to her, surprised. "You think this has something to do with the murders?"

Surrounded by the people she'd trusted with her life for years, she felt no comfort. Something in these woods was malevolent, and it didn't want them here. The hairs on the back of her neck rose again. Jorge caught her eye, and from his expression, Maria knew he felt it as well.

She cleared her throat, willing her voice to work. "Yes. I have no idea what, but I think it does."

CHAPTER FIVE

Her heart pounding, she retreated until her heel connected with nylon. She spun around, fumbling with the zipper. It was stuck. Mad with terror, she clawed at the tent, but her fingers scrabbled futilely over the slick surface.

Behind her, the squelching noise grew louder.

She didn't want to see it, but somehow hearing it without knowing where it was coming from was worse.

Reluctantly she turned.

The bloody mass of tissue had only one appendage that remained recognizable – a single hand. It was flat as an X-ray but still a hand, a hand that gripped the nylon floor of the tent and pulled itself toward her.

"Hhhhelp me," it whispered, a writhing, bubbling pool of gore. She saw what she took to be several shiny bits of rock, and then realized in horror they were teeth. The thing that had been Kira slithered closer and closer, until Maria thought her heart would stop. Surely no one could survive this level of fear.

Kira's organs gleamed with blood and something else Maria dared not put a name to. The girl's heart still beat. Her deformed hand reached for Maria's boot, touching the toe.

"Ssh, Maria. Maria! Stop screaming."

The Kira-thing had hold of her entire foot now, and as she continued to scream, it shook her by the leg with surprising strength.

"Maria, wake up!"

Wake up?

Her eyes fluttered open and focused on the concerned face of her husband.

The adrenaline surged through her as she searched the room. Her hand went to her hip but found only the soft cotton of her sweatpants.

"Are you okay?"

Her feet were in his hands, causing her to return to reality. She must have fallen asleep while he was massaging them. The television flickered in the corner, showing an eighties teen comedy, but not the one they'd started watching together at the start of the evening. Ben had changed the movie while she'd slept. The upholstery of the old sofa was familiar underneath her, reassuring. Her pulse throbbed behind her temples, and she was willing to bet her blood pressure was through the roof. It had been so real.

She could feel the nylon of the tent against her back. She could still hear that terrible squelching sound.

"Maria?"

"I must have fallen asleep. I'm sorry."

He winked, waggling his fingers. "It's my magic hands. Works every time."

"Still." She reached for him. "I'm sorry."

If there was anything Maria hated about her job, it was how often her husband and daughter suffered for it.

"I was worried you were going to scare Heidi. I'm glad I was able to wake you up."

Their eight-year-old daughter hated bedtime with a passion. Getting her to settle down was a fight every single evening. Thankfully, once she was in bed, she was a sound sleeper. Poor thing was probably chronically exhausted.

"You must have been having one heck of a nightmare. I've never heard you scream like that before."

And she'd never dreamed about one of her crime scenes before. Not that she could remember.

"Hey, Earth to Maria." Ben jiggled one of her feet. "You all right?"

She began to tell him things were fine, must have drunk too much coffee at the office, blah blah blah, but stopped herself. A lot of the cops she worked with were divorced, and there were many reasons for that, but there was one she'd witnessed time and time again.

Officers tended to shut out their spouses. They had good intentions. They didn't want to hurt or upset them, or drag them down into the dark hell cops sometimes live in. But it was ultimately a mistake, because cops have to talk to *someone*, and usually that someone is another cop, the only person they believe really understands them. It doesn't take long before confiding in someone other than your spouse, especially if that someone is regularly sharing adrenaline-charged experiences with you, becomes something intimate. Officers didn't always have physical affairs, but if the person you turned to whenever you were struggling was someone other than your husband, that could be even more damaging.

Maria refused to let that happen with Ben. Her husband was a sensitive soul, a high school art and music teacher who intentionally surrounded himself with beauty. When they'd started dating, she'd warned him that he was making a huge mistake. He sought the light when her life was about the dark. He'd shrugged, smiled in that hopeful, whimsical way she'd quickly grown to love, and said, "Opposites attract."

Still, she couldn't tell him how Jessica and Kira had died. That would give *him* nightmares. Instead, she filled him in on the basics and then told him what was bothering her.

"I can't explain it, but something about that place is off. Being at that campsite made my skin crawl."

Most people would say there was something wrong with her if she hadn't found the campsite eerie, considering three people had died there. But not Ben. Her husband was a firm believer in intuition.

He also knew she didn't freak out easily.

Ben resumed the foot massage while he waited her out. They'd been married long enough to understand each other's patterns. There was no point pressuring her to talk, or asking a lot of questions. She had to tell a story her way, in her own time.

"I heard someone tell me to leave, Ben. I swear he was right behind me. I could feel his breath. But when I turned, he was gone."

Maria shivered at the memory, pulling her afghan tighter and remembering how Reese had done the same with the fireman's blanket. Had he encountered the same person? Was it the killer?

"That's creepy. What do you think it was?"

"I'm not sure. I know what I heard, but I have no idea how someone got away that fast without any of us seeing him."

"Did the guys see anything?"

She shook her head. "Not a thing."

When her husband tactfully kept his silence, she felt the need to defend herself. "I can guess what you're thinking, but it wasn't the wind, and it wasn't my imagination. Someone said, *'You're not welcome here,'* and they said it practically in my ear. And that's not all – I sensed someone was watching us the entire day."

"Hey, if you say you heard something, you heard something. I believe you."

Maria hadn't noticed she'd been holding her breath, waiting for his reaction. The tension in her chest eased a little, and she knew talking to Ben had been the right thing to do. "Jorge felt it too. At one point, I was sure someone was in the bush, but when we gave chase, no one was there. We did find the strangest tree, though."

She told Ben about the black tree and how it appeared to have exploded from within. "Have you ever heard of anything like that?" Ben was the one with the green thumb, but she wasn't surprised when he said no.

"It sounds like a spooky place. Have there been any murders there before?"

"Not that I know of." She settled back into the couch cushions as Ben started on her other foot. Meow Mix, their silver tabby, jumped onto her lap and promptly began arranging the blankets to her liking. "But it's worth checking out." Maria smiled as she scratched behind the tabby's soft ears and was rewarded with a purr. Between hanging in a bar with her colleagues and going home, she'd choose home every time.

"You'll figure it out, Maria. Those kids are lucky to have you on their side."

He spoke out of kindness, but she wished he hadn't brought them up. She winced as she recalled Jessica's expression of horror, Kira's brain matter splattered all over her tent. *Lucky* was not the word she'd use to describe them.

CHAPTER SIX

Someone tapped on my door. It was the gentlest of knocks, but I jumped from my chair in shock, spilling coffee all over my desk.

"Shit!" I swiped at the liquid with one of the three blankets wrapped around me, frantically trying to build a barrier between the coffee and my computer.

"Reese, honey?"

Continuing to mop up the mess, I ignored her. How many times did I have to tell her I wanted to be left alone?

"Someone's here to see you."

Unfortunately, Mom was as stubborn as me. Guess it had to come from somewhere.

"Well, I don't want to see them. So you can tell whoever it is to fuck off."

"I think you should make an exception for me," said a smooth voice I didn't recognize. "Unless you'd rather we had this conversation in a prison cell."

The door opened, and I whirled around to find a man in a pinstriped suit standing with my mother. He had that impossibly perfect skin that always reminded me of babies, and his tie was pink. I hated him instantly.

"Who the fuck are you?"

"Reese!" my mother scolded, her mouth pursed into a frown, as if she didn't use that word on a regular basis herself. "Language, please."

"I think I have a right to know who's in my room. Especially when I've said *several* times that I don't want to talk to anybody." My blanket was soaked now, but it appeared my computer would be safe, so I stopped swabbing at it like an idiot. I was tempted to throw the soiled blanket at my mother, but this guy looked like the type who would make a big deal out of something like that.

"I'm Gregory Vincent Prosper, Esquire. Your parents have hired me to represent you." He handed me a white card with the impossibly long name of a law firm embossed on the front. It reminded me of the business card scene in *American Psycho*, and it took every ounce of self-control not to crumple it.

"Thank you, but I don't need a lawyer." I shot my mother a look of disgust. "I haven't been charged with anything."

"Yet." Gregory Vincent My-Shit-Don't-Stink moved a pile of clothing to one side before taking a seat on my bed, crossing his ankles and folding his hands as if he were at a goddamn tea party or a polo match. Smug bastard. "You haven't been charged with anything *yet*. But from what your mother tells me, it's only a matter of time."

Mom's eyes welled with tears, and I glared at her, hoping she got my message loud and clear. "I really don't care what my mother told you, *Greg*, but I'm innocent. I didn't do anything wrong, and the cops know it. Ask that investigator—" *Shit, what was her name?* "She believes I'm innocent. She's the one who let me come home."

The man laughed, a sound so brimming with condescension I wanted to pop him one. "Who said anything about innocence? Or guilt, for that matter. No one cares if you're innocent or not, Reese. Can they pin it on you? That's what they care about."

I thought about the detective who'd questioned me. She'd acted tough initially, but by the end, she'd appeared to feel sorry for me. I couldn't believe she was that good an actress. But then again, Mr. Gregory Vincent Whatever probably had a lot more experience with this stuff than I did. What if she'd only been nice to trick me into saying something incriminating? Everyone knew about that Good Cop, Bad Cop routine.

"They can't. So I stand by my original statement. I don't need a lawyer."

If I'd hoped that was enough to send Mr. Pompous Ass on his way, I was disappointed. The man didn't budge, which sucked, because I was really tired of standing, but there was no way in hell I'd sit next to him and my chair was still wet.

"Let's see." He held up a hand, ticking off the facts of my case on his fingers. "You illegally break into a campsite. Speaks to character. You deface said campsite by cutting down a tree from a protected forest and destroying a sign. Speaks to character again. You were arguing with your girlfriend right before her death. That's motive. And out of the four, you are the sole survivor. That, my friend, is highly suspicious."

"I'm not your friend," I said automatically, but cold terror had seeped into my gut at his words. Could I actually go to jail for this? I'd rather stick my head in the oven.

"Once you wake up and realize how deeply you're mired in shit, I'll be the only friend you care about."

"None of that stuff means anything." My mother was wringing her hands like some woman in a Shakespearean play. It was obvious she wanted me to play nice with this overdressed windbag, but why? Did *she* think I was guilty? Was that what she and Dad had been whispering about? Well, fuck them. "It's circumstantial."

"Do you have any idea how many people get convicted on circumstantial evidence every day? Do you know how many 'innocent' people have been executed because of the same? Circumstantial evidence is all they need to send you away for life."

At least they couldn't fry me. Minnesota didn't have capital punishment. But to say my relief was fleeting would be an understatement. Being stuck in a classroom for hours was enough to make me lose my mind. I couldn't handle prison.

"The justice system is not 'As Seen on TV'. People have been locked away forever on a lot less evidence than you have against you."

I would never have admitted it, but Mr. Pompous had my attention. Leaning against my desk for support, I said the only thing I could think of, but then cringed at how whiny it sounded. "But I'm innocent."

The lawyer smirked. "Aw, and you think people will care. That's cute. You'd better grow up in a hurry, kid. And you better stop talking to the cops. From now on, keep your big mouth shut."

"Why? I have nothing to hide." I couldn't believe my mother had gone along with this. Didn't she want to catch the person who'd killed Jess? I was the only witness, not that it meant much, but I couldn't stop talking to Detective Greyeyes. She wanted the same thing I did – justice for Jessica, Kira, and Dan.

"It's not as if your friends were smothered with pillows. They were *slaughtered*. One of them was in a two-man tent with you, inches away from where you were sleeping. And you're telling me you didn't hear anything?"

The room spun, and I gripped my desk chair, feeling nauseated even though I hadn't eaten. The thought of Dan and how his head had rolled toward me stole my breath. I gasped for air, sinking onto the floor as my knees gave out. Mom came over to help but I wouldn't let her touch me.

"H— how do you – know about that?" I said between breaths. Except for my official statement, I hadn't talked about what had happened or what I'd seen. Forcing it out of my mind was the only way I could cope.

The lawyer offered his hand. I hated to take it, but it felt sillier to lay curled in a ball at his feet. He was surprisingly strong, hoisting me upright like I was a puppet on a string. "Clear Springs isn't the Big City. People talk. And that's why it's so important we get them saying the right things."

I eased myself onto my bed, holding an arm across my stomach as if that would prevent me from throwing up. Closing my eyes, I leaned my head against the wall, hoping they would get the hint. "I'm not feeling well." I waited for them to leave.

"Before I go, I want to hear the truth."

I squinted at him. "The truth about what?" My mother inched toward the door. Clearly she wasn't keen to hear this part of the conversation.

"About what happened that night. If I'm going to represent you, I'll need to know the truth, no matter what it is."

"That's a big if. I'm still not sure I need a lawyer." My stomach lurched, and I groaned. "And I don't know what happened. When I went to bed, everyone was alive and when I woke up, they were dead."

Darts of pain shot across my forehead, and I buried my head in the pillow. *Why won't this go away?* All I wanted was for the universe to grant me one gigantic do-over. I'd listen to Jessica and drive away from that campsite as fast as I could. Maybe I'd even patch things up with her.

Mr. Pompous leaned so close to me our noses almost touched. I could smell mint on his breath, but under that, something else – something unpleasant, something stale. My stomach growled a warning.

"You don't expect me to believe that bullshit, do you?" he asked so warmly you'd think he'd inquired about my health. "You *must* have heard something."

Didn't he think I'd tortured myself enough over this? Jess and Kira had taken this ridiculous self-defense course together. They'd shown me their moves, which consisted of a few kicks, punches, and elbow strikes while screaming, "No! No! No!" Neither would have died quietly, and Dan was a farm boy who'd spent his summers working for his dad. I'd seen him toss around one-hundred-pound hay bales like they weighed nothing. Whoever had killed them had to have taken them by surprise. Unless our beer had been drugged.

"Test our beer bottles." I felt optimistic for the first time since I'd woken up yesterday. It had never occurred to me before, but it made perfect sense. "Maybe they were tampered with."

Mr. Pompous didn't appear impressed with this new theory. "What, you think McGraw slipped you a roofie and then gave himself one for good measure?"

I remembered Dan joking about *Brokeback Mountain* with me before he died, and my heart ached. I used to think that heart-hurting thing was a figure of speech, but I knew better now.

Dan had been a good guy. Maybe we'd met through our girlfriends, but we easily could have been buddies, given time. Now that would never happen. I decided not to dignify Prosper's insulting question with a response.

"It's worth a check, isn't it?" my mother asked, and I heard the same hope in her voice that I'd felt when I'd thought of it. "It's a possibility. It would explain why he didn't hear anything."

"I'll look into it. Where are the bottles now?"

My cheeks flushed. "We threw them in the fire."

Prosper groaned. "Great. Well, I'll see what I can do. How many did you drink?"

"Just one each. The girls didn't have any." I considered telling him how pissed off they'd been with me, but decided against it.

For a moment I thought he was leaving, but before I could sigh in relief, he turned to study me. His eyes were the color of a glacier and just as cold.

"You're absolutely certain you didn't hear anything that night? No strange sounds, no scuffling, no one coming into the tent?"

I was about to say no, when I remembered.

In spite of the warmth of my room and the several layers of clothing I wore, I began to shake. My teeth chattered.

"Reese, what is it?" My mom hurried to the bed. "What's wrong?"

Unable to speak for a moment, I stared at Prosper and nodded.

"There was something. Didn't think of it before."

The lawyer seemed oblivious to my reaction. "Yes? What was it?"

"It was a voice. He said—" I paused for a second to think. *What had he said?* Stay away? No, not that. Go away? No, that wasn't it....

And then it came rushing back to me like I still stood in that campsite. "He said, '*You're not welcome here.*'"

My mother's face paled, but the lawyer remained expressionless. "And you think it was Dan?"

I shook my head and immediately regretted it. The room blurred in front of me. "No. No, it definitely wasn't Dan. I don't know *who* said it, because when I turned around, no one was there."

Tears spilled from her eyes onto her cheeks, and in that moment, I forgave her everything. She believed me.

We both startled when Prosper began to laugh. He laughed so hard he had to hold on to my dresser for support. If I'd been stronger, I'd have given him a kick. "You've got to be kidding me," he said once he'd recovered. "Don't tell me you think anyone is going to buy the Bushy-haired Stranger defense."

"What are you talking about?" Through the pain in my head and my dizziness, I heard my voice from a far distance, as if I were speaking under water. Staggering to my feet, I made my way to the door. "I never said he had bushy hair. I don't know what he looked like. I never saw him."

"It's an expression. Whenever someone wants to cover up a crime, they claim a stranger did it. Often as not, it's a bushy-haired stranger."

"I don't want to cover up – oh God, wait a sec, I'm gonna—"

The meeting with my new lawyer came to an abrupt end when I puked all over his Hugo Boss suit.

CHAPTER SEVEN

Groggy from lack of sleep, Maria blinked to bring the crime-scene photos back into focus, and then wished she hadn't. They were every bit as horrific as she'd remembered. Wincing, she spread the photos across her desk until she found the ones of Dan McGraw. It said a lot that the decapitated camper's pictures were the tamest of the bunch. Which might speak to the killer's motive. The men obviously weren't the focus of the attack. McGraw's death, while brutal, was a walk in the park compared to what the women had suffered. And then there was Reese, who didn't have a scratch on him.

We have a woman hater on our hands. Great. So what else was new?

"Detective?"

James Archer loomed in the doorway. He was the last person she wanted to see. Cops tended to be smart-asses in general, but Archer unleashed his inappropriate humor at the most inopportune times. However, it was his cruel streak that really bothered her. She smiled weakly, hoping it looked more genuine than it felt. "What can I do for you?"

"DCB's here to see you."

She bristled. "I wish you wouldn't call him that."

Crazyhorse was an Elder of the Strong Lake Band, and as such, he was entitled to respect. Unfortunately, he also had a drinking problem, which had earned him his nickname at the department. DCB, short for Drunk Crazy Bastard.

Archer shrugged. "He's insistent on seeing you. Says he can help you with your latest case. He's made a bit of a scene. I'm surprised you haven't heard the commotion."

She'd been so fixated on the case materials she hadn't noticed a thing, but now that he mentioned it, she could hear the familiar voice.

"Get your hands off me, you Nazis! I need to see Maria." The last few words slurred so they were strung together. Maria wanted nothing more than to lock her door and pretend she wasn't there, but Crazyhorse never stayed long. He just needed to talk to someone who'd listen. For whatever reason, she was usually that person.

She sighed. "Okay, send him in."

Like a vulture spotting carrion, Archer detected her reluctance. "Do you want me to kick him out, Detective? Because it would be my pleasure."

I'm sure it would. The guys were careful to avoid using racial slurs around her, but their disgust was harder to hide. "We're here to serve and protect every member of society, Archer. Not just the rich white folks."

"As you wish," Archer said in an obsequious tone, but she didn't miss the sneer that twisted his upper lip, turning him ugly. Sighing again, she wished she were a drinking woman. She settled for chewing gum, packing three pieces of Bubblemint into her mouth before Crazyhorse stumbled into her domain.

"Good morning, Detective."

"Good morning, Crazyhorse." Maria held his regular chair for him so it wouldn't slide away as he more or less fell into it. "What can I do for you?"

Wow. His breath was enough to stop a truck, and from the smell of it, he'd pissed himself as well. Instead of revulsion, she felt only sadness, sadness that a man who'd once been a well-respected Elder had fallen so far.

Still, it was best to breathe through her mouth while Crazyhorse was there.

"It's not about what you can do for me. I've come to do something for you. I've heard about the killings at Strong Lake, and I know who did it."

Used to his grand proclamations, she concentrated instead on the part of his statement that shocked her. "How did you hear?" The media hadn't gotten wind of it yet, which was helped by the fact that the only 'media' of record in Clear Springs was a small, community newspaper. Once Minneapolis got their hands on the story, it would spread like oil. She'd steeled herself to deal with the reporters, but to say she wasn't looking forward to it would be the understatement of the decade.

The man leaned toward her, his long, black hair streaked with gray and wild around his face. "Maria Greyeyes, I'm surprised at you. You know it's part of the Strong Lake community."

Of course. The campsite butted up against Crazyhorse's reservation. In spite of her heritage, her knowledge of Native American territories was sorely lacking.

"They are treaty lands, but you won't find anyone from my community anywhere near there. It's a bad place."

"Bad place? Why is that?" Her mind was already wandering. Once Crazyhorse got into the superstitions of their people, she tuned out. There was enough tangible evil in her world without chasing boogeymen.

"Land's tainted," he said in his thick accent. Sometimes she suspected her colleagues were uncomfortable around him simply because they couldn't understand him. They didn't want to look foolish in front of someone they considered beneath them. "Always has been. Lots of sad things happened there, going back to the beginning."

"Really?" History was more tangible than the boogeyman. History was something she could use. If there had been more murders at the camp, maybe it was the work of a serial. Maybe someone from the Strong Lake Band resented the near-constant presence of drunken teens and twentysomethings. "I've never heard of anything."

"'Course not. This is not the knowledge of the white man. It is the knowledge of *our* people." Crazyhorse narrowed his eyes at her and she squirmed, feeling ashamed. Why should she be ashamed that this man was disappointed in her? It was beyond her, but she did. He had once accused her of betraying '*the Native within*' in order to get ahead in a White Man's world, and she guessed she had. The truth was, she had never felt connected to her culture. Her family tended to ignore it. They'd raised her to be like 'everyone else', and to them, 'everyone else' was white.

"Enlighten me."

Crazyhorse coughed. "A cup of coffee would be nice."

"Of course." Her cheeks grew warm. The man loved her Keurig, which might be the only luxury he experienced this week. She couldn't believe she hadn't offered. The lack of sleep had affected her more than she'd thought. "What would you like?"

He smiled, and it was a smile that lit up his face despite the cracked and missing teeth. She'd often thought he should be on the cover of *National Geographic*. The lines that scored his cheeks and forehead told a vivid story. "What do you got?"

"Oh, you're in luck today. I've got new stock in. I have Irish Cream, French Vanilla, Hazelnut Mocha, Cinnamon Twist, and plain old dark roast."

Crazyhorse puffed his cheeks and rolled his eyes to the ceiling, pretending to be deep in thought while she pretended she didn't know what his answer would be. He always had the same thing. "I think I'll try that French Vanilla. That sounds real nice."

"Good choice," she said, putting the little container of coffee into the machine. She made sure never to run out of French Vanilla.

It took her a few minutes to make two cups, enough to fill the oversized mug she used for Crazyhorse. She'd noticed a couple of years ago that his hands shook too badly to manage anything with a small, delicate handle, so she'd bought him this bruiser. The weight of it helped to stabilize his tremors.

He took it from her with both hands, trembling as he brought it to his lips. As was his habit, he smelled the drink before he sipped. "Ah, that's good stuff. This is the best coffee I've ever had."

She'd brewed herself a cup of the Hazelnut Mocha, wishing she enjoyed it half as much as Crazyhorse loved his. They sipped in silence. Then she caught a glimpse of the case folder on her desk. It was thin – *too* thin.

"What do you know about the campsite?"

"I know it's a place of evil. A place of darkness. Have you heard of the wendigo?"

"Sure. It's like a Native American boogeyman, isn't it?" She recalled some scary stories from her youth, but she'd never paid much attention to that sort of thing.

"No, it is not a 'boogeyman'," Crazyhorse said, resting his mug on her desk so he could make quotes in the air with his fingers. "Wendigos are the spirits of people, *bad* people. People with a taste for human flesh."

Images from the crime scene flashed through her mind. No one had been nibbled on, as far she could tell. The coroner had warned there was no chance of putting Kira together again. Maria prayed the parents would agree to cremation once the coroner had finished with Kira's body, so there would be no risk the family would see what had become of her.

If parts of Kira were missing, it would be extremely difficult to tell.

Maria mentally slapped herself back to reality. Was she actually entertaining the possibility that a *wendigo* was responsible?

"You need to talk to my friend, Chief Kinew. He'll tell you what's going on out there."

As much as she thought the idea of wendigos was preposterous, Maria made note of his friend's name. Aside from questioning conservation officers for the twentieth time and asking the friends and family whether the deceased had any enemies, what other leads did they have?

Perhaps there was a grain of truth buried within the legend and lore.

Crazyhorse rose from his chair, handing her his coffee cup with reverence, as if it were a great treasure instead of a dollar-store mug. She'd once suggested he take it with him, but he insisted on keeping it in her office.

"I need to let you get to your investigatin'. You're a busy lady."

"Thank you. I'll go see your friend today." *And hope he doesn't waste my time with a bunch of wendigo bullshit.*

"Good. Good. The chief hates cops, but he won't have a problem talking to you."

She was careful to keep her expression neutral, but inwardly she cringed. It saddened her how many of her people distrusted cops. The police were supposed to be there to help. Unfortunately, she was willing to bet Chief Kinew had his reasons.

Crazyhorse paused at her door, holding on to the frame for support. "I can tell you one thing."

"What's that?" Now that he was on his way out, she was impatient to return to her work. There were many calls to be made before she could visit the chief.

"Those kids messed with something they should have left well enough alone."

The vehemence in his voice caught her full attention. Crazyhorse was many things, but angry was not one of them. "What are you talking about?"

"The tree. They never should have touched that tree."

CHAPTER EIGHT

Every time I closed my eyes I saw Jessica's face.

Not the ugly mockery that had been my last image of her, but the real girl. Snarling, pouting, arguing, and occasionally smiling. Damn, she'd been beautiful when she smiled.

Unable to stand it anymore, I jumped in Mom's Toyota. The cops were still 'processing' my truck, but I couldn't understand why. It wasn't like anyone had died in the Silverado.

I'd only met Jess's parents a couple of times, but they'd seemed like nice people. The least I could do was express my sympathy and pay my respects. Selfishly, I also hoped that being around other people who'd known her would help ease my own pain.

The driveway of the two-story house was empty, the street eerily quiet. For a moment I thought about getting back in the car, but since I'd come this far, I might as well knock.

After rapping on the door, I turned to leave. I'd convinced myself the McCaffreys weren't home, and never thought the door would open behind me.

Mrs. McCaffrey stood on the step, staring at me with red-rimmed and puffy eyes. She looked like hell. I instantly knew this had been a mistake.

"Reese. You're the last person I expected to see. Bruce, come see who's here," she called over her shoulder.

"I'm – I'm very sorry for your loss." Fumbling over the words, I wished I'd planned what to say.

"I'm sure you are."

I was taken aback at the hostility in her voice. She'd always treated me well.

Just when I thought it was only her grief talking, I saw Jessica's father. The man's chest heaved as he glared at me. He looked like a half-crazed dog that would rip me to shreds as soon as he escaped his leash.

"What the hell are you doing here? You must have a death wish."

What? What was he talking about?

"I don't uh – understand. I came to tell you I'm sorry about Jessica. But I can see I came at a bad time. I'll go, and—"

"A bad time? Don't be silly. We're always willing to talk to the psycho son of a bitch who murdered our daughter. By all means, come on in."

Stunned, I moved away from him, stumbling off the step. The full-body shaking that had only recently quit started up again.

"That's it, run like the coward you are. Killing two defenseless girls and a young man in his sleep. Bet you feel real proud of yourself. Bet you feel like a real man, huh?"

I wanted to tell McCaffrey he had it wrong, that he had *me* wrong, but the words stuck in my throat. All I could do was stare at them. Jessica's mother held her husband back, serving as his remaining link to civilized society, but I could see her grip was tenuous. There had to be some part of her, probably a large part, that wanted to let him go, to watch as he tore me apart.

"I need to know why. I need to know why you did this." Her eyes filled with tears, and I couldn't stand it anymore. I couldn't fathom how I'd thought this would make me feel better. Their pain was too raw, too intense. Before I could run to the car, her voice stopped me.

"What did she ever do to you? She loved you, Reese."

Loved me? I didn't think so. Jess and I'd had a certain chemistry, and when she was in a generous mood, we'd had some fun together. But she hadn't loved me. I was pretty sure about that.

However, I wasn't about to stand on the woman's doorstep and tell her my big love affair with her daughter had only lasted as long as it had because we both enjoyed fucking each other senseless.

"I didn't touch her. I never hurt her, Mrs. McCaffrey." And it was true. On that last, grim night, I couldn't even summon the courage to break up with her. The irony was that if I had, she'd be alive. She would have insisted on leaving the campground, or maybe not going at all, and she'd have been free to find a new boy toy for her amusement.

The realization tightened my chest to the point I could barely breathe. Perhaps I hadn't killed her, but my cowardice had certainly played a role. A vision of Jess's battered, nude body impaled on the tree flashed through my mind without warning

Jess. I'm sorry. My God, I'm so fucking sorry.

"You're lying," Mrs. McCaffrey said, and I noticed how much she resembled her daughter. Or, I guess, how much Jessica had resembled her. They could have been sisters if her mother hadn't aged twenty years overnight. "The cops told us you were going to break up with her. Why couldn't you have done it? Why couldn't you have let her go if you didn't want her? You didn't have to kill her."

She sobbed then, knees buckling, and her husband automatically reached out to keep her from falling, as if he'd already done it several times.

Her words had shocked me into silence again. Why on earth had Greyeyes told them? The last thing they needed to know was that their daughter's boyfriend had considered her expendable.

"Get out of here," Mr. McCaffrey said.

"But I didn't hurt Jessica. I could never have done that. I—"

Say you loved her, you idiot. That's what they want to hear. That's what their daughter's boyfriend should say.

"She was a great girl," I finished lamely.

Honesty had always been one of my best qualities and my biggest flaw.

Mr. McCaffrey shook his head at me before guiding his wife inside. Still sobbing, her face pressed to her husband's shirt, she couldn't even look at me.

It took ten minutes until the trembling eased enough for me to drive home.

Tears stung my eyes, but I couldn't let them fall. If I did, I was afraid they'd never stop.

CHAPTER NINE

The chief was nothing like Maria had pictured. His hair was cropped close to his head and its tight wave spoke of its tendency to curl. He wore cowboy boots and a Western-style shirt, and his painted-on jeans were held in place by the type of dinner plate-sized belt buckle most often seen at rodeos. The belt itself was completely unnecessary. He'd need a crowbar to get himself out of those pants.

The bored woman at reception lost her sullen attitude fast when she saw Maria. She'd scurried to the chief's office like a frightened weasel, and Kinew appeared before the second hand of Maria's watch had managed a full rotation.

The chief's brow furrowed, but the lines crinkling around his eyes suggested this was not his typical expression.

"What can I do for you, Officer?"

As soon as he spoke, she knew this was a man who had only received bad news from her colleagues. Both the office she ran and the company she kept were suspect. It didn't matter that she was also Native American. She was a cop, and therefore not to be trusted.

Before she could answer, he added, "It's Kevin again, isn't it? Little bastard is always getting into trouble."

"No, not Kevin." She was quick to reassure him, glad to be able to give him some good news before the bad. Her eyes flicked to the dispatcher, who clung to Maria's every word like Saran Wrap. "Is it possible to speak in your office? This is of a sensitive nature."

He sized her up for a moment before nodding and turning on his heel. She hurried to follow before he could change his mind.

She'd expected his office to more or less match the reception area, which hadn't been updated since the seventies. But instead of the faux-wood paneling so popular in the disco era, the walls were lined with bookshelves, which were crammed to capacity with every conceivable type of volume. At a glance, there were atlases, Farmers' Almanacs, hunting and fishing manuals, travel guides, mysteries, true crime thrillers, graphic novels, and a few Stephen King and Ray Bradbury dog-eared paperbacks. Piled on a chair in a precarious stack were the novels she'd always meant to read and had never gotten around to: *War and Peace, Crime and Punishment, Roots,* and *The Collected Works of William Shakespeare.*

"Before you ask, yes. I've read every one of them."

If possible, his posture stiffened even more, and Maria wondered how many people had insulted him with that question.

"I wasn't going to ask. I was just admiring your collection." He grabbed a couple of books off a chair and gestured for her to sit down. "I'm a reader too, but I don't think I've read as many books in my life as you have in this room."

She forgot everything else she'd planned to say when she spotted the book on his desk. The cover featured a young, blonde woman wearing a ceremonial headdress with her lips parted and her head thrown back, presumably in ecstasy. Grasping her around the waist was a Native man who sported an overdeveloped physique not common to their people. *Captured by the Savage,* the title proclaimed in lurid purple.

Kinew noticed her noticing and tossed the book onto the shelf behind him, but he didn't look embarrassed. "My daughter's. I was desperate. It gets pretty quiet out here."

That was her cue. "Sorry to tell you, but your days of peace and quiet have come to an end."

He raised an eyebrow. "Oh?"

"We had some trouble at the Strong Lake campground."

"What kind of trouble?"

He sounded interested, but not concerned. He'd shown more of a reaction when he'd thought she was visiting on behalf of Kevin, whoever he was. Maria supposed he'd had to deal with plenty of drunken exploits at the campsite over the years. He'd have no idea what was coming.

"A triple homicide."

Kinew's face remained impassive. They could have been talking about books.

She tried again. "I'm surprised you didn't hear about it. We've had officers up there since yesterday morning. We've got the campsite completely barricaded."

"I let the conservation officers handle anything to do with the campground."

His attention drifted to the nearest stack of books, and she swore she saw *longing* in his eyes. She was shocked when she realized he was bored. Did he consider a triple homicide 'quiet'?

"I was told the campground is on your land."

For once she had his full attention. It was an unnerving experience, and it took all her willpower not to squirm as he stared her down, his irises going from brown to almost black.

"Conservation. Will. Handle. It," he said, as if speaking to a child.

"We would have involved you from the beginning, had we known the murders occurred on treaty land. Once we received the report, things moved quickly, as I'm sure you can understand. I'm assuming the tribal police will want to participate in the investigation."

He shrugged. "Do what you need to do. If Conservation has a problem, they'll let you know."

Whatever had caught his interest for that fleeting moment was gone. He stared out the window, and Maria suspected he was waiting for her to leave. "Don't you need to know what's happening with the investigation?"

"Nope." Kinew focused on the window with such intensity she had the urge to look too. Then she remembered Jessica McCaffrey and her friends. She could feel rage bubble in her throat like heartburn.

"Well, we could use your help. We'll need to question your people, and it would be most appreciated if you would ask them to be cooperative."

"You're wasting your time. My people don't go up there."

"Not even your youth?" This surprised her. Strong Lake was a beautiful spot with the kind of isolation that was usually a siren song for teens. At least, it *had* been beautiful. Before it had been turned into an abattoir.

"My people don't go up there," he repeated.

"With all due respect, Chief, three people were slaughtered on Strong Lake Band territory. I will need to interview everyone in the community."

He shrugged again. "Suit yourself, but you're wasting your time."

"What if I told you three of your own people had been killed?"

"I'd know you were lying."

Fuming, she contemplated an obstruction of justice charge when he finally faced her again.

"I bet I can guess who ran into a bad end out there. They were young, they were white, and they were from the city."

"And because they're white, they're expendable?" Her temples throbbed and she forced herself to relax her jaw.

Kinew laughed. "Oh, like they think of us? No, I'm not that cold."

"Forgive me for calling you out in your own office, but you seem damn cold to me. If it were my land—"

He held up a hand, cutting her off. "But it's not."

"I would feel a duty, an *obligation*, to assist with this investigation any way I could."

"Forgive me for calling *you* out, but I'm not about to risk my life or the lives of my people for the sake of three dumb kids who were fooling with something they should have left alone."

The hairs on the back of her arms prickled as they stood at attention. "Do you know something I don't, Chief?"

"I'm sure you're aware the campground was closed for the season. Those kids had no business being there."

"Are you saying someone would have felt strongly about their trespassing?"

"I don't know how many times I have to repeat myself, Officer—"

"Detective."

"Fine, Detective. I suspect you are smarter than your questions would suggest. But I've now told you more than once that none of my people so much as stroll past that campground. Not to mention they are not murderers."

"Sometimes people act out of character. Especially if they're angry."

"Not in this case."

She'd never met anyone quite so blasé when confronted with the news of a triple homicide. A triple *unsolved* homicide. "I'm still going to need to interview everyone."

"If you want to waste your time, that's your prerogative." He rose from his chair. "I think we're finished here."

In desperation, she played her ace. "Crazyhorse said you would tell me what happened out there. He said you'd tell me about the history."

With a sigh, Kinew sat back down. "Would you like to go for coffee, Detective? This is going to take a while."

CHAPTER TEN

She was unnerved when Kinew drove past the reserve limits and kept on going. She wasn't proud to admit it, but a little flicker of doubt insisted on sparking dark thoughts in her brain. *You don't know this man. Where is he taking you? You should have brought your own vehicle.*

Pushing her fears aside, Maria concentrated on that horrific vision of the victims. If this man could help her find the killer, it was worth a bit of risk.

If she'd dared to hope the mention of Crazyhorse would open the chief up, those hopes were dashed, but it did spur him to usher her out of his office in a hurry.

"I'll talk to you," he'd said, reluctance lending a certain heaviness to his words, as though it would be a great sacrifice. "But not here."

She'd gladly agreed to leave his shrine to the written word, especially since it appeared to prove such a huge distraction for him. She'd even agreed it would be easiest if he drove, since he knew the way. The cop part of her worried that she was now at the mercy of a man she didn't know, who was mysterious at best and evasive at worst. Not only that, she stupidly hadn't told anyone in the department where she was going, so tracing her whereabouts would be left to a rambling alcoholic whose theories would no doubt be mocked by her colleagues.

The female part of her insisted that no one with that many smile lines could possibly be evil.

And yet, she sighed with relief when Kinew pulled alongside a cluster of clapboard houses and businesses that could only generously be called a town. At least it wasn't some remote corner of the forest.

"You hungry?" He popped the door on his side like the answer was a forgone conclusion.

It was then she realized she hadn't eaten a thing since yesterday morning. A strange, hollow emptiness had contrived to fill her stomach, tricking her body into thinking it was full. "I could eat," she said, trusting it was true as she followed Kinew into a diner with the optimistic name of *Happy's*.

Those expecting to find a cheery place behind the flickering neon sign would be disappointed. Rather than the promised exuberance, Happy's appeared to be a place of despair with its stained, plastic tables, white walls streaked brown from time and water leaks, and world-weary waitresses.

Most of the other patrons didn't bother to acknowledge their presence, in spite of the bell over the door announcing their arrival. They continued to study their food, heads lowered, picking and prodding rather than eating.

It wasn't a ringing endorsement for the cuisine.

The few that did glance over narrowed their eyes as soon as they caught sight of her. While she was used to this – her era was one where even children greeted cops with suspicion instead of a friendly wave – here it made her feel ashamed.

Kinew nodded to someone she guessed was the proprietor, a stocky, grim-faced man who studied her from behind the counter, spatula held out like a weapon. Happy, she presumed?

In that No Man's Land of cracked chairs that listed to one side as if hungover, Kinew managed to find a booth. The vinyl on the seats bled stuffing, but the booth was remarkably comfortable all the same.

Happy's was the kind of establishment where laminated menus, their edges curled, were wedged in between the napkin holder and the salt and pepper shakers, and where the salt was speckled with rice grains that looked like maggots. A waitress trudged over long enough to set two thick, plastic glasses of lukewarm water on the table.

"The usual?" she asked Kinew, ignoring Maria completely.

"Give us a minute," he said. It was not a request.

He handed Maria a menu. "They grind their own chuck here, and the turkey is roasted in-house, so the sandwiches and burgers are good. So is the trout. But stay away from anything fancy. If you order the crab stroganoff, you're flirting with death."

A dimple made a fleeting appearance in his cheek, vanishing from sight so quickly she wondered if she'd seen it at all. *Did Kinew actually make a joke?*

"I'll take that under advisement," she said, amused to see *Entrees* was one of the menu categories, along with *Sandwiches, Nibbles,* and *Sweeties.* They did indeed have crab stroganoff.

The waitress rematerialized the second their attention drifted from the menus. She was attentive, if nothing else. "What can I getcha?" She looked to Kinew initially, of course, but he inclined his head in Maria's direction, forcing the waitress to be polite against her will. She looked as pleased about this as expected.

"The hot turkey sandwich, please." She hadn't thought to ask Kinew how the gravy was, but if they roasted their own turkeys, it should be safe.

"Salad or fries?" The waitress scribbled on a red-lined notepad reminiscent of the one Maria had carried around during her own stint in the hospitality industry. Guess some things didn't change.

She'd started to say salad when Kinew pressed his foot into her calf. Startled, she met his eyes across the table and instantly understood. "Fries, please."

"White, brown, rye, or sourdough?"

"Sourdough."

"And you?"

"The usual. With a Coke. No ice."

Maria usually stuck with water, but lukewarm it held little appeal. "I'll take a Coke too, please."

"You want ice?"

Glancing at Kinew, she detected no further issues, so she nodded. The waitress shuffled off, scribbling.

"The salad isn't great, I take it?"

"This isn't a place where vegetables arrive at the peak of freshness. No one orders the salad here."

"I see. Thanks for the warning."

Kinew tipped his head, which was clearly as emotive as the man was going to get.

"What's the usual?" She was curious, but her curiosity mostly stemmed from the fact that he would come to this place often enough to *have* a usual.

"Plain burger."

Sitting across a table from the chief was proving to be twice as awkward as sitting across a desk from him. Once they'd ordered, the conversation died a predictable death, if one could call Kinew's insights about the menu a conversation.

Since the chief appeared to be more comfortable with silence than she was, rather than 'beating around the bush', as her mother might say, Maria charged right through it.

"Why did you bring me here?"

"You wanted to talk."

"Seems your office was the most likely place for that talk. I suspect you didn't come here for the food."

A glint of amusement touched his eyes before they grew serious again. "I don't believe evil just happens. I believe we invite it in."

"And talking about this crime will invite it in?" She would have laughed at such superstition if she hadn't seen the manner in which Kira and Jessica had died.

"Maybe it will, and maybe it won't, but why take chances? If we're going to bring something into the open, I'd rather it be here."

"I'm sure Happy will appreciate that."

Kinew laughed, which shifted the planes of his face, turning a merely handsome man into a beautiful one. "There is no Happy. There is only Harry, and the grouchy old shit would be thrilled if the place burned to the ground. Then he could collect the insurance money and retire instead of spending his days cooking for people he doesn't like."

Maria checked over her shoulder, but the disgruntled man with the spatula was nowhere to be seen. "I'm surprised he doesn't set fire to it himself." Surely there was enough grease soaked into the walls that it wouldn't take much encouragement to make the place light up like a Roman candle.

"He's no criminal, only a man who knows he's made himself a bed and now has to lie in it, just like the rest of us."

"That's a depressing view of life."

"Not if you have a nice bed." He smiled, and her face grew warm. *Is he flirting with me?*

Thinking of Ben, she returned to the subject at hand. "So who do you think caused what happened at the campground this weekend?"

Kinew shrugged. He did it so often she was beginning to think the gesture was a tic. "No one knows."

Wow, thanks. That's enlightening. She was about to give him shit for wasting her time when the food arrived, and she discovered that in this particular instance, her surly new friend had been right. The sandwich was layered so thick with juicy slices of turkey she couldn't see the bread, and the gravy was pale enough to be the real thing. As the rising steam reached Maria's nose, her stomach growled in anticipation.

Kinew laughed. "Did you hear that?" he asked the waitress. "You can tell Harry that Minnesota's finest appreciates his cooking."

If their server was amused, she managed to hide it. "Need anything else?"

Maria said no, while Kinew ordered milk to go with his meal. When he'd ordered a 'plain burger', he'd meant *plain* – as in no pickles, no cheese, no tomatoes, no mustard, no soggy leaf of lettuce. Not even a desultory squirt of ketchup. There were no sesame seeds on the bun.

To her delight, her gravy was savory, soothing, and tasted of Thanksgiving. The ultimate comfort food. Once Kinew had his milk, she was about to continue grilling him when he shook his head.

"Not now. Not while we're eating. There will be plenty of time when we're finished."

Resigning herself to a silent meal, she was startled when he asked, "How long have you been a cop?"

"Twenty years."

His eyes widened in the manner she'd become accustomed to whenever anyone discovered her age. She took it in her stride, knowing that someday she'd probably miss the reaction. "You must have started when you were a baby."

She smiled. "Almost."

"Do you mind if I ask why?"

"Why, what? Why I became a cop?"

He nodded, and she struggled not to take offense. Often that question was paired with something like, *"You're too pretty to be a cop,"* or *"Isn't that a little violent for you, sweetheart?"* But he'd said neither, and she would give him the benefit of the doubt as long as she could.

"My dad was a cop. Initially, I didn't have any interest in the 'family business', as he called it. I wanted to be a teacher. But when I was halfway through college, someone took him from us." Even though her dad had died years ago, it wasn't easy to talk about. "I figured becoming a police officer was the best way to honor him. As long as a Greyeyes wears the badge, his memory is alive and well."

Maria had high hopes for Heidi. She'd been working on her daughter since the girl was two, dressing her as a cop for Halloween and buying her the Fisher-Price police station, the one where the little cars lit up and had actual sirens. Ben had tried to counteract her influence with a toy guitar and a miniature violin, but Maria suspected he'd accepted he was fighting a losing battle. Police work was in her blood.

"I'm sorry," Kinew said. His voice softened considerably. "Is it okay to ask what happened?"

Tia Montrose. Maria would never forget how the woman had chewed on her quivering lip throughout her trial, how her voice had been stifled for so long that she could barely speak in her own defense. Or how she'd clung to Maria's mother, sobbing, and how her mother had cried with her, forgiving her instantly. It was a little more difficult for Maria.

"It was a domestic. Neighbors reported hearing gunfire, and by the time Dad and his partner arrived, the husband was lying dead in his front yard. The partner wanted to wait for back up, but my dad went inside, and as soon as he walked into the house, a woman shot him."

Though the words were bitter and tasted of bile, Maria made herself say them. "She didn't mean to. She'd had the shit beaten out of her for years, and finally snapped. When she heard my dad come into the house, she'd thought it was her husband, returning to settle the score. She fired before she could see his face. It was a lucky shot, but not for my dad. One bullet to the heart was all it took."

"I'm sorry, Maria."

It had taken her a long while to figure out how to respond to expressions of sympathy. She couldn't say, "It's okay," because it would never be okay.

"Thank you."

They didn't say much for the rest of the meal, the specter of her father looming large between them. When the waitress asked about dessert, Kinew recommended the pie, but Maria shook her head. As a cop, she'd had enough diner pie to last her a lifetime. Not to mention she'd lost her appetite. She settled for coffee.

"Have you heard of the Donner Party?" He had that far-off look again, but this time there wasn't a readily available window to gaze out of.

"Of course." She suspected most Americans were aware of the ill-fated pioneers.

"What about the lost tribe?"

She thought for a moment, even though she could have answered immediately. "Sorry, no. I haven't."

He smiled, but there was no joy in it. "Shows you how important we are to the education system, doesn't it? Thirty-nine white people die, and generations later, we're still mourning the tragedy. Hundreds of our people disappear, and no one hears of it."

Aside from Sitting Bull and Crazy Horse, the most she'd learned of her people's history in school was that they were savages who'd terrorized the settlers with their wild ways. "Dwelling on that stuff will get you nowhere."

"Maybe not, but someone has to remember." Kinew pushed aside his lemon meringue pie after taking two bites. The meringue was weeping, glistening tears dotting its surface. "The so-called lost tribe was a thriving society. It was also a matriarchy. The nation boasted highly successful hunters, farmers, and fishermen. Their land had some valuable mineral deposits, and the people had learned how to mine them. By all accounts, they had a strong government as well."

"And they lived near here?" *How could I have never heard of them?* Maybe she hadn't been taught about them in school, but she did a fair amount of reading and research on her own.

"Right at Strong Lake, where the campground is now." His eyes locked with hers. "A group of settlers heard of their success. They wanted to meet with the people, to learn from them. Only, when they arrived, no one was there. The tribe had vanished."

Maria felt a draft, and wished she'd brought her jacket. "There must have been some sign of what happened to them?"

"None. Everything was gone: their dwellings, their caches of food, the minerals. Gone. The only clue they had ever been there was a few shards of pottery."

"Maybe they had to relocate?" It happened, due to drought, flood, and wildlife leaving the region. It was certainly possible, and in that era, it would have been difficult to leave a message.

"You would hope so. You might even believe it, if it weren't for what happened to those settlers."

Another chill. Even their waitress was keeping her distance, as though she suspected they were discussing something she didn't want to overhear. Maria waited, sipping what was left of her cold coffee, knowing Kinew would continue when he was ready.

"There are several diary entries suggesting the majority of the settlers didn't want to stay in the area, not even for the night. Something spooked them, but I haven't seen any documentation that explains what. It would have been insanity for them to leave. There was no settlement close by, and it wasn't safe to travel at night. So they cut some wood, made a fire, and set up camp as best they could.

"Weeks passed, and the rest of their colony grew resigned to the fact that their brethren had perished somewhere along the journey. Just when they'd convinced themselves they would never see their kin again, a man returned. It was their minister, a fellow by the name of Thomas J. Babbit."

Kinew lowered his voice. "Good ol' Thomas J. was a little the worse for wear. Truth be told, he was barely alive. One of his arms hung by a thread and his face had been mutilated. He was missing his nose and an ear, as I understand it, and his clothes were soaked with blood."

"What on earth happened to him?"

"He babbled about monsters that had torn his fellow settlers apart while they slept, but no one believed him. His people thought he was delirious, and soon after that, he died. Haven't you wondered why Strong Lake isn't a state park?"

The thought had occurred to her. Usually reserve lands were the worst of the worst. The beautiful parks and campgrounds belonged to the government.

"They didn't want it," Kinew continued before she could answer. "And my ancestors didn't want it either. They argued against it. Already there was talk that the land was cursed."

"Were the rest of the settlers ever found?"

"Eventually folks discovered good ol' Thomas J. had been telling the truth about what became of his party, if nothing else. By then, animals had had their way, so there wasn't much left to find, but it was clear something terrible had taken place. Omens and portents were respected back then. A lot of my people still respect them. I challenge you to find one person from our community who is willing to spend the night in that campground."

"Seems like a weird place to designate as a campground, doesn't it? Or did you figure tourists wouldn't care about a few scary stories?"

Kinew pressed his lips together. A muscle twitched in his cheek. "The campground wasn't our idea. We fought it. But apparently, even though it is 'our' land, the government has a say. They liked the idea of 'lessening our dependence' on them." He made quotation marks in the air. "But when they tried to make us wardens, that's where we drew the line."

"That's why Conservation takes care of it."

He nodded. "Yes."

"I'm sorry about what happened to the settlers, and to the lost tribe, assuming they didn't relocate. But those are old stories. I'm not sure I understand why people still talk about them."

Kinew stared at her as if she were insane. "We still talk about them because the killing hasn't stopped."

CHAPTER ELEVEN

"I can't believe you're sleeping. You must have no conscience."

With her arms folded across her chest and her foot tapping with impatience, Jessica was a caricature of a furious woman. Nothing about it was funny, though. Her eyes blazed with rage.

"Of course I have a conscience. I feel terrible about what happened to you, to *all* of you." I could see Kira watching me from behind Jess. *Where is Dan?*

"And yet, you're sleeping like a baby. Thanks for the concern, Reese. Nice of you to feel so terrible. Nice of you to care so much."

I recoiled at the pain in her voice. It sharpened the edge of her words, and she used it to cut me raw. "I didn't fall asleep so much as collapsed. What did you expect me to do? Stay awake forever?"

"You could have had the decency to join us. Especially since this was your fault."

"Yeah, Reese," Kira chimed in. She looked cute as ever, but something was off. The spark in her eyes was no longer mischievous. Now it seemed…*malevolent.* "That's the least you could do."

"What do you mean, it's my fault? I didn't do anything."

Jessica's face twisted in anger. She rushed me. I tried to get away, but there was nowhere to go. No matter how much I sidestepped, there she was again, jabbing her finger against my chest. "*You* chose the campsite, even though it was closed. *You* cut that tree. *You* left us alone to die."

"Hey, I didn't leave you alone. That was your choice."

"It wasn't like I was going to share a tent with you. How would you like it if I'd been making the moves on Dan all night? Would you have wanted to sleep with me?" She rolled her eyes. "Never mind. You'd probably see it as a challenge or something."

"I d-don't know what you're talking about. You were pissed at me before the trip started. That's why you stayed in the tent with Kira."

But I could see from the girls' expressions that I was convincing no one, least of all myself.

"Stop the lies, Reese. I've told her everything. She knows about us," Kira said, smirking.

At that moment I hated her, dead or not. "I don't know what you're on, but there *is* no us. There never was."

"Don't bother. You know how I can tell you're lying? Your lips are moving." Jessica jabbed me in the chest again, and her nail was sharp. A few more times and she'd break the skin.

"Oh, for fuck's sake. I thought she was cute, that's it. It's not like it's cheating to *look.*"

My girlfriend sneered, her face becoming hideous. "Cheating begins in the mind. You were planning to dump me and go after her. *Admit it.*"

Out of all her accusations, this was the one that truly shocked me. They wanted honesty? Fine, they would get honesty. "Fuck no. That bitch would have driven me crazy. I just wanted to ball her."

Mad with fury, the women bared their teeth and lunged at me, more animal than human. Unable to run, I stood my ground, fists raised. I'd never hit a woman before, but it didn't count if they were dead, did it? Froth dripped from Jessica's mouth and I shuddered as she pounced, fangs curving toward her chin.

Fangs?

Before they could reach me, a man stepped between us. He was tall and powerfully built, his shoulders so broad I could no longer see the girls or whatever it was they had become. His bronze skin was covered with tattoos, but other than the body art, his only adornment was a small cloth around his waist. He carried an ornate walking stick, which he brandished at them.

Jessica hissed, but Kira whimpered like a kicked puppy.

When he turned to me, his face was stern. "What are you doing back here? I told you, you are not welcome. Leave and never return, not even in your dreams."

"You! You're the one who talked to me that night," I said, remembering his words more than his voice, which had only been a whisper. Surely I'd remember seeing a man who looked like him. Wouldn't I?

"Smart people only need to be warned once," he said. When I didn't react, he scowled and I felt a stabbing pain in my head. "*Go*. And don't come back. You are not welcome here."

The barrier that had kept me from leaving was gone, and I ran down the gravel path as fast as I could, convinced the girls were chasing me.

I sprinted through the dark until I thought my lungs would burst. Finally I stopped to catch my breath, bent over and gasping.

Something brushed against my arm.

I screamed.

"Hey, take it easy. It's me, Dan."

And it was Dan, his head thankfully reattached. His face was as round and white as the moon, his eyes bulging. "You've got to get me out of here. Take me with you?"

I checked behind him, but no large native man loomed out of the darkness. Neither did those things Jessica and Kira had become. Dan *sounded* normal, even though he looked terrified. Still, I wasn't sure bringing a dead guy with me was the smartest thing to do. What if he turned into a monster too?

"Reese, it's *Dan*. I'm your friend. I'm not going to hurt you." His eyes begged me for compassion, and I could feel myself weakening. He'd always been my favorite of the three. "Are you seriously thinking of leaving me out here? I wouldn't do that to you. You *have* to come get me."

"What do you mean, 'come get you'? I'm already here."

He shook his head. "No, you're not. It feels like you are, because you left us here. You'll keep coming back, night after night, until you get me out."

Did he look a bit crazed now, or was it only the clouds skittering across the moon, casting shadows on his face? I couldn't tell.

"Don't leave me here, Reese. *Please*."

I opened my eyes.

I heard a harsh sound in the darkness and almost cried out before I realized it wasn't the pant of an animal.

It was my own breathing.

Dan needs me.

I had to get to him.

Had I been wrong? I'd been sure Dan was dead. I mean, his blood had been everywhere. It had covered the inside of our tent.

Maybe it wasn't his blood.

I'd seen his head separated from his body. It had rolled over to me and hit me on the leg. But maybe, somehow, the paramedics and doctors had saved him.

Could someone live through that?

I didn't think so, but I wasn't a doctor, so what did I know? I'd just seen him, and he needed my help. That was all I knew, and it was enough.

Fumbling in the dark to get dressed, I pulled on a pair of sweats and a T-shirt that was lying rumpled on the floor. I crept down the hallway to the kitchen, grabbing Mom's keys and a light jacket. The damn cops still had my truck. Getting to the campsite without four-wheel drive was going to be a problem, especially if the gate remained shut. I'd have to walk in.

My hand was on the doorknob when a voice made me pause.

"Where do you think you're going?"

Dad flicked on the light, blinding me.

"Out for a drive. I can't sleep."

"I know you're going for a drive. I can see the keys in your hand. That's not what I asked."

He sat in the living room in his old terrycloth robe, looking like he hadn't slept in years. My father used to be a robust man, but lately, time had caught up with him and then some. An empty highball glass rested beside him on the end table, but I could guess what had been in it – a Black Russian. Dad rarely drank, but when he did, it was always a Black Russian. He thought they helped him sleep.

"Where are you going, son?"

"No particular place. Just going to drive around for a bit, clear my head."

"Why don't we try that again, without the bullshit?"

My mouth went dry. Dad seldom engaged in more than small talk with my brother and me. Mom was the one who did the talking, too much talking. When I'd discussed my family with Jessica, she had laughed at me. "What are you, Goldilocks?" she'd teased. "Everything has to be just right?"

No, not everything. But it would be nice if something were.

Wait, why was I lying to him, anyway? It wasn't like I was a little kid who needed to ask permission. I was a grown man. I could do whatever I wanted. "I thought I'd go to Strong Lake, take a look around."

"That's what I thought. Sit down."

"Dad, I really have to—"

"Sit your ass down and have a drink with your old man."

He shuffled over to the bar cabinet where he kept the liqueur and vodka.

"No thanks, Dad. I don't want anything."

He considered me with a weary eye, and poured us both a drink anyway. Handing a glass to me, he went back to his chair, gesturing to my mother's. "Go ahead, sit down. It's not like what's out there won't keep."

I wasn't sure about that. I thought of Dan, his face drawn and pale with fear. *You have to get me out of here.*

Dad tipped his glass at mine like a toast before slugging back half his drink. I sniffed the concoction and wrinkled my nose. I didn't like coffee liqueur, but how would he know? He didn't know the slightest thing about me.

"Go on. It'll put color in your cheeks."

Feeling shaky after my dream, I figured it couldn't hurt. I tried not to taste the alcohol going down, but the flavor of coffee filled my mouth and started a slow burn in my throat. I coughed.

"Never took you for a lightweight," my dad said, and at that moment I hated him.

"I'm not. I don't like Black Russians."

"No accounting for taste, I guess." He frowned. "Now why in hell would you want to go back to that campsite? That's where your friends died, isn't it?"

Something kept me from telling him about Dan. He'd think I was crazy, and I wouldn't be able to help anyone if I were in an asylum.

"I need to figure out something. I have to go back for a bit."

Dad shook his head like he'd heard nothing so stupid in his life. Sighing, he asked, "Why would you want to do something like that?"

"I can't explain it." *Especially not to you.* "It's what I need to do."

"It's a crime scene, son. Don't you get it? The police won't let you anywhere near it."

Oh. Now I did feel dumb. I hadn't thought of that, but he was probably right. What had once been our campsite was now the center of an investigation. Even if the cops had gone home for the night, there would be crime-scene tape and barricades everywhere. And what if I ended up leaving new evidence behind, like some of my hair or a shoeprint? Things would be even worse for me than Gregory Pompous had predicted.

There was no choice but to risk it, though. I couldn't leave Dan out there.

"I have to go." I rose from the chair, putting distance between the hateful Black Russian and me. I couldn't stand the way it smelled. How he could drink that crap was beyond me. "It may seem stupid to you, but I have to see it again."

I have to make sure Dan's okay. I wanted to say it, but I couldn't. Dad would tell me Dan was dead, that his body wasn't at the campsite anymore, that my vision had been a bad dream, likely brought on by survivor's guilt. It was probably true, but it hadn't felt like a dream. I'd never forgive myself if Dan needed me and I didn't go.

"At least wait until morning." Dad checked his watch. He was one of the few people on the planet who continued to wear one. "That's not far off, only a couple of hours. You can wait a couple of hours, can't you?"

The thought of returning to that campsite at all, let alone in the dark, gave me the creeps. I wanted to help Dan, but if he were really there, he'd be there in a couple of hours, wouldn't he?

"Get your mother to call that lawyer of yours. He should go with you. Otherwise, it'll look suspicious." He drained the rest of his drink and wiped his mouth with the ever-present handkerchief he kept in his robe pocket. "Everyone knows the killer always returns to the scene of the crime."

My body stiffened. I couldn't have been more hurt if he had belted me. "I didn't kill anyone."

Instead of reassuring me, he studied my face. Finally he nodded. "I believe you, son. But you better start telling the truth."

Rage festered inside me until I thought I would scream. "I *am* telling the truth."

"Maybe your lawyer believes that shit. Hell, maybe even your mother does. But I talked to that lady cop. What was her name, Running Waters? She told me those girls were torn apart. Ain't no way you slept through that."

My legs lost their strength at the thought of Jessica and Kira's suffering and I slumped into the recliner again. I hadn't seen Kira that morning, and I was glad I hadn't. Seeing Jessica and Dan had been enough to give me nightmares for the rest of my life.

I'd racked my brain ever since I'd awakened in that tent to find the world as I'd known it had changed. Once I'd gotten over the strangeness of sharing a tent with another guy, it had been kind of fun. Dan had cracked jokes about Dutch ovens and *Brokeback*, and I'd actually been relieved I was bunking with another dude instead of dealing with Jessica and her melodrama. If I'd had any doubt about ending things with her, they'd vanished when she'd decided to spend the night with Kira. My heart ached with guilt when I thought of the speech she would have received if she'd lived.

It's not you; it's me. I'm sensing we want different things. Perhaps I would have thrown in *I hope we can still be friends* for good measure. That would have been a laugh. We had never been friends.

Dan had me giggling like a kid at a slumber party, and it must have been annoying, because one of the women had yelled at us to "Shut the fuck up!" I was pretty sure it had been Jessica.

I wasn't proud of it, but I'd been tempted to keep the party going out of spite. Who were they to kick us out of our tents and then tell us to shut up? What made them think they could control everything?

As always, Dan had been the voice of reason.

"Maybe we should call it a night, huh? Don't want those two to miss out on their beauty sleep."

I snorted. "They could use it. Especially Jess."

"Oh hey, she's not so bad." But from his expression of sympathy, I could tell none of our mutual animosity had gone unnoticed.

"Compared to who? Hitler? Lizzie Borden?"

Dan chuckled. "You guys got on each other's nerves today. You'll feel better tomorrow. Sleep *and* space, that's the key."

He had settled in for the night, fluffing the top of his mummy-style sleeping bag to make a pillow. Thinking about it now, he might as well have been lying in a down-filled coffin. Those bags are impossible to get out of in a hurry.

"I hope you're right."

My own bag was nothing fancy, just two pieces of poly-filled, flannel-lined cotton stitched together, which meant I wore several layers of clothes to bed. Dan could get away with a pair of boxers. When I saw he'd already closed his eyes, I switched off the Maglite, plunging us into darkness. I never got used to how dark it was in the woods, and for a moment, I was tempted to sleep in the truck. But I didn't want Dan to think I was a coward.

"Good night."

"Good night, Reese."

Shutting my eyes, I tried my best not to think about the voice I'd heard. I thought of the girls in the tent by themselves. What if something happened to them because Dan and I weren't there? *Maybe I should have told Jess about it.*

My brain was spinning, and just when I'd thought there was no way I'd ever get to sleep that night, my eyelids got really heavy. The Sandman was dragging me under.

"Reese?"

Dan's whisper jolted me back to consciousness. "Yeah?"

"I wish I knew how to quit you."

We both burst out laughing.

"You all right, Reese?"

I brushed away a tear before my dad could see it and start with that *Real men don't cry* crap. "No, I don't think I am. I get how crazy it sounds, but I swear I didn't hear anything. I just woke up and found them like that."

The last thing I remembered was rearranging my hoodie, which I'd been using as a pillow, so the zipper didn't dig into my face. I must have crashed after that, because the next thing I'd heard had been the rain.

Drip, drip, drip.

No, not rain.

Dan's blood.

Falling from the ceiling.

"Your mother says you told the lawyer someone talked to you that night, tried to scare you off."

You're not welcome here.

I shuddered, snagging the blanket Mom kept on the couch. "If you can call it talking."

"Well, there you go. He has to be the killer."

Actually, I thought whoever it was had been trying to warn me, but I couldn't tell Dad that. I wasn't sure how I knew. It was just a hunch.

CHAPTER TWELVE

Something brushed against her and she cried out, whipping around so fast she nearly toppled her chair.

Ben threw his hands up in surrender. "Don't shoot, Officer."

"Very funny. You scared the shit out of me." Her heart pounded so hard it made her feel dizzy.

"I'm sorry. I didn't mean to." Her husband looked so contrite that she tried not to be angry with him, but it was tough. She hated getting spooked. "I was wondering if you're planning on coming to bed soon."

He waggled his eyebrows at her, and a week ago she probably would have laughed. However, that was then, and this was now.

"It won't be for a few hours yet."

Kinew had been tight-lipped about the modern catastrophes that had befallen the campsite, and she was curious to see what she could find out. It had taken her so long to drive home from her meeting with Kinew that she'd started late.

"A few hours? Honey, it's already midnight."

"Three college students were torn to bits at the campground, Ben. Can you think of a better reason for overtime?"

His response could go one of two ways. Either he'd start in about how there would always be something pulling her away from him and Heidi, or he'd understand. Whichever direction he decided to go would impact how much work she'd get done. After a fight with Ben, she was pretty much useless. Maria dreaded confrontations, which she figured others would find strange, given her line of work.

Without saying anything, her husband gently turned her chair around so she faced the window. He rubbed her shoulders until she moaned, stretching her neck from side to side until the joints popped.

"You're working so hard," he said.

"I really want to solve this one."

"I know."

There weren't many homicides in her county, thank God, and there had never been one like this. Not that she was aware of – the tribal and state police usually investigated crimes on treaty lands. She wasn't sure why this one had been left to her. Because the victims were Caucasian?

"I miss you."

Her husband's attempts to relax her failed with those words. Feeling the tension return to her shoulders, her reply sounded harsher than she'd meant. "Don't start."

"What? I'm being honest. I *do* miss you, and Heidi does too."

His hands sought the tight muscles at the base of her neck, but she pushed them away. "Nice. Thanks for the guilt trip. That's the last thing I needed today."

"I wasn't trying to make you feel guilty. I only wanted to let you know we care about you. If you feel guilty, maybe it's your own conscience nagging you."

She whirled to face him. "What are you talking about?"

"Nothing, other than the fact you were having dinner with another man when you could have been home with us."

"I wasn't 'having dinner' with him. I was interviewing him, remember?" Maria often regaled Ben with funny stories about her day, but perhaps the humor of Kinew's tight pants was more subjective than most. And she never should have told her husband about the 'nice bed' remark. "Don't tell me you're jealous of him."

"Why not? He's spent more time with my wife this week than I have." Ben's face reddened while she gaped at him. Her husband was the most mild-mannered man on the planet. Occasionally he got upset if the job took her away from home too much, but even then, he was always upset *for* her, never at her.

"That's not true. And I only spent as much time as I did because he insisted on stonewalling me. I didn't know we were going to eat until we arrived at the diner."

Seen through her husband's perspective, she wondered if Kinew's reluctance to talk had had a nefarious purpose behind it. "What's really going on, Ben?"

He lowered his eyes, unable to face her. "Those nightmares you've been having. Barb thinks there's something you're not telling me."

Barb. The dreaded sister-in-law. She was older than Ben by five years and absurdly overprotective. Most days Maria cut her a lot of slack because her coddling came from a good place. But sometimes she had no patience for Barb's unerring ability to stir up shit in their marriage, and this was one of those times.

If Barb wasn't feeding Ben crazy ideas, she was asking him for money. She was one of those people who couldn't hold down a job if her life depended on it. Her latest gig had been at a so-called 'wellness' institute whose services included Reiki, phrenology, cupping, Tarot-card readings, and dream analysis.

Ben was smart, but he was also creative, and it didn't take much to get him imagining various worst-case scenarios.

"Barb thinks every police officer in the world is hiding something. Ben, I saw a young woman turned into a *puddle*. Tell me who wouldn't have nightmares after something like that."

Ben grimaced. He was happy to hear about her job, but he couldn't handle the gore. She figured that if he were going to accuse her of infidelity, he deserved everything he got.

"I wish you'd cut her off when she starts going down that road. She always ends up causing problems between us."

She had long suspected Barb was jealous of their relationship. The woman had been divorced three times and was currently single. Maria wished Barb would stick to one of her many dating stories when she phoned. They were infinitely more entertaining.

"So you're not hiding anything?"

"Well, I am, but it's not what you think. And this has nothing to do with your sister's accusations, so don't you dare give her credit."

A ghost of a smile creased her husband's face. "Fair enough. I promise."

And then Maria told him about Kinew's stories of the lost tribe and the slaughtered settlers. Ben's eyes widened.

"Do you think there's some truth to it?"

"What happened to the settlers is definitely true. I verified it with a quick Google search. As for the lost tribe, that will be harder to prove."

"That's certainly disturbing. Please don't take this the wrong way, but what does that have to do with the murders?"

"Kinew says his people believe the campground is cursed,

something to do with what happened to this so-called lost tribe. He says the deaths of the settlers prove it."

"But the settlers could have been killed by bears, or wolves, or some other kind of predator. It's creepy, sure, but that doesn't mean it's supernatural."

"I didn't say it was. I'm telling you what Kinew's people believe," Maria snapped.

Ben recoiled. "No need for hostility."

"You're right, I'm sorry." She hugged him, relieved when he wrapped his arms around her as tight as ever. "This is difficult for me, but I don't mean to take it out on you."

"Apology accepted. I'm sorry for psychoanalyzing you with my crazy sister."

"That's okay. I probably need to be psychoanalyzed."

"Did this guy Kinew have a theory?" His anger forgotten, Ben's words tumbled over each other in his excitement. Now that they were discussing a case, he would do his best to help her figure it out. Everyone liked to play detective.

"From what I can tell, he stands with his people, believes the land is cursed."

Ordinarily she'd never share that with anyone who *wasn't* a dream analyst at a New Age clinic. But since Ben was non-judgmental, she trusted him to keep an open mind.

He didn't let her down.

"Is that what you think?"

"I don't know," she admitted, resting her head against his chest. "It's a strange place. I don't like being there. But is that the place itself or the horrific things that have happened there?"

"I've never heard you entertain any supernatural explanation before."

He stroked her hair, and she felt her lids growing heavier. It would be nice to follow him to bed. The case file would be there in the morning.

"Something's got you riled up," he said.

"That would be Kinew," she admitted. "He claims there have been several deaths at the campsite in the past twenty years, but I haven't been able to find mention of one before this."

"Can I help you look? With two sets of eyes, it'll go a lot faster."

She hugged him tighter. If you needed to find something online,

Ben was your man. He'd been that way since the days of AOL and Webcrawler. If he hadn't set his sights on becoming a music teacher, he could have founded Google. "That would be great, but you should get some sleep. You have school tomorrow."

"If I start to nod off, I'm sure the Zimbowski twins will wake me."

She laughed. The Zimbowski twins had an extraordinary talent with the violin. As Ben had once put it, "I don't understand how they make that instrument sound like cats in heat and air-raid sirens simultaneously. It's a gift."

Before she could protest, Ben took a seat in front of his laptop. "What are we looking for?"

Leaning back in her own chair, Maria smiled. He was right – things were always better with two. "Any news you can find on Strong Lake. If there have been other murders out there, someone must have written about it."

Especially if things were as bad as Kinew had made it seem.

She ordinarily preferred silence while she worked, but in this case, the sound of Ben typing was reassuring. There was something about researching that godforsaken place when she was alone that gave her the shivers. Her husband's companionship was most appreciated.

Understanding her need for quiet, Ben didn't speak. An hour went by, and then two. Maria could barely concentrate on the screen anymore, and her mind wandered.

"This is interesting...."

She jumped. Ben hadn't said anything for so long that she'd almost forgotten he was there. He patted her hand.

"Sorry, didn't mean to scare you. Again."

"It's okay. Whatcha got?"

"Strong Lake Band challenges Minnesota State in land dispute," Ben read aloud.

"That's not a surprise. It seems like there's always a land dispute going on somewhere." Disappointed, she rested her head on the desk, closing her eyes. "This is hopeless. Let's go to bed."

Her husband nudged her. "You don't understand. This dispute wasn't because they *wanted* the land. It was because they didn't."

Her ears perked up. She rolled her chair over to Ben's, scanning the article on his screen. He was right. Kinew's people had tried to hand Strong Lake over to the state, but the state didn't want it.

"It's the oddest thing I've ever seen. If they didn't like the idea of managing a campground, either side could have split the property into waterfront lots and made a fortune." Ben put his arm around her so she could rest her head against his shoulder. Though it was the closest thing they'd had to a lead that night, it hadn't cured her exhaustion. "What do you think it means?"

"Kinew told me conservation officers patrol it. He said his people won't go anywhere near it."

"Because of a curse?" Maria could hear the disbelief in her husband's voice, open minded or not. "I can't believe everyone in the community would go along with something like that. It's not the Dark Ages anymore."

She thought of Kinew, who'd appeared as rational and sensible as anyone else until he'd taken her to a diner because he didn't want their conversation about the campground to 'taint' his office. "I'm not sure, but something has definitely spooked them."

"It looks like you're going to have to pay the chief another visit."

Even as she teased him about sending her into the arms of another man, she knew her husband was right. If there had been other murders at Strong Lake, why hadn't anything been written about them?

This time she didn't refuse her husband's invitation. She gladly followed him to bed.

Unfortunately, they were too tired to do anything more than sleep.

CHAPTER THIRTEEN

At the sound of the engine, her partner groaned. "Don't tell me there's another one."

Straightening from where she'd been crouching near the girls' tent to study the blood spatter, Maria shielded her eyes from the sun. The day was unseasonably hot, which had done nothing to prevent the chills that periodically crept over her spine.

The car wasn't marked, and no police officer drove an Audi – not in this town. "Looks like it."

"Fucking vultures," Jorge said. "Sometimes I wonder about people."

She raised an eyebrow. "Only sometimes?"

It had been a rough day. They'd had to chase three different SUVs full of teenagers and one very determined woman away from the crime scene. News of the murders had hit the media, and the locals were smart enough to read between the lines and figure out where the 'unspecified campground' was. Maria found the disruptions irritating, but they drove Jorge into a state.

"I'll go this time," she offered, but he caught hold of her arm before she could move.

"No, wait. Maybe they'll cross the tape and we can haul their asses in for obstruction," he said, an optimistic gleam in his eyes.

She didn't recognize the man who got out of the driver's seat. He was ludicrously out of place in his three-piece suit. His hair was so blond it was nearly white, and the sharpness of his features was exaggerated like a model's. She disliked him instantly.

"What in the fresh hell is this?" Jorge muttered.

The passenger door of the glossy car opened, and she was shocked to see Reese emerge.

"Hey, isn't that the—?" Jorge asked, but she was already walking to meet them.

Reese couldn't possibly have lost a noticeable amount of weight in the couple of days that had passed since she'd last seen him, but he looked diminished. He scuffed his sneakers through the gravel as he moved, keeping his head down. His hands were stuffed in the pocket of his hoodie, and the hood was up, as if he wanted to hide his face.

As soon as she got a good look at him, any fleeting suspicions that might have lingered vanished. This kid wasn't guilty. This kid was suffering.

"Reese, are you okay?"

She reached out to touch his sleeve but the man he was with stepped between them.

"Officer Greyeyes, I presume?"

"Detective."

"Detective, then." The man stuck out his hand, and although she was loath to take it, she couldn't see any way around it without being rude. He was one of those men who got manicures, she noted.

She'd never trust a man with a manicure.

"Gregory Vincent Prosper, attorney at law." He pressed an embossed business card into her hand, and she was gratified to notice her dirty fingerprints adhere to its surface. She tucked the card into her back pocket, not bothering to acknowledge it. "Mr. Wallace here is my client."

Reese lawyered up?

As if he'd read her mind, Reese lifted his head, an expression of misery on his face. "It was my mom's idea."

"I thought we agreed it would be better if I did the talking, did we not, Mr. Wallace?" the lawyer said.

Reese lowered his eyes. Where was the feisty smartass she'd met the other day? Even after receiving the shock of his life, there was no way *that* kid would have put up with this shit.

"I'm surprised to see you here, Reese. Did you come to talk to me?" If Maria had been a civilian who'd found her friends slaughtered in their sleep, you wouldn't have been able to drag her out here again no matter what you did. Whether fair or not, she blamed the lawyer, which pushed her instinctive dislike closer to revulsion. The possibility Reese would *want* to come out there never occurred to her.

"We have strong reason to believe there may be important evidence here, evidence that will exonerate my client," Prosper broke in before Reese could speak, puffing himself up to full self-importance.

What was this guy up to? And why on earth would Reese's mother hire such an awful man? She could hardly bear to share airspace with him. "Your client isn't under arrest, Mr. Prosper."

"Even so, we think it's prudent to collect this evidence, if you'd be agreeable to letting us through."

She stared at him, aghast at his arrogance. "This is a crime scene. Of course I'm not going to let you through. As a lawyer, you should know that."

Jorge appeared at her side as though summoned. "Is there a problem here?"

"Not yet," she said. "Reese, can I talk to you for a sec?"

Reese lifted his head enough to meet her eyes before glancing at his lawyer.

"Anything you can say to my client you can say to me," Prosper said.

"In that case, I'd rather say nothing." She felt sorry for the kid, but his mom had made a tragic mistake that was going to cost him. As long as he had a lawyer in tow, she wasn't allowed to say anything to him. She'd already crossed a line by asking to talk to him privately.

"It's okay. I want to talk to her alone," Reese said.

Maria expected his lawyer to put up a fuss, but the man merely shrugged. "Whatever," he said, studying his nails. "It's your funeral."

As she led Reese away from the crime scene toward another campsite, she gave Jorge a meaningful look. He tilted his head in response — message received. He would keep a close watch on the lawyer.

Once they'd moved far enough away to have a little privacy, Maria stopped walking. "Okay, what's going on? Why do you have a lawyer?"

"My parents thought it would be best. Since I was the only survivor."

"I guess I can understand that. It's a shame, though. We'd expected to get your cooperation with this investigation. We're working hard to find whoever killed your friends."

Reese looked startled. His mouth hung slack, what Ben called the 'fish out of water' expression when he saw it on his students. "But that hasn't changed. I'll still cooperate."

"Maybe you want to, but in my experience, lawyers don't let their clients talk to the police very often. Even to give statements." She was giving the kid a hard time, but she couldn't help it. She was pissed – if not at Reese, then with his parents. The last thing they needed was a barricade between the investigation and the only living witness.

"He's not going to fuck this up. I won't let him."

Some of Reese's spirit had returned, and she was grateful. As long as he called the shots, they'd be okay. Maria believed he really did want to find out what had happened to his friends. It was hard to imagine the horror of what he'd experienced, waking up in that tent, not having a clue what he was about to discover. "What are you doing here, Reese? What are you looking for?"

Reese's fingers clutched at the cuffs of his hoodie and he pulled the sleeves over his hands. It was a warm day, but he was shivering. She wondered if Reese had always been cold, or if this was a side effect of the trauma he'd gone through.

"Um...remember I told you Dan and I had a beer that night?"

"Yes?"

"Prosper thinks there might have been something in them."

Her expression must have betrayed what she was thinking, because he rushed to explain.

"We were normal one minute, laughing and shooting the shit, and then I just passed out. I don't remember falling asleep. My lawyer thinks maybe we were drugged."

It wasn't a bad theory, save for the fact that beer bottles were nearly impossible to tamper with before they were opened, unless the baddie happened to own a bottle-recapping machine. "Do you remember anything strange about the beer? Did the cap hiss when you twisted it? Was the beer flat?"

Reese toed the dirt with his sneaker, which was getting grimier by the second. "It wasn't flat, but I can't remember if I heard a hiss. The sound of the fire probably covered it if there was. It was pretty loud because the wood was so dry."

"Where did you leave the bottles?" It was a long shot, but this crime was already so strange, who could tell what was relevant and what was not? Maybe the kid's fancy-ass lawyer was on to something.

"We threw them in the fire."

Great. "I'll find them, and as long as the glass isn't shattered, we might be able to get some readings off it. Okay?"

He nodded, still looking like he wanted to sink into the soil and disappear.

"Now why don't you tell me why you're really here?"

She'd anticipated a few protests, or at least an attempt at ignorance, perhaps a few wide-eyed *What do you mean's?* or *I don't know what you're talking about's.* But once again, she'd misjudged him.

"It's going to sound stupid."

"Try me."

"I've been having nightmares." Reese's voice dropped so low it was nearly a whisper. He was also jumpy, as though afraid something was sneaking up behind him. No one could blame him. The kid had balls to come back here; she'd give him credit for that. It had been tough enough for Maria to return and it was her job.

"Nothing stupid about that. You saw something beyond ghastly, something no one should ever have to see. I'd wonder if you *weren't* having nightmares."

The image of the Kira-thing from her own dream came to mind, but she forced it aside. She had a feeling Reese was trying to tell her something important, but what?

"These – they, oh Christ, they're not ordinary nightmares. They're too real."

The kid was shaking all over now. She patted his arm, wishing she could do more to comfort him. "What are they about, Reese?"

He raised his gaze to hers then, and she was troubled to see his eyes were full of tears. "I saw Dan. Dan was alive, and he begged me to come back for him. He needs help."

Her heart twisted. *Poor kid.* "Reese, you know Dan isn't alive," she said as gently as she could. "No one could survive what happened to him."

"I *know.*" Reese swiped at his wet cheeks with his sleeve. "It doesn't make sense. But I couldn't leave him out here. I had to come. I wanted to last night when I woke up, but Dad wouldn't let me. He said it would look bad, like I was guilty. He made me bring Prosper."

"Your dad was probably right." She didn't think Reese was guilty, but even she would have had to wonder if he'd been brave enough to return at night. At the very least, it would have looked strange. "But it's okay you waited, because Dan isn't here."

She began to tell him the bodies had been taken to the morgue, but bit her lip before the words could escape. Telling him would be worse than senseless. It would be cruel.

Reese appeared to understand without her saying the words. "Can I see the tent again? I keep thinking I must have missed something."

Her initial impulse was to say no, to protect the crime scene at all costs. But the techs had finished processing the tent where Dan and Reese had spent the night.

The one that had held Kira's body would take a lot longer.

"Follow me. I can let you look inside, but you can't touch anything or go inside it, okay?"

He nodded, falling in behind her without a word of protest. She hadn't expected one. The forensics people had no choice but to go in there, and even they hadn't wanted to. With the sauna-like effect of the nylon accelerating decomposition, the place stank like a slaughterhouse.

"I'm taking him to see the tent," she told Jorge as they passed. The lawyer was trying to chat with him, but her partner had never been much for small talk. "We'll be right back."

After snapping on a latex glove, she held the tent flap open for Reese so he could look inside. The odor was stronger after another day in the sun, but the kid didn't appear to notice. He certainly didn't react, just stared inside for a few minutes, searching for something he couldn't explain and probably didn't understand. Maria was thankful the tent was such a dark shade of blue. It intensified the sun's warmth, but it also made the blood harder to see. The only place the carnage was obvious was on the mesh window. Brown droplets splashed across the white material like an abstract painting, and she suspected that's what Reese would focus on.

"You weren't hurt during the attack." It was more statement than question. The preliminary results had begun to come in, revealing that all the blood in the tent was Dan's.

"Wait a minute. What's that?"

Moving as carefully as she could, she held the tent's other flap aside. "What do you see?"

"Over there – in the corner. That's not blood."

Among the pools of gore and fluid not yet dried, and thick flakes of the stuff that had, was a small object. At first she didn't see it, since it was a similar shade of reddish brown, but moving the tent flaps had let a little more light in.

She pulled two shoe covers out of her pocket and slipped them on before going inside. The techs had supposedly finished with the tent, but it was always better to be overcautious when working a crime scene. However, she wore the booties mostly out of respect. Breathing through her mouth, she duck-walked to the item so she wouldn't touch the tent's roof with her head. The ceiling was coated with Dan's blood.

Initially, she'd thought the object was a rock. She was careful to grasp it by its edges as she removed it from the muck.

It was an arrowhead, and from what she could tell, a very old one, skillfully chipped from stone.

How in the hell did that get there? There was no way forensics would have missed it. It must have fallen from Dan when his body was removed. Maria felt claustrophobic, and hurried to join Reese on the outside.

"You have good eyes." Sealing the arrowhead into an evidence bag, she lifted it to show him.

Reese held out his hand, and she gave him the bag, watching for his reaction. If he recognized the object, he didn't show it.

"Did Dan mention finding an arrowhead out here?" she asked.

The kid shook his head, turning the bag so the relic glittered in the sun. She was no authority on arrowheads, but her dad had owned a small collection. Maria was pretty sure this one was museum quality.

"Can I have this?"

"Sorry, Reese. It's evidence."

Reese gave her a skeptical look. "Don't tell me you think this was the murder weapon."

"Well, no, but it could be a clue to our killer. Maybe he's a collector of some sort, or an archaeologist."

She didn't really believe the murderer could be an archeologist. In her experience, scientists were a quiet, cerebral bunch, not the type who would go for this kind of bloodbath. The only sadistic archeologists she'd encountered were in *Indiana Jones* movies.

"When you've finished the investigation, I'd like to have it."

"Okay, I'll see what I can do. Can I ask why?"

Reese returned the bag. "I'd like something. Some...*reminder*, I guess. You know, something to remember Dan by."

"Do you think this was his?" She made a mental note to show the arrowhead to Dan's family.

"If it was, he didn't mention it. Maybe he found it here but didn't want to get guilted into giving it up." Reese's lips curved in the faintest smile. "I think he would have liked it, though. The guy loved his tools."

"I'll ask his family to consider letting you have it, assuming we don't need to keep it. If it weren't for you, we'd never have found it. Not until we moved the tent."

Everyone dealt with grief in different ways, but Dan's family had been the most inconsolable. His mother had started screaming and hadn't quit until someone gave her a tranquilizer.

"Ms. Greyeyes...sorry, *Detective*. I've been meaning to ask you something."

"Go ahead."

"Why did you tell Jessica's parents I was going to break up with her? Now they think I killed her." His voice wavered.

Shit. "I'm sorry, Reese, but I never told them anything of the kind." Jessica's parents had been difficult. They were obviously grieving, and it was hard enough to deal with the death of a child without having to cooperate with an investigation, but their level of hostility had surprised everyone in the department. "Did they name me specifically?"

"No. They said the cops, and I figured it was you. I never talked to anyone else."

"I'll speak to my team this evening. I apologize. That is not appropriate, and it never should have happened."

She could imagine her boss bellowing at her, demanding to know what in the fresh hell she thought she was doing. Cops were never supposed to apologize to civilians. It made them liable, as he'd told her again and again, but fuck it. Cops were also human, and in this case, they were at fault. "Would you like me to speak to the McCaffreys?"

This time his smile looked more genuine. "Nah. I don't think they liked me much to start with."

"From what I can see, you're not missing out." As soon as the words escaped, she longed to take them back. "I'm sorry, I should not have said that."

These people had lost their daughter in the most atrocious, brutal manner, and she'd just insulted them? *What on earth is* wrong *with me?* She really needed to get more sleep.

Reese shrugged. "That's okay. If it makes you feel better, it's not just you. They've always been…challenging. Jess was like that too."

Maria shifted her weight, fidgeting. Criticizing Jess's parents was bad enough, but she wasn't about to speak ill of a murder victim. Especially not to the guy who had planned to break up with her while scoping out her friend. Reese hadn't admitted to any involvement with Kira, and the girl's family certainly hadn't been aware of any — they didn't even know who he was — but the truth had been written on his face that morning. She'd seen it. Something had shifted in his eyes when he'd said her name. "Did you get what you needed?" she asked, hoping it was sufficient enough to change the subject. "We're probably going to take the tent down this afternoon."

"Yeah, I think I'm good." But he choked on the last word.

She rested a hand on his shoulder. "Dan isn't here, in body or in spirit. You understand that, right?"

"I guess."

She could tell he didn't believe her, but she didn't know what else to do. It wasn't like she could channel Dan's spirit and get him to weigh in. "You've been through a massive trauma, Reese. Do you want to talk to somebody? I know a good pers—"

He cut her off. "No thanks. I'll be okay, really. I have nothing to complain about. I mean, out of the four of us, I'm the luckiest, right?"

"I'm not so sure about that." She loved her life, but given the choice between oblivion and finding her friends massacred, she knew which one she'd choose.

Tears spilled over Reese's cheeks, and this time he didn't bother brushing them away. It was a start.

"You should go home, and I don't want to hear that you came back here, okay? It's not healthy."

"Okay, Mom." But he smiled in spite of his tears.

"If you need something, call me. I gave you my card."

"Or I guess I could always talk to my *lawyer*." The way he said the word left no doubt how he felt toward Prosper.

"Better you than me."

Without warning, Reese wrapped her in a bear hug. Startled, she hugged him back. When he released her, his eyes were red and swollen.

"You take care of yourself, Reese."

"I'll try, Detective."

She couldn't say for certain who was happiest to see them return, Reese's lawyer or her partner, but it was a close contest. Once Mr. Fancy Pants had bundled his client into the Audi and backed out of the campsite, she showed Jorge the arrowhead.

"Where'd you find that?" Yanking the bag from her, he held it up to the light for a better look.

"In the tent." She gestured to Dan's so he would have no doubt which tent she was referring to.

"But that's impossible. We went over that tent with a fine-tooth comb for hours. Forensics took samples from every square inch. Where was it?"

"In the southwest corner. Reese found it."

Her partner raised an eyebrow. "Are you sure he didn't plant it?"

"Of course I'm sure. Why on earth would he plant an arrowhead? What good would it do him? Actually, he wants to keep it once we're finished with it."

Jorge ran his fingers over the surface of the arrowhead, tracing it through the plastic. "This is well made. Probably the finest one I've seen." He handed it back to her. "Just watch yourself, Maria. I don't trust that kid."

CHAPTER FOURTEEN

"What's this?"

Maria turned from the stove, where she was making pancakes with Heidi. Since she was home for dinner for a change, she'd left the menu up to her daughter, but she didn't think Ben would mind. Who didn't love pancakes for dinner?

Her husband held up the plastic evidence bag, his nose crinkled in distaste. The interior of the bag was littered with flakes of dried blood. Dan's blood.

"Oh shit. I meant to drop that off at the station." The lack of sleep had clearly made her senile.

Hearing a gasp from her daughter, she tensed, but Heidi only stared at her with those big, dark eyes that were so much like her own. "You said a bad word, Mom."

Relieved, Maria exhaled with a sigh, feeling her body go limp. She hugged the girl close for a moment, stroking her fine, black hair. Someday soon, Heidi wouldn't want to be held anymore. She was already getting so big. "Sorry, baby. It won't happen again. Mom's tired."

Now it was Heidi who crinkled her nose. "I'm not a baby. I'm *eight*."

"It's a term of endearment, sport," Ben said, setting the plastic bag with the arrowhead on top of the fridge after giving Maria a look of warning. Her job was something you didn't bring home. "I call Mom 'baby' all the time, and she's even older than eight, if you can believe it."

Maria swatted her husband with the nearest dishtowel. He was a year younger, and he never let her forget it.

"You guys are laughing at me." Their daughter's lower lip protruded, and Maria braced herself for a possible tantrum.

"Not laughing at you, laughing with you. It's a fine distinction," Ben said, picking Heidi up and tickling her with his beard until she squealed. Crisis averted. Although her husband drove her crazy sometimes, there were other times – like now – when she loved him to distraction. When it came to their daughter, he hit all the right notes, while she often felt out of tune. Ben said the two of them were too alike to get along, and maybe he was right. Still, shouldn't that mean they understood each other more, not less?

"Now do you want blueberries in those pancakes, or chocolate chips?" He used his most boisterous voice, the one he tended to reserve for firing up his students or distracting their daughter.

"Blueberries," Heidi shrieked, showing off the gap where her front teeth should have been. The Tooth Fairy had done a brisk business at their house this week. Maria's husband looked so crestfallen that she laughed.

"Don't worry," she told him. "You can still have chocolate chips in yours."

Later that evening, she apologized.

"I don't understand what's gotten into me. I thought I'd dropped it off, honestly. You know I don't normally bring that stuff home."

Ben rubbed her back, which made her want to purr along with the silver tabby on her lap. They were sacked out on the couch again.

"It's okay. I just didn't want the girl to get her hands on it. And you know she would have."

Much like her hair, eyes, and copper skin, Heidi had inherited her curiosity from her mother. After each new disaster, Maria could almost hear her own mother saying, *"Payback time!"*

She shuddered at the image of her daughter trotting into the living room holding the arrowhead, her fingers stained with Dan's dried blood. "What's this, Mom?" Or, even worse, she might have managed to stab herself with it. (The klutziness she had inherited from her father.) "Good catch. Thank God someone is getting enough sleep for both of us."

"Mmm-hmm." Ben's eyes were already half closed. She envied him – she still had a ton of paperwork to catch up on. "That was from the triple homicide?"

"What else? Weirdest thing too. Reese came to the campground today and he was the one who found it. In one of the tents, the same one our techs had spent hours going over."

"Reese?" Her husband straightened, no longer looking sleepy. "Isn't he the—"

"The survivor, yeah. Why? What does that matter?"

"You're the professional dick, honey. I'm a rank amateur, but—"

"Ha ha."

"—isn't it possible he could have planted it in the tent himself?"

Her eyes widened. "What is it with you guys? Jorge said the same thing."

"Yeah, well, Jorge is a smart man. How else could your techs have missed it? They're trained to find a single hair in a shag carpet. I'm sure they could find an arrowhead in a tent."

"I don't know. I assumed it fell off the body when the coroner took Dan to the morgue." She frowned. "Why would Reese plant it? How could it possibly benefit him?"

"Maybe that's not Dan's blood on it. Maybe it's someone else's. Some foreign DNA to lead you guys on a goose chase."

"That doesn't make sense. Reese isn't even a suspect. Besides, he didn't go inside the tent – I did. He only pointed it out."

Ben stroked his beard like he always did when he was deep in thought or wanted to appear that way. It was the same fiery shade as his hair. "Could he have thrown it in the tent?"

She considered the possibility for a minute before shaking her head. "I don't think so. I kept a pretty good watch on him."

"So what were his reasons for revisiting the crime scene? Please don't tell me he wanted his tent back."

Maria swatted his leg. "Don't be silly. No, he's been having nightmares."

"Ah, I see." Ben cocked an eyebrow. "A guilty conscience, I presume."

The subject had rapidly lost its appeal. "Maybe *you* should be Jorge's partner. You two certainly think alike. I don't feel Reese did anything wrong."

He squeezed her foot. "I hope you're right, honey; I really do. But I have to wonder about a guy who slept through three brutal murders, one of which happened right beside him. You have to wonder about a guy like that."

★   ★   ★

The snow had hardened into a crisp crust overnight, and Lone Wolf moved across it without breaking through. His footsteps vanished with the wind.

"Are you the shaman of this tribe?" His voice thundered across the camp and everyone stiffened in fear, from the women who were beating dried berries with meat and fat for pemmican, to the men who sharpened their weapons as they sat around the fire.

Lone Wolf's question was not for them, and neither was his anger, which gave them some comfort. But they feared for their chief.

"I am not. I am chief of this tribe. The title of shaman goes to you." Chief White Fox lowered his head in deference, even though he was the chief. His people understood he was their leader in name only. Lone Wolf had the ear of the Creator, so he must be obeyed in all things.

Crack!

The women gasped as Lone Wolf's hand shot out, striking Chief White Fox across the cheek. The smaller man fell to his knees, his face blooming red in his humiliation.

"Then why do you disobey me? I gave you a direct order, which you ignored. You are putting our people in danger with your foolish actions. You will be the death of us."

Chief White Fox cowered on the snow, holding up his arms to deflect a second blow. "They...they were starving. I did not have the heart to turn them away."

"They are not our brothers. If *our* children were going without, do you think they would inconvenience themselves for a second to come to our aid? They would *NOT*."

Although he was smaller and the powerful shaman terrified him, White Fox was still a chief. He picked himself off the ground and brushed the snow from his furs. "The same Creator made us all. I will not let them starve in our shadow."

The tall shaman stared at the chief, narrowing his eyes until they were slits. Finally, he spat at the leader's feet. "Then you will die."

He turned on his heel and stalked over the snow the same way he had come. Within minutes, he was gone. Everyone in the settlement began to talk, men and women, young and old alike.

The chief jumped at a soft touch at his elbow. He looked into the eyes of Little Dove, his third wife. "You shouldn't have angered him," she said, her voice as youthful as a child's. "The people are afraid."

"He is wrong, and he needs to be told so. We've let him have his way for too long." The chief looked over to where his men huddled by the fire. *How had everything gone so wrong?* The shaman was supposed to heal them, protect them, chase the drought and bring forth the harvest. Instead, he had turned into a tyrant.

"How can the Creator be wrong?" The confusion was too much for Little Dove, whose face scrunched up as if she might cry. She was still so young.

"Perhaps he doesn't speak through Lone Wolf," White Fox said. "Perhaps he speaks through me."

His words inspired another flurry of whispered conversation.

It was a bold pronouncement, but his people didn't believe any of it. Not for a second.

*   *   *

Maria's mouth tasted horrible. As she raised her head, she realized she'd fallen asleep at her desk – *again*. Before she'd followed her father into the family business, she wouldn't have thought it possible. When she was a child, and especially a teenager, she'd loved sleep. Without her ten hours, she'd been a miserable crank. Now she was lucky if she got five.

Something pinched her face, and she pulled off the Post-it note that had adhered to her cheek. The ink had smeared to a barely legible scribble. It would have been funny if it weren't so depressing. Another wild and crazy Friday night for Maria Greyeyes.

She vaguely remembered the dream. It had been winter, and there had been something frightening. Some kind of threat? She rubbed her forehead, but it was no use. Nothing was going to straighten out the mess in there but twelve to fourteen hours of uninterrupted sleep.

When she pushed away from her desk, something crawled across her chest. A small cry escaped her lips as she swatted at it, swinging her arms around like hornets pursued her. Then she caught sight of her hands. Her fingers were covered with blood.

A late-season mosquito? But mosquitoes didn't crawl; they bit. She hurried to the bathroom, holding out her bloody hands, terrified at what she would see in the mirror. The insect moved against her breastbone. It took every inch of willpower she had not to swat at it again, but if she touched its hard, loathsome body, she *would* scream. And neither her husband nor her daughter would be happy about having their beauty sleep disturbed.

She switched on the bathroom light, but its warm glow hardly comforted. Easing the door shut – the better to muffle her shouts and prevent whatever the heck it was from escaping into the rest of the house – she faced the mirror with her eyes squeezed shut. Slowly, she opened them in increments, like a kid watching a scary movie.

When she finally got a good look at the intruder, her eyes flew open. She blinked hard, unable to believe what she saw.

And then she blinked hard again.

The arrowhead hung from her neck on a rawhide cord. Its tip glistened as if it were wet. She ripped some toilet paper from the roll and wrapped it around her hand as a makeshift glove, the word *EVIDENCE* blazing through her brain, not that it mattered anymore. If there had been any fingerprints on it, surely they were already compromised.

The macabre pendant had a sharp smell, like damp river rock and old pennies. The glistening hadn't been an illusion – the arrowhead *was* wet. No longer covered in dry, flaking blood, it was instead coated in fresh.

As she stared in horror, a perfect drop formed at the point of the arrowhead and then plummeted, splashing against the sink.

CHAPTER FIFTEEN

When the alarm I'd optimistically set went off for the third time, I almost threw it against the wall. It would be great to have one of those clocks you *could* throw — those ones shaped like baseballs, for instance. Instead, it was an old thing of my mother's (an *antique*, as the woman never failed to remind me), and if I did what I very much wanted to do, it wouldn't bounce. It would shatter.

Too bad I hadn't asked her how to turn it off.

Burying it under a stack of pillows, I yanked the duvet over my head. Ever since I'd had that nightmare about Dan, I'd been exhausted. It didn't seem to matter how much sleep I got. Nothing was ever enough.

On the night table, my phone buzzed. *Shit.* Before I could answer, the alarm started again. This time I shoved it between the mattress and the wall, but it fell through the gap and smashed against the hardwood with a fatalistic clanging. *Whoops.* Oh well. I'd just have to buy Mom a new one.

"'Lo?"

There was silence on the other end, and for a moment I thought it was the delay before a telemarketer came on the line. I nearly hung up…and then I heard breathing.

"You disgust me."

If the caller had been speaking a foreign language, I would have understood the gist of what she'd said. Revulsion dripped from every word.

"Mom?" I asked, angling for a laugh if nothing else, but this chick was too far gone for that.

"Asshole," the girl said, and hung up.

I shut the phone off before tossing it on the pillows, just in case the sweetheart wanted to make a follow-up call.

What was that about? I stared at the ceiling, following the brown water stains with my eyes. It was pebbly with popcorn stucco, the kind that rained down on your head in a light mist if something tapped it. My parents were the only people I knew who still had ceilings like that.

Maybe I should have thrown the alarm clock up there, convinced them to spring for an upgrade.

For one heart-splitting moment, I'd thought it was Jess on the phone, giving me grief about one transgression or another. And then I'd remembered.

Jess was never going to give me shit about anything again.

If someone had asked me a few days ago if that would bother me, I would have laughed in their face.

I knew better now.

"What are you going to do?"

I grazed my lip against her lower abdomen, knowing full well it drove her crazy. Peering at her through my beer haze, I winked. "Wouldn't you like to know?"

She shot out her foot, catching me in the gut.

"Oof!" I immediately felt something not very pleasant churn to the surface. "Don't do that again. Unless you want to wear everything I've consumed during the last twenty-four hours."

Ordinarily she'd make a face at a remark like that and call me revolting. But not this time. My shoulders slumped as I recognized her expression. Jessica wanted to be 'serious'. I couldn't understand why she set such stock in being serious. It was really only worrying with a different name, and it wasn't like it accomplished anything.

In contrast, if we'd followed *my* plan for the evening, we both would have had orgasms. There was no question which option I would have chosen.

She propped herself on her elbows, the better to dissect me with her eyes. I touched my tongue to her smooth skin again, attempting to rush my way down to the sweet spot before she could stop me, but she threw her legs sharply to the right, practically breaking my neck in the process.

"Ow! What's with the violence?" I rubbed my neck while glaring at her.

"I was trying to get your attention," she said, yanking down her skirt while she lifted herself into a sitting position. It wasn't an easy move to pull off with grace, but she managed it. "You weren't listening to me."

"I was listening. I just wasn't in the mood for talking."

"Don't you think we should discuss our future?"

I groaned, letting myself fall over on the bed. If I hadn't already lost my erection, that would have done it.

"Be serious." She gave me a playful shove. Well, to the outside observer it would have appeared playful, but Jessica wasn't the play-wrestling type. She tended to use aggression to send a message, and I got her message loud and clear. "I want to know what your plans are."

Rolling over, I buried my face in her pillow. It smelled like a cupcake. Her entire fucking apartment smelled like vanilla – girl must have bathed in it. "Give me a break, Jess. We graduated two minutes ago."

"It's been two weeks. Then it will be a month, and then it will be a year. Can we please talk about this for a second, like adults?"

'Like adults' was one of her favorite expressions, along with 'be serious'.

"I don't feel like adulting right now."

The guys had invited me over to watch the game, and I'd let my dick convince me otherwise. Now I greatly regretted that decision. When had Jess quit being fun?

She folded her arms across her chest. "So you don't see a future for us." Her casual tone was cultivated, but I could hear the hurt woven through the things she didn't say.

"That's not true." I reached for her hand, but she pulled away from me, getting up from the bed and smoothing her skirt. "What is your problem? Why are you letting yourself get worked up? I thought we were going to have some fun."

That was clearly the wrong thing to say, as Jessica's eyes snapped sparks at me. "That's all I am to you, isn't it? Some kind of good-time girl."

"What? What the fuck are you talking about? What did I do wrong?"

She ran a brush through her pale blonde hair and applied a fresh coat of strawberry-colored lip something-or-other, which I was sure would taste like vanilla. "You didn't answer my question. That's what you did wrong."

"Fine. *Fine*. Ask me whatever you want, and I'll answer." I wished she wouldn't ask so many questions about our future. We'd only recently started dating. How was I supposed to know how I felt this soon?

Problem was, I *did* know. I just didn't want to admit it to her – or to myself.

"What are your plans? What do you want to do next?"

This again. "I thought I'd told you. I'm thinking of going to business school, getting my MBA."

She leaned against her dresser, facing me, and I was relieved to see the angry light had left her eyes. "Yeah, that's step one, Reese, but what's after that? What do you want to do with your MBA?"

"I'm not sure. Start some kind of business, I guess."

"You want to be an entrepreneur?"

I shrugged. To be honest, I hadn't thought about this stuff yet, but an MBA would open up a lot of options, and that was appealing. Getting my BSc had been difficult enough. Did I *need* another plan already?

"Are you planning to go to business school here?"

"Um…." Everything I'd read recommended doing your MBA at a different school from where you'd gotten your bachelor's degree. There were some great business schools out there, and whenever I *did* think about this stuff, which wasn't often – not yet – they seemed like good enough places to be. "I'm not sure."

"Aren't you going to ask about me and what I want to do?"

I started to shrug again, but caught myself before she saw it. "Sure, I just haven't had a chance yet."

"You don't give a shit, do you?"

Ah, crap. She had seen it.

Her face turned a dark and ugly color. "The only thing you care about is what's between my legs. What's between my ears doesn't matter."

Neither location was giving me a lot of joy right then, but I certainly wasn't going to tell her that. "You know that isn't true, Jess. It's just – we've talked about your plans a lot already. I feel like I know exactly what you're going to do. You're set."

Hopefully she did something about her temper before she got her degree and started teaching little kids. Otherwise, she was going to destroy a whole lot of childhoods.

"Are you telling me the truth? Because I feel like every time I try to talk to you about our future, you check out."

There was no point trying to keep the peace anymore, so I decided to be honest. At least then I could use this conversation as a chance to improve things between us. "Maybe that's because I don't like being criticized."

"What are you talking about? I don't *criticize* you."

Dumbfounded, I was at a loss for words. I'm sure my jaw dropped. "Jess, you're the most critical person I've ever met. You criticize everything, including me."

She rolled her eyes at me before turning back to her mirror. "You're too sensitive."

"Yeah, that's what people usually say when the object of their criticism has a problem with it. You haven't let up about this college stuff for months. Nagging me about it isn't going to make me give you the answer you want."

Jess winced as if I'd hit her. The truth was, *she* was the more sensitive out of the two of us. She didn't realize I'd figured that out. "I wasn't nagging you. I was trying to get you to think about it."

"Which, when repeated over and over again, constitutes nagging." Giving up on the idea of the evening going anywhere good, I got out of her bed and tugged on my jeans. I didn't miss that her gaze strayed to my crotch, but instead of turning me on, it pissed me off. "I don't understand where your head is at these days. We've been fooling around for what – two, three months? And it sounds like you have our whole lives mapped out for us, down to the two-point-five kids and the white picket fence."

"Don't flatter yourself." Her lip curled into a sneer.

"Then why do you care what I do after graduation? Why do you care if I get an MBA or try out for the NBA? What does it matter?"

"Maybe I wanted to know if there was any potential here, okay?" Her voice rose in volume. I hoped her roommate wasn't home. "Maybe some of us don't want to waste our time."

"We've been having a great time, and now you're telling me it doesn't amount to anything if it doesn't result in a ring on your finger?" I was incredulous. I'd heard about girls who were desperate to get married, but Jess had never struck me like the type. Besides, she barely knew me. How could she consider the prospect of a future together so soon?

"I don't think we're on the same page, Reese."

"No, we're definitely not." Grabbing my phone from her night table, I checked it before turning it off and shoving it in my back pocket. "Look, it's past midnight. I'm going home to get some rest. We can talk about this on the drive over tomorrow if you want."

"In front of Kira and Dan? Yeah, that's a great idea. I'm sure that fits into their idea of a fun weekend."

Shit. I'd forgotten I was supposed to pick them up too, but I wasn't about to admit it. "I meant on the drive to get them. Dan lives across the city."

"Oh, so you're willing to give our relationship a whole fifteen minutes of discussion? That's big of you."

My jaw tightened. I had to get out of there or it was going to get ugly. "Nothing I say is going to make you happy tonight, so I'm going to go, okay? We can talk about it on the way or not talk about it. It's up to you."

Jessica snatched a textbook from her dresser and flopped down on the bed, using the book's cover to block me from view. "I assume you can show yourself out."

"With pleasure." I slammed the door behind me.

And that was the charming kickoff to our first and last camping trip.

Since we hadn't dated long, I didn't have any proper photos of Jess, just some crappy shots I'd taken with my phone. But anything was better than picturing how I'd last seen her.

Scrolling through the images, I slowed when I got to the ones from the beginning of our relationship, if you could call what we'd had a relationship. She'd been softer then, almost beautiful. She'd been too smart to let me take any nudies, or to send me so much as a risqué selfie, but now I was glad for it. It was ironic that only now, after her death, I was able to feel romantic about her.

I'd taken my favorite photo of her at a folk music festival. She held a straw cowboy hat on her head while looking at me over her shoulder, laughing. The sun lit up her hair and face, turning her into some kind of bohemian-cowgirl goddess.

Someone had killed her. Not only killed her, but *tortured* her. I knew from experience that Jess could be harsh. She'd made more than her fair share of enemies. It wasn't unusual for us to bump into someone Jess wanted to avoid whenever we left campus, and there were quite a few on campus too. What if what happened to us hadn't been random? What if Jess had finally crossed the line with someone crazy enough to want to hurt her?

But that didn't make sense. Why would someone set on killing Jessica murder Dan and Kira too? If it were a matter of eliminating witnesses, that didn't explain why I was still alive.

Whoever had slaughtered my friends hadn't done it out of necessity. There was too much overkill for that. Whoever had murdered them had *liked* it.

"Who was he, Jess?" I whispered to her smiling face. "Was it someone you knew? What on earth did you do to him?"

The answer was a loud knock on my bedroom door. "Reese, are you awake?"

Dad. I was surprised. Usually Mom was the one who took it upon herself to drag me out of bed. "Yeah. I'll be out in a minute."

"I think you better get out here now, son. There's something you have to see."

I'd fallen asleep in the same clothes I'd worn yesterday – good enough. Smoothing my increasingly shaggy hair, I left the bedroom and went to the kitchen, where I figured my parents would be waiting.

It was empty.

"Dad?" My voice echoed through the kitchen.

"We're in the great room. Hurry."

I could hear a bunch of people talking, but I assumed my parents had the TV on. Mom was on her cell, her eyes wide and frightened. When she saw me, she covered the receiver and said, "I've already called Mr. Prosper. He's on his way."

"Wha—why? What's going on?"

Dad peered through the curtains, which were drawn for some reason. The television was off, the steady hum of strangers' voices coming from outside.

"Who's in the yard?"

"Show him, Eloise. He needs to know."

Mom handed me a newspaper. I was startled to see my own face on the front.

Real-life horror story, the headline screamed. *Survivor or killer?*

Police expected to make arrest today in triple-homicide case.

"This is crazy. Detective Greyeyes told me I wasn't a suspect. How can they print this? And how can they use this photo?"

I recognized it right away. It had been taken at a barbecue that summer. I had a beer in one hand, and my arm was slung around a buddy's shoulder. I'd cropped it to use as my Facebook profile picture. The bastards had lifted it from my own Facebook page.

"Vultures," Dad said. He couldn't stop staring out the window, and now I was pretty sure who was out there. More reporters, determined to get their own scoop of the day. Well, I had a quote for them. It was a short one too. "That's what they are. A bunch of blood-thirsty vultures."

Pounding at the back door cut his rant short. Before we could debate whether or not to answer it, a loud male voice slashed through the murmur of the reporters.

"Police. Open up."

CHAPTER SIXTEEN

Kinew appeared as happy to see Maria as she was to see him. His receptionist hadn't bothered to summon him this time. She'd gestured to the hallway behind her, saying, "You know the way."

The man was reading, his boots propped on his desk. He didn't hide his disappointment when he saw her, making a big show of how much effort it took to put his book aside.

"You lied to me."

"I told you I didn't want to discuss this in my office, Detective."

"Tell me, what is it? Some long-running gag, a silly story to tell the outsiders so you can see how far they'll run with it?"

"I don't know what you're talking about, but if you don't change your tone, I'll have to ask you to leave. This has always been a place of peace, and I'd like to keep it that way."

"If you value your peace, don't lie to a police officer. That's the most valuable piece of advice I can give you." She was determined to remain calm, but the insolent disrespect emanating from the man made that impossible. Even now, his attention strayed longingly to his books.

"If it's too difficult for you to focus here, I'd be happy to take you to my office, Chief. I'm positive you'll find my décor less of a distraction."

Kinew raised an eyebrow at her. "Am I under arrest, Detective?"

Maria moved a stack of books to the floor so she could sit down. "No, you're not under arrest. But I can't understand why you told me those tall tales. I'm a detective, not a child, and it's in your best interest that I catch the guy who did this."

He steepled his fingers together, resting his chin on them as he studied her. "Why do you think it was a man?"

"Men are typically the perpetrators of sex crimes of this nature, not to mention the immense strength it would have taken—"

"You misunderstand me. Perhaps what I should have asked was why you think the one you are seeking is human."

She snorted. "Please don't tell me you're going to start crying curse again. Next you'll be claiming the boogeyman did it."

To his credit, Kinew looked confused, a slight frown creasing his forehead. "Not a boogeyman, no."

"I believed you. I did my research, okay? I couldn't find a single report of a suspicious death at Strong Lake. Hell, I couldn't find a report of *any* death at Strong Lake...until now."

"I never told you there had been deaths at Strong Lake, Detective."

"But you told me, 'The killing never stopped.'" She stared at him. Was he going to deny it? Did he think she'd forgotten?

He exhaled loudly. "Once again, you misunderstood me. It is not what happens *at* the campground that concerns my people, but what happens after."

"What are you talking about?"

Kinew rolled his chair to a small filing cabinet that crouched in the corner by his desk. She hadn't noticed it before, since, like every other surface in his office, it was covered with books. "This time I will save you some trouble, Detective." He retrieved a fat manila folder and handed it to her. "As you will see, I have done your research for you."

Flipping through it, she found dozens upon dozens of newspaper clippings. Strangers smiled back at her, their faces transcribed into black-and-white dots. Most of them were heartbreakingly young. Teenagers, with maybe a few in their early twenties like McCaffrey and her friends. Several of the stories were about families with young children and Maria thought of Heidi. She closed the folder, put it back on his desk and pushed it toward him.

"These are stories of car accidents."

He nodded once, the grimace returning to his face. "Some, yes. Some are stories of aneurysms and heart attacks in otherwise healthy people. Then there are home invasions that turned violent and an inexplicable amount of suicides." Kinew tapped the folder with an index finger. "Those ones are in my notes, as the papers don't find self-inflicted death newsworthy."

"You're telling me all of these people stayed at the campground?"

"Right before they died, yes. Most didn't make it twenty-four hours."

In spite of her skepticism, he was getting to her. "How do you know they stayed at Strong Lake?"

Kinew rose from his chair, displaying another pair of obscenely tight jeans. He strode to one of his many bookcases, hauling down at least ten thick, leather-bound ledgers the size of briefcases. "We track it. Everyone who stays at Strong Lake is required to give us their name, address, phone number, and driver's license. This is then checked against the ID they present when they pay for their campsite."

Slapping the ledgers down in front of her, he ran his fingers over the leather cover of the top book. "You're free to take these with you. If you cross reference them with the articles, you will find I am correct about the dates."

"But why—" She picked up a ledger, and scanned its pages. Hundreds of addresses were crammed into the lines, row upon row of personal history inscribed in blue ink.

"People aren't as likely to trash a place if they know we can track them down," he said, forgoing the chair to sit on the corner of his desk. One long, denim-clad thigh was close enough to touch. "That's why Conservation thinks we do it, in any case."

"But in reality...?" It was disconcerting, having to look up at him. She wished he'd go back behind his desk.

"In reality, we noticed a trend. A trend that troubled us. My people came to me, and I agreed to be their eyes. The result of my watch is in that folder." He indicated it with a tilt of his head.

"There's no trend here, Chief. The deaths aren't even related." Retrieving the folder from his desk, she thumbed through the articles again, careful not to bend or smudge the old newsprint. "Car accidents, suicides, and here's one of a girl who died in her sleep. It's just a coincidence."

"When does a coincidence become more than a coincidence, Detective? When it happens a dozen times? Twenty times? How about two hundred and fifty times? Is it more than a coincidence then?"

The persistent chill along her spine had returned. She resisted the urge to check behind her. "You're not serious."

"Sorry, my mistake. It was actually two hundred and *seventy-seven* at my last count." He turned to the final page of the newest-looking ledger. "A family of six died of the chicken pox. Can you imagine dying of the chicken pox in this day and age? And of course, your three makes it an even two hundred and eighty." His eyes were grave as they met hers. "Since the campground was closed, they didn't sign in."

She leaned back in the chair, mind reeling. It was impossible, yet the proof was there. She didn't need to go through every ledger to know he'd told her the truth. "When did this start happening?"

"We started to pay attention in the early eighties, but I believe it was going on long before then. That campground has always had a reputation. Warnings to stay away from it were passed along by my father's generation, and his father's generation before that."

As she flipped through the clippings, something struck her. There was a general sameness about them, as if she were paging through the records of a single unfortunate family. "These people are all Caucasian. Have there been any—"

"Deaths among my people? No – at least, not yet. But like I've said, we've always kept our distance."

Her brain had been trained to detect patterns. She definitely saw one here, but didn't understand its significance. "What do you think is going on out there, Kinew?"

He walked to the window, where he pulled back the thick Navajo-inspired curtain and stared outside. The day was overcast, as bleak and dreary as Maria felt, and no sun dared to brighten the room. "I think that place is evil. The kind of evil that doesn't stay put, the kind that will follow you home." He turned. "You've been there. Didn't you feel it?"

You're not welcome here. The memory of the whispered warning came into her brain so unexpectedly it was like she'd heard it all over again.

Kinew's sharp eyes missed nothing. "Something happened to you out there. What was it?"

Now it was her turn to be evasive. "I was investigating the worst homicide of my career. Three young people were brutally murdered. There would be something wrong with me if I *hadn't* felt the presence of evil."

"No, there's more to it than that. I can tell. What happened, Detective? It's important you tell me."

She looked away, feeling foolish. "It was probably my imagination."

Kinew gave her a wry smile. "I think you can feel confident that I'm not going to mock anything you tell me about that place. I understand your conviction that the dark feelings you experienced stemmed from the murders, but I can tell you evil lived there long before this."

"I didn't feel anything unusual, aside from horror over what had happened to the victims...."

He nodded.

"But while I was there, something strange happened. Someone told me to leave. 'You're not welcome here,' is what he said. His voice was quite distinct. I heard him clearly. However, when I turned around, no one was there."

Kinew frowned. "Was anyone else with you?"

"Yes, my partner, the coroner, and a few other officers. Why?" She sounded defensive. She'd let her guard down, and now he was going to tell her that her partner had said it, as if she were too stupid not to recognize Jorge's voice.

But, as usual, Kinew surprised her.

"Did any of them hear it?"

"No, just me. I think that's why it frightened me so much." That wasn't the only thing that was frightening – a strange expression had come over Kinew's face, one she couldn't read. "What is it? What are you thinking?"

"I'm thinking you were very lucky, Detective Greyeyes. Tell me, is your partner a white man?"

"No, he's Latino."

He looked relieved. "That's good. Since you were so kind as to give me some advice, I will give you some. Keep everyone you love away from that campground."

"I don't think that will be a problem." She gathered the articles into a neat stack before returning them to the manila file. "Is it all right if I borrow these?"

"Of course. You're the reason I saved them."

"You saved them for *me*?"

"Well, someone like you. I knew the police would become interested in our cursed little campground eventually. It was only a matter of time." Kinew shrugged. "It's my hope your investigation will help me get the place shut down. It's not safe."

He picked up the ledgers, insisting on helping her out to her car. As Kinew held open his office door for her, he gave her a funny look. "That's an interesting necklace."

She didn't understand what he was talking about for a second, but then she remembered the arrowhead hanging around her neck. Her initial attempts to remove it had been unsuccessful. Every time she'd tried, she'd been overwhelmed with nausea.

Kinew moved closer, peering at the grisly pendant, and she stiffened, wondering what he would see. Would he accuse her of disrespecting the artifacts of their ancestors? How would she convince him it hadn't been her idea?

"It's a good replica," he said finally.

"It's not a replica — it's the real thing. It's probably hundreds of years old."

The chief shook his head slowly with a sorrowful expression, no doubt believing she'd been ripped off. "Afraid not. It's far too new-looking for that. Authentic arrowheads aren't shiny."

"What are you talking about? It isn't shiny." She felt more than a little self-conscious as Kinew leaned in, studying the pendant on her chest.

"Wait a minute. What is this?"

As soon as he touched the arrowhead, a tremendous shockwave of electricity forced them apart.

Kinew's body slammed against the doorframe of his office, his eyes wide and startled. The ledgers fell from his arms and scattered around his feet.

Maria was dazed herself, but rushed to help him. "Are you okay?"

Shaking his wounded hand, he nodded. "I think so, but I'd take that off, if I were you."

He showed her what had provoked him to touch the arrowhead.

His fingers were wet with blood.

CHAPTER SEVENTEEN

As the cop slammed me against the wall, my mother screamed.

"Take it easy! He's not resisting you," my dad protested, and it was the only time I'd heard my old man sound defeated. "Why are you doing this to him?"

"Reese Anthony Wallace, you're under arrest for first-degree murder. You have the right to remain silent." The cop had me pinned, my cheek pressed against the drywall. He snapped the handcuffs painfully tight around my wrists, giving them an extra twist. I recognized him from the night I'd given my statement, and I'd noticed even then he'd seemed mean as fuck.

"Anything you say may be used against you in a court of law."

"Where's Detective Greyeyes? I want to speak to Detective Greyeyes."

The cop swung me around by the arm. He obviously loved every minute of this and made no attempt to hide it. "Detective Greyeyes is busy right now, but I'll tell her you send your regards. You have the right to consult an attorney before speaking to the police, and to have an attorney present during questioning now or in the future."

When he shoved me toward the door, making me stumble over my own feet, his partner reached out to steady me. "Ease up, Archer," the man said, his forehead creased in concern. "He's cooperating."

"This sack of shit murdered three people. I'm going to show him the same amount of consideration he showed them." Archer punctuated the statement with another shove. The handcuffs were so tight I worried my arms would be ripped from their sockets. "If you cannot afford an attorney, one will be appointed for you before any questioning if you wish."

As his words sunk in, I struggled to face him, wrenching my neck. "Wait a minute. There has to be some mistake. I didn't kill anyone."

If anything, the sadistic cop's hold grew tighter, and I noticed his partner was gesturing at me, trying to get my attention. "I'd keep your mouth shut, kid," he said.

"No, let him talk. He can tell us his story on the way to the pen. This oughta be good." Archer laughed, and at that moment, I hated him with a ferocity I'd never experienced before. "If you decide to answer questions now without a lawyer present, you have the right to stop answering at any time."

"He's got an attorney." My dad trailed us to the door and then onto the front walk. "Reese, don't say anything. Prosper will know what to do, just stay quiet. They can't force you to talk."

"Did you hear that? Kid's lawyered up already. What a surprise." Archer shoved me inside the cruiser with such force I toppled over on my side. The cop tried to slam the door behind me, but his partner stopped him.

"His belt isn't fastened."

"Who cares? Let him get tossed around like trash, 'cause that's exactly what he is." The cop leered at me, and for a horrifying moment, I thought I was going to piss myself. Thankfully, the sensation passed, but aside from that dreadful morning in the campground, I couldn't remember ever being so scared.

"It's the law," Archer's partner insisted. He reached inside the car and pulled me into a sitting position. His movements were careful rather than rough, so I decided to plead my case with him.

"Can you loosen the handcuffs, please?" My voice cracked. "They're hurting."

"Are you actually asking for mercy, you shit? After what you did? You have no fucking shame." Archer kicked my foot, which jostled my shrieking arms and shoulders enough that pain ricocheted through my upper body.

"That's it, Archer. Back off," his partner snapped, and I was relieved he used his body to shield me.

"I think you're on the wrong side, Markham."

"I don't care what you think. You're a hothead. Do you want to get sued for police brutality? His parents are watching, for Christ's sake." He gently pushed me forward and sucked in his breath. "Jesus Christ. Give me the keys."

"I didn't realize you had such a soft spot for murderers and rapists. Maybe I should request a new partner."

"If you don't, I will. Now give me the damn keys."

I flinched when the tangle of metal came flying at my savior's head, but I needn't have worried. The cop called Markham snatched it out of the air. As he fit the key in the lock, he said, "Christ, kid, you're trembling. I bet we don't need to use cuffs on you at all, do we?"

"No sir."

"If I take these off, do you promise to sit quietly?"

My fevered assertions could barely be heard over Archer's swearing. Markham removed the cuffs and fastened my seatbelt before shutting the door. I'd watched enough crime shows to be familiar with the good-cop, bad-cop routine, but at this point I didn't care if it was an act. If it weren't for Markham's kindness, I'd still be in excruciating pain. As I rotated my wrists and rubbed them together to get the blood flowing again, my mind raced. *How can they arrest me for murder? I didn't do anything wrong.*

"I'm driving," Markham insisted, and I was beyond grateful, even though it would leave Archer free to sneer at me through the partition. "You need to calm your ass down."

"I bet you feel like a real big man, protecting a murderer. I hope you can sleep at night." For a moment I thought Archer was going to refuse to get inside the vehicle, and that would have been fine with me. But then he spat on the driveway and climbed in, slamming the door. "You're a fucking pussy, Markham."

"Yeah, it takes a real hero to beat the snot out of a kid in handcuffs," Markham replied, starting the engine. "I'm sure the mayor will give you a medal."

"Fuck you," Archer said, and I recoiled at the venom in his voice. I had no doubt Officer Markham would pay dearly for his kindness.

"Thanks for the offer, but you're not my type."

When Markham shifted into reverse and backed out of my parents' driveway, I leaned my head against the seat and shut my eyes, ignoring the reporters who surrounded the car, begging for a quote.

For the first time since I'd met him, I looked forward to seeing Prosper.

Detective Greyeyes arrived before my lawyer. Overwhelmed with relief, I rushed to the bars. She retreated a step at my approach, and I hesitated, confused. I'd been sure she would tell me it was a mistake, that she would get me out of here, but I could tell from the coldness in her eyes that wasn't to be.

"Please tell me what's going on, Detective. I've been here for over an hour, and no one's told me anything." I wasn't sure how long I'd been locked up, since the police had confiscated my phone when they'd booked me. It had to have been an hour at the very least. It felt like years since they'd thrown me in this stinking cell, my only company a muttering drunk sleeping it off.

"I'm sorry, but I'm not at liberty to discuss the case with you."

How could she pull this formal shit on me now? "I've always been honest with you. I've always cooperated. You know I didn't kill Jessica, or Kira, or Dan. What's going on?"

"Are you waiving your rights, Reese? Would you like to give a statement?"

The question startled me. "Do you think I should?"

"No, I think you should keep your mouth shut until your lawyer gets here. You're going to dig yourself into a deeper hole."

When she turned away, waves of claustrophobia hit. I gripped the bars, pleading for her to wait. "I don't understand why I'm in *any* hole. What happened? What changed?"

"What changed is I realized I was an idiot to have believed your story." Greyeyes shook her head. "After all these years, you'd think I would know better by now."

"But I've told you the truth. I've told you everything I know." *Everything except my feelings for Kira that night, and my suspicion that they were returned.*

It must have shown on my face, because her jaw tightened. "That's what I'm talking about, right there. You're *still* hiding something from me."

"Nothing about...about what happened. Only something personal. Something that isn't relevant."

"That's the problem, Reese. In a homicide investigation, nothing is personal and everything is relevant."

As she started to leave, I saw something hanging around her neck. I didn't believe it, couldn't believe it. I had to squint and rub my eyes before I was certain. "Why are you wearing that?"

She glanced at her chest, only to start at the sight of the arrowhead, as if she hadn't expected it to be there. Grabbing the rawhide thong she'd used to tie it around her neck, she dropped the pendant inside her shirt.

I was dumbfounded. "That's *evidence*. How can you wear it?"

"It's not what you think, Reese."

"Of course it is. I found it, remember? I know exactly what it is. It might be the thing that clears my name."

"I doubt that."

"I can't believe you're doing this. I trusted you."

She snorted. "You're a fine one to talk about trust."

Before I could respond, I heard the sound of someone hurrying down the corridor. It was Prosper, looking as flushed as I'd ever seen him. "Are you talking to her?" He glared at me. "Did I just catch you talking to a cop?"

"Don't worry," Detective Greyeyes said. "He's sticking to his story."

Prosper waited until she was out of earshot before he spoke again. "Are you mad? Do you want to spend the rest of your life in prison? You have to start keeping your mouth shut, Wallace."

"But this is a mistake. I'm not supposed to be here. I didn't do anything—"

"*I didn't do anything*," my lawyer simpered in a childish falsetto. "Give me a break, kid. If we have any hope of preparing a defense for you, you've got to do better than that."

"But I really didn't do anything. I told you what happened. I told you—"

Prosper charged the bars, scaring the crap out of me. I was glad there were bars between us; I only wished I was the one on the other side. "For fuck's sake, kid, they've got your DNA. So it's time to cut the crap." His eyes flicked to my roommate. I wouldn't have thought it was possible, but he turned a whiter shade of pale. "What's up with that guy? Is he listening to us?"

"No. He's passed out cold."

"How do you know?" Prosper tipped his head at the unfortunate man. "Give him a kick, see if he moves."

"I'm not going to *kick* him." Where in the hell did my parents find this guy, the yellow pages?

"Well, we can't discuss your case under these conditions. Let me talk to them, see what I can do."

"Okay." Prosper seemed crazy, and DNA evidence? *What* DNA evidence? I'd hung out with those people, shared a meal and beers with them, slept in a tent with one of them. Of course my DNA would be at the scene, but that didn't mean anything. It certainly didn't mean I'd killed them.

"You should start telling your lawyer the truth, kid," my cellmate slurred from his bunk. "A weasel like that ain't got no room to judge."

CHAPTER EIGHTEEN

The coroner's words kept swirling in Maria's brain as she drove. They gave her a headache.

We've found some DNA and there's a match....

Three people were brutally murdered. One person survived.

One of the victims had suffered a violent sexual assault.

Guess whose DNA was found in her vagina?

How could I have been so stupid?

She'd been surprised when the judge signed the warrant. After all, Reese had been intimately involved with the victim. They had his statement that he hadn't had sex with his girlfriend that night, or the night before, but he could easily say he'd gotten the dates confused.

But she didn't think he had, and evidently, neither did the judge. For now, everything they had was circumstantial, but juries had convicted on less. The search warrant hadn't resulted in much, but maybe she'd be able to get him to confess. With a confession, they'd have a much better chance of putting that monster away for life. Never mind the fact that they still didn't know how he'd killed Kira – the poor girl had been ground into hamburger.

If only Maria hadn't believed him. If only she hadn't been irresponsible enough to get emotionally involved.

She slammed her hand on the steering wheel, making her Suburban swerve. *Get a handle on yourself, Maria. Everyone makes mistakes.*

Not cops. Cops weren't allowed to make mistakes. When they made mistakes, people died.

The darker her thoughts, the heavier the arrowhead weighed around her neck. She loathed it, but she was afraid to touch it. The last time she'd tried, she'd experienced more than quivers of nausea – she'd puked, and quite violently. Best not to do that while speeding down the highway.

For once in her life she was glad Heidi would be in bed when she pulled into the driveway. She couldn't deal with her daughter's exuberance, her stubbornness, or her questions. Not tonight.

As she dragged herself up the front steps, the door opened, warm, yellow light spilling into the dark and enveloping her husband in its halo.

"Hey there. Are you all right? You sounded terrible on the phone."

She flung herself into his arms, sending him back a few inches. For some reason she didn't understand, she felt like bawling. It had been years since the job had made her cry.

"Ouch!" Ben moved away, wincing. He looked down at his chest, where a dark spot was forming on his grey T-shirt.

"What's wrong?" She was so raw that she took his withdrawal as a rejection, even though she could see something else was going on.

"What the—?" Taking off his shirt, Ben stared at the scratch on his chest. He pointed at her pendant. "That thing cut me."

"I'm sorry. It wasn't intentional." She was stung by the anger in his voice.

"It's okay, it's just a flesh wound." Balling up his now-stained T-shirt, Ben pressed it to his bleeding chest. "Why are you wearing that thing anyhow? I thought it was evidence."

She wasn't ready to admit she'd woken up in the middle of the night with the repulsive thing around her neck. Ben liked to tease her about her forgetfulness. What if this made him think she was senile? Or worse, insane? "This is a replica Chief Kinew made me. Cool, huh?"

Ben gave her a rueful smile as he dabbed at his chest. "I guess that's one way of putting it. But I'm surprised you took it, honey. I thought cops didn't accept gifts. Couldn't it be seen as a bribe?"

"Oh, it's different on the reserves. You have to accept gifts or it's an insult." She had no idea if that were true or not, but she was also pretty sure Ben wouldn't know. And he wouldn't care enough to check. "Besides, why would he bribe me? He doesn't want anything from me."

"You never know. It doesn't hurt to have a police officer in your back pocket. Especially a beautiful one." Ben protested when she smacked him on the arm. "Hey, no fair. I'm an injured man."

"Actually, now that I'm home, I'd really like to take it off. Would you help me?" Mindful of what had happened to Kinew when he'd touched the arrowhead, Maria presented her husband with the nape of her neck, hoping he could untie the cord without making contact with the pendant.

She heard her husband suck in his breath, as if he'd spotted a particularly big spider crawling across the floor. Goose bumps broke out on her arms. "What? What is it? What's wrong?"

"Well, I don't quite understand how you managed this, but your hair is caught in the rawhide."

"So pull it free. I don't care, I can handle it."

"It's not that easy, hon." She felt his tentative fingers at her neck, gently tugging at her hair. Since the hairs there were fine and short, every time he pulled it was like getting pricked with a fine needle. "This is a bad tangle. I might have to cut it free."

"What? It can't be that bad."

"Remember the time Heidi got gum caught in her hair and we had to give her a pixie cut? This is worse."

Slowly, she moved her hands to join her husband's, terrified at what she'd find. She gasped when she discovered the mess. Her usually smooth, well-behaved hair was a snarl of impossible knots. She tore at it, using her fingers to separate the strands, her eyes burning with tears at the pain.

"Stop. You're only making it worse."

"What am I supposed to do? I can't leave it."

"Wait a minute. Stay right there." Ben disappeared into the kitchen, leaving Maria with her hands hopelessly tangled. She didn't have long to wonder what he was doing, for he soon returned with a pair of kitchen scissors.

"You're not going to cut my hair?" She hated the whine in her voice.

"Nope." Before she could protest further, Ben stepped behind her. She heard a snipping sound. She also felt a huge release, as if she'd been carrying a ten-pound weight around her neck all day and he'd just taken it from her. Her husband yanked at something in her hair, which hurt, but nowhere near as much as the tearing she'd been doing. At last the severed rawhide cord came loose, and with it the arrowhead, which clattered on the floor.

Ben handed her the ruined cord, but she didn't want to touch it.

Instead she threw her arms around his neck. "Thank you so much. You're a genius. Why didn't I think of that?"

"Probably because you didn't want to ruin your necklace. Sorry about that, babe. I'll replace it. I think our art teacher has some of this cord. I'll see if I can buy a bit off her."

Maria rubbed her neck, surprised and not surprised that her hair felt smooth again. The nasty snarl she'd struggled with seconds ago was gone. She hoped her husband wouldn't notice. "Actually, I'm glad to have it off. Don't worry about the cord. I don't want to wear it."

"Won't the chief be offended?"

"He'll get over it. I don't know when I'll see him again, anyway."

"Okay." He bent to retrieve the arrowhead, and she almost screamed for him to leave it, but nothing happened. Ben held it out to her, and she was relieved to see it was an old arrowhead again, like thousands of others. "Are you sure this isn't the one you found at the campsite? It looks really old."

"Appearances can be deceiving." When he tried to give it to her, she gently pushed his arm away. "Would you mind throwing it out for me? Not in the house." Taking him by the shoulders, she turned him to face the door. "Can you throw it in one of the cans on the curb? Please?"

He stared at her as if she were someone he didn't quite recognize, someone who could very well have lost her mind, and she couldn't blame him. "Why?"

"I don't like it. This may sound silly, but I don't want it in the house."

Maybe it was the cut on his chest, or the drama of freeing the cord from her hair, but Ben appeared to understand. "I don't like it either." He took the cord too.

After she'd enjoyed a boiling-hot shower and filled her stomach with the pasta and marinara sauce Ben had made for dinner, Maria felt a lot better. Once they'd resumed their usual positions on the couch, she was strong enough to tell her husband about Reese's arrest, and how betrayed she'd been when she'd gotten the DNA results.

"This isn't my field of expertise, but why does finding his DNA make him guilty? He admitted he was fucking her, didn't he?"

She wrinkled her nose at him. "Nice. You definitely have a way with words. He did admit it, but said they hadn't been active for several days before she died. She suffered a violent sexual assault, and all the lab could find was his sperm."

"Couldn't it be old sperm?"

Wiggling her feet so he'd remember he was supposed to be giving her a massage, she considered his question. It was strange – she'd been convinced Reese was guilty earlier that day, but now she wasn't so sure. She thought of how terrified he'd looked in the cell. Christ, he was more of a kid than a man. "The coroner didn't think so, but maybe it's worth looking into. It's not my area of expertise either."

Ben grinned. "I'll say," he said, caressing her feet. "It's been a while since either of us practiced our expertise."

"Sorry. Working a case like this doesn't exactly put me in the mood."

"I get that." The atmosphere in the room grew heavy as they thought about what had happened to the three young victims. "But your instincts are good, honey. I've never seen you wrong before. You were convinced the kid was telling the truth. What made you change your mind?"

"I don't know. But I think I've changed it back."

★   ★   ★

The woman staggered into camp with a bundle in her arms. Her garments, which had always been much too light for the climate, were torn and tattered. As the people watched in horror, she began to fall. They heard a thin cry, the cry of a child. Little Dove ran to catch the woman. The bundle of rags was an infant, skinny and starved, and the chief's wife sucked in her breath when she beheld his tiny face. He was as pale as Death.

Little Dove looked up to see the woman staring at her, and she recognized the desperation in the stranger's eyes. Before she could move away, the woman seized her hand.

"Please help us." Her teeth chattered so violently she could barely speak. "We are starving. My baby needs food or he will die. Please help him."

Before Little Dove could protest, the infant was thrust into her arms. She cradled him to her, this child who was not hers. She couldn't very well let him fall to the ground. In his weakened condition, such a fall might kill him.

She had a new child of her own, snuggled securely on her back. She knew she could easily give this woman's baby what it needed, but would the stranger agree to it? Little Dove put a hand on the woman's arm, feeling the bones that nearly protruded through her skin. It was as if the woman and her child were already dead. The thought made her shiver.

The stranger's eyes were red and crusted with old tears. Little Dove gestured to her chest, and the woman nodded, an expression of gratitude softening her face. That was all Little Dove needed. She rearranged her hides and furs in order to bring the starving child to her breast.

"What are you thinking, Little Dove?"

The chief's wife spun around to see Red Sky Dancer glaring at her. The rest of the women clustered behind, banding together for courage. It wasn't working. Little Dove could smell their fear.

"I will not let this child starve." As Little Dove tucked the infant under her furs, Red Sky Dancer moved forward to grab her wrist, twisting it.

"Did you not hear what Lone Wolf said? We weren't to speak to these strangers anymore. And now you're *feeding* them."

Little Dove moved away from the other woman, clutching the cold child to her warm skin. She'd been afraid the infant was already too far gone to suckle, but she was a natural mother. She soon felt the baby latch on and smiled. The child would be fine now. Her milk was strong.

Red Sky Dancer didn't have a family of her own. That was why she was so angry, Little Dove thought.

With the infant safe against her breast, its tiny fingers clutching her skin, Little Dove felt a rush of sympathy for its mother. She surveyed the women from her community with disgust. "Have you no soul? Help her."

Red Sky Dancer blocked their path. "Are you willing to send us to our deaths? This pathetic creature is not our sister."

Soaring Hawk pushed her way forward. Most of the people called her Grey Mother, as she was the matriarch of the nation. In spite of her extended age, she remained tall and proud. If anything, the years had strengthened rather than diminished her. Her kind face was tight with anger. "Have you no heart, Red Sky Dancer? The woman and her child are dying. We cannot leave them to the elements."

The lovely woman scoffed, and as she did so she greatly resembled her brother, Lone Wolf. "And why not? They are not our kin. They would abandon us without hesitation."

The stranger was too weak to protest. She lay on the snow, but at Grey Mother's signal, the other women scooped her up, wrapping her in their furs.

"Take them inside and warm them. Running Deer, Waning Moon – get some food together. Enough to see her people through to the next cycle."

"Yes, Mother."

"You are dooming us, old woman," Red Sky Dancer said as the women scurried around her, careful to stay out of striking range. Like her brother, Red Sky had a reputation for cruelty.

"It is a shame your great beauty is only on the outside. You have a hideous soul, and that can never be cured. Not even by a man as skilled as your brother."

Red Sky Dancer's eyes narrowed as she looked down at the older woman. "You believe I care what you think of me? I do not. You are all fools, and you will learn the wisdom of my brother's warning soon enough."

"I would rather be a fool than a vessel of emptiness," Grey Mother said, and turned her back on the female warrior to show she had no fear. Holding her head high, she hastened to the lodge, grateful that the winter wind carried Red Sky Dancer's curses safely away from her ears.

The women clicked their tongues as they stripped away the stranger's garments. They rubbed her poor, stiff body to warm it, making sure she was close enough to the fire to get her blood flowing. Grey Mother shook her head when she saw the woman's feet. She hoped it wasn't too late to save them. The woman might lose some fingers as well.

The woman was unconscious, but Grey Mother could see some color returning to her cheeks. Once she awoke, she would be in terrible pain. The matriarch ordered Running Deer to mix a drink of willow bark and other sacred herbs. Otherwise, the stranger's hands and feet, so cruelly treated by the harsh winter, would feel like they were on fire.

"Look!" The woman's threadbare hood had slipped aside, revealing an astonishing amount of yellow hair. "She has hair of gold. I wonder if it's valuable?" Waning Moon bounced the curls in her hand with a childish grin.

"Stop that foolishness," Grey Mother said. "She is a mother, and she is worthy of our respect. She is not a plaything for you to toy with."

Ashamed, Waning Moon released the curls and slunk into the shadows. Her sisters dared not say a word.

"How is the child?" The matriarch waited while Little Dove withdrew the infant from her robes. The baby had finished feeding, and was now asleep. Like his mother, he had new color in his cheeks.

"He is fine. He is a strong one." Little Dove smiled at the child, who – weakened from near-starvation – was half the size of her own son.

"Then throw him into the fire now, before it is too late."

The women gasped to see Lone Wolf at the door. But not Grey Mother, who rose to meet him, chin raised.

"Shame on you. This is the women's lodge. How dare you think yourself welcome?"

"I have not entered, Grey Mother, merely darkened your doorstep. My sister warned me of your foolishness, but so assured was I of your wisdom I had to see it with my own eyes to believe it." He sneered at the child, and at the women who hastened to hide the stranger's exposed skin from view. "Already I have seen enough to discourage me from ever tarrying with you again."

The group around the fire protested, but Grey Mother held up a hand, silencing their cries. "It is of no consequence. My skills with medicine are a match for yours, Lone Wolf. We have no need for such a shaman, a man of 'healing' cowardly enough to fear a half-dead woman and her babe." She turned away, leaving no mystery as to what she thought of the medicine man, whose expression grew dark.

Little Dove tugged at Grey Mother's skirt, urging her to sit down, to end the conflict with Lone Wolf before it grew into a battle. But the older woman waved her off. "We do not need him, child," she said, the resolve in her voice strong.

"It is not the woman and child I fear, but what they represent," the shaman said through gritted teeth. "You are at the end of your life, Old Woman, while I am at the peak of mine. Who will help your daughters when you are gone? Who will attend to their suffering? Do you care for the strangers enough to sacrifice your own people?"

"I will have more strength on my deathbed than you will demonstrate during your finest day as a warrior."

The man's face darkened further, and for a moment, the frightened women who clustered around the fire feared he would commit a terrible act of violence. Instead, he lowered his head in acquiescence. "With those words you seal your fate, Old Woman. I pray you do not live long enough to realize your mistake."

As he disappeared into the growing storm, the women started a flurry of whispered conversations. Grey Mother sagged onto the furs near the fire as if she had aged ten moons.

Little Dove brewed her some healing tea, and as the older woman sipped, she lifted a hand to touch the girl's smooth cheek. "You have the heart of a warrior, my dear. More importantly, your actions are always sweet and true."

"I do not mean to question you, Grey Mother, but was sending Lone Wolf away the best thing to do? Many of the sisters rely on him." The soft-spoken woman's voice broke, but she swallowed her tears. Before the medicine man had gained his powers, several of their women had died in childbirth, screaming their torment at the stars. Both men and women had perished in battle, and the slightest bite of tainted meat had brought death on swift heels. She dreaded returning to those treacherous days. As unyielding as Lone Wolf was, he had brought the power of the Creator with him, and now she feared he had taken it away again.

"Bah! Only because they did not care to trouble me. Perhaps they felt I am too old." She chuckled. "Don't worry. There is no method of healing that is beyond me. I will attend to our women myself."

"And what if..." Little Dove hesitated, not wishing to offend.

"What if I myself grow ill? What if my own moon is waning, as Lone Wolf oh-so-subtly implied?" Grey Mother caressed Little Dove's face once more. "Then you will take my place, cherished daughter."

Little Dove's eyes widened. "Me? I am no healer."

"Ah, but you are, sweet girl. Trust me, and I will show you that you've been a healer since the day you were born."

★   ★   ★

Maria's eyes flew open. She stared at the ceiling, expecting to see thick smoke billowing towards a hole in the fabric. She could still smell it, cloying but sweet, and feel the soft fur enveloping her in a warm embrace.

The mattress beneath her was as foreign as it would have been to Little Dove. Maria didn't know the woman, but she knew Little Dove was as real as the husband who snored beside her. In some ways, Maria was closer to the delicate-featured woman with the braids, because she had experienced Little Dove's terror as if it were her own. Her heart had pounded in rhythm with the woman's.

Who is she, and why do I keep dreaming of her?

It was the memory of the smoke that made her jump out of bed, convinced her own child's life was in jeopardy. But as soon as her bare feet touched the freezing hardwood, she realized the truth. The blaze, however real it seemed, had been a figment of her imagination.

She checked on Heidi anyway, scooping her daughter's favorite teddy bear from the floor and tucking it in bed with her. Maria had never understood why her child loved that ugly thing, and understood even less why she'd named it Edgar, but whatever made her happy. Brushing Heidi's fine hair back from her face, Maria kissed her forehead. Her daughter's skin was cool against her lips, and the child murmured in her sleep, tugging the blanket up to her chin.

"Good night, sweet girl," Maria whispered, and padded to the bathroom for a glass of water. Her T-shirt and shorts were damp with sweat, and her neck ached as if she'd strained it. The scent of hickory smoke clung to her nostrils, and she wondered if the neighbors were having a bonfire. If so, she hoped they were obeying regulations this time. She hated having to play the heavy.

Leaning her head against the wall, she held her fingers under the tap, waiting for the water to reach a desirable frostiness. Finally it was cold enough to drink, and as she gulped it down, she caught a glimpse of herself in the mirror.

The glass fell from her hands and shattered in the sink.

Around her neck, pulsing like a blood-filled tick, was the arrowhead.

CHAPTER NINETEEN

"What are you in for?"

The old man leered at me, showing off the grim results of a life without proper dental care. His words were no longer slurred, but he had a thick accent that made him difficult to understand.

Flipping over on my cot so he faced my back, I hoped he would get the hint.

He didn't.

"Come on, the hours are long in this place without someone to talk to. What are you in for?"

Sighing, I decided to give up on the prospect of sleeping. I wasn't tired anyway, and the mattress was as comfortable as concrete. "What are *you* in for?"

"Public drunkenness," the man said, as if it were a source of pride.

"You don't say." I rolled my eyes, feeling innately superior to this poor slob.

"Hey, at least I'm not in for murder."

I bolted upright and the old cot creaked in warning. "How did you know?"

The old man shrugged. I could swear he was smirking at me. "Hey, I'm a regular," he said, displaying his palms in a don't-shoot-the-messenger gesture. "A guy hears things after a while."

"Not that I have to defend myself to you, but I'm innocent." The 'unlike you' hung in the air between us, unspoken but clearly heard.

"Yeah, that's what they all say." The man grunted, scratching his greasy hair, hair that looked like it had never met a comb. "Not me, though. I have a little drinking problem. No sense saying different."

"Why don't you get help, then?" I didn't bother to keep the disgust out of my voice. Maybe if he got mad at me, he'd quit talking. Then again, he could have a shiv he'd draw across my throat while I slept, but at this point, that might be a blessing. A single day in this cell had lasted a million years. I couldn't imagine surviving a lifetime.

He chuckled. "And who's gonna help a guy like me? Rehab is for fancy white boys like yourself, who can afford feather beds and pretty nurses who hand you 'pensive pills in a paper cup. For me, that would be like going to heaven. Ain't no one gonna pay to send *me* there."

"There has to be some kind of help for the—" I groped for the least offensive word, "—indigent."

"Have you seen those places? Bedbugs and fleas, no thanks. I'd rather take my chances on the street with the rats. I may get my teeth kicked in now and then, but it's better than staying at the shelter."

"You're homeless?"

The man straightened, attempting to smooth his threadbare pants, but it was hopeless. "What, you think you're better than me?"

My cheeks flushed. For some reason I couldn't understand, I felt guilty. "No, not at all. It's just – it's going to sound stupid, but I've never known anyone homeless before."

"It's okay." My cellmate shrugged. "I've never known an over-privileged white boy before. Oh, wait a minute...." He pretended to think, tapping a finger against his temple. "Yes, I have. I've known far too many."

"You think *I'm* over-privileged?" I gestured at our surroundings. "Would I still be in here if my family had a lot of money?"

The man took in the peeling paint, the stained floor. "You have a point. But trust me when I tell you there are much worse places to stay."

Whether he'd meant to or not, the vagrant had put my own problems in stark perspective. What had happened to me was inconvenient and scary, but it was also a mistake. Sooner or later, the cops would figure it out, and I'd go home to my parents' house, which was the Taj Mahal compared to this place, while this guy would return to the streets.

"Do you mind if I ask why you're homeless?"

He gazed out beyond the bars, the smirk gone from his face. "Told you already. I've got a little drinking problem."

"But before that – you must have had a home, right? What happened to it?"

"What makes you think something happened?"

I suspected I'd made him uncomfortable, but he'd had no problem putting *me* on the spot. Besides, I was curious. "Well, something had to have happened. No one is born homeless."

Even before he raised an eyebrow at me, I got how stupid a statement it was.

"And that, my friend, is white privilege."

"You were born on the streets?"

He shook his head, smoothing his pants again. His hands were trembling. "No, had a good home. A good family."

"Did something happen to them?"

"No. Something happened to me."

The silence between us grew heavy as I waited for him to continue his story. Finally, he seemed to make up his mind about something. "The church took me and my siblings away. Said they'd give us an education, make sure we were 'properly integrated' into society."

I could hear the bitterness in his voice, but I couldn't understand it. "Isn't education a good thing?"

"Oh, they educated us, all right. They sure did." The man leaned against the wall, his face darkened by the memory. "If we spoke our language, they beat us. If we said we were homesick or missed our families, they beat us. And some of those priests, well – you better believe they were messing around with us the first chance they got."

"That's disgusting." Studying the man across from me, his wild, graying hair and missing teeth, the filth caked on his skin, I had a difficult time picturing him as a defenseless child. A child who had, assuming he was telling the truth, been beaten and abused.

"Disgusting ain't the half of it. I've often wondered if they hired those monsters on purpose, or if a large percentage of them happened to be attracted to the job."

"Wasn't there someone you could have gone to for help? A nun, maybe?"

He laughed. "The nuns were even worse. Most of them didn't diddle with us, but they loved to beat us black and blue. All part of converting us from 'savages' to upstanding white folk. But we could never be upstanding white folk, no matter how hard we tried. From the start, we were doomed to fail."

It was difficult to accept his story. He told it with conviction, but why would a church do such horrible things? It went against everything they claimed to stand for. "Couldn't your parents help?"

The man's expression softened a little, and I could have sworn a tear ran down his wrinkled cheek before he ducked his head. "Here's the clincher. All this time, all these years we're getting beaten and messed with, they told us our parents didn't want us. We were too much trouble to raise. They let us believe our folks didn't love us anymore, that they'd given away their children the way you might get rid of a turtle that grows too big for its tank.

"I ran away from the boarding school when I was twelve years old. It took a long time, but I found my way back home. My parents weren't there, but a woman who had been like a grandmother to me told me the truth. The church *stole* us from our families. They ripped us from our mothers' arms and told them they had no choice, that it was the law." He shook his head. "Even worse, our families had no idea where we were. They'd accepted they were never going to see us again."

I suspected I didn't want to know the answer, but I had to ask. "*Did* you see your parents again?"

"Nope. By the time I got out, they were both gone," he said, his voice breaking. "My father, he never recovered from losing us. He started hitting the bottle hard, and I heard there were other women too. One day he hit my mother instead of the bottle, and she left him. He drank himself to death and she died of cancer while I was rotting in that godforsaken place."

"I'm so sorry."

He acknowledged my apology with a nod, never lifting his eyes from his dirty hands.

"But you still have family, right? What about your siblings?"

"My brother, he never made it out. He hung himself when he was ten years old. And my sister, she lives on the res." The man attempted a smile, but it was a poor imitation of his earlier grin. "At least her trailer is nice. She lets me stay sometimes."

I was at a loss for words. I'd heard sad stories before, of course, but never anything like this. I'd considered lying down on the cot again, trying to get a couple of hours of sleep, when my cellmate spoke.

"I told you my story. Now I want to know yours."

"I don't really have one. Before this happened, I would have said I led a boring life."

"You do have a story. You must have, or you wouldn't be sitting here now."

Goose bumps broke out along my arms. "What do you mean?" As I asked the question, I thought of Prosper and his warnings. Was it possible the old man was a plant, put here to earn my trust and record a confession? Could he have created that sad story to force a bond between us?

No. His tears were real.

The man leaned forward, pinning my eyes with his own. "What is it that's different about you? Why did they let you live?"

I felt a chill. "Do you know something I don't, old man? Do you know who did this to my friends?"

Somehow the man managed to appear proud and terrified at the same time. "'Course I do. Everyone knows what's wrong with those woods. It's the wendigo."

"Wendigo?" *Is he pulling my leg?* "What's a wendigo? I've never heard of it."

He opened his mouth to enlighten me, but before he could say a word, someone else answered.

"A child's fairy tale, that's what it is." Startled, I looked up to see Detective Greyeyes standing at the door to our cell. I'd been so engrossed in the man's story I hadn't heard her approach.

"Wendigos are as real as the two unfortunates sitting in this cell. I hope you'll never have to pay for your skepticism, Detective," the man said.

"I'll take my chances. Did you get anything to eat, Crazyhorse?"

He lifted his hand, and I saw how bad his trembling was. The man wasn't just shaking; he was full-on vibrating. "Can't. Couldn't get the fork to my mouth, and it's only going to get worse. Can you help me?"

"I'll see what I can do." She barely glanced in my direction, but I had nothing to lose.

"I didn't lie to you, Detective," I said, moving closer so she could see my face. "I've answered your questions as truthfully as I could. I want to find out who did this to Jess, Dan, and Kira as much as you do."

"I believe you," she replied, startling me so much I almost tripped over my own feet hurrying over to the bars.

"You do?"

"Yes, I do. I don't think you should be in there. I'm going to see what I can do to get you out."

Relieved, I rested my forehead against the cool metal of the bars that separated us. In my wildest dreams I hadn't dared to hope it would be that easy. As much as I hated to admit it, Mom had been right. When it came down to it, Prosper knew what he was doing. "What did my lawyer say to convince you?" I asked, dying to find out what clever strategy he had invoked in my defense.

She frowned. "Prosper? Not a thing. I haven't seen him since we booked you."

"Was it the beer bottles? Did you find something?"

"Sorry, no. The results were negative. We couldn't find anything unusual."

Now I was the one confused. "What was it, then? What happened to change your mind?"

The detective studied me for a moment, as if deciding whether or not she could trust me. Finally, reluctantly, she removed something from the collar of her shirt.

"It was this."

The rawhide cord was gone, replaced by one that appeared to have been braided from human hair. But that wasn't the worst of it.

The arrowhead no longer looked like rock. It was as swollen and glossy as an overfed beetle. I reached through the bars to touch it, but before I could, it moved. Something was alive under its surface. With a cry, I snatched my hand back.

"What is it?" I asked, grateful when she tucked it under her shirt again.

When she met my eyes, her own were wide with fear. Finally I noticed how exhausted she looked. "I don't know. But I can't get rid of it."

CHAPTER TWENTY

Maria put more pressure on the gas, praying the drivers ahead of her would move out of the way.

For the most part, they did, although a few were stubborn enough to need a blast of her horn as well. Her fingers tightened on the wheel, and as she squinted at the road, she forced herself to take several deep breaths.

Damn Jorge. Any hint of intrigue sent her into a tailspin, and yet he'd refused to tell her what was going on.

"You'd better get down here right away," was all he'd say.

A red Volvo in front of her hesitated before the railroad tracks and almost got rear-ended for its trouble. Maria considered pulling over the elderly gentleman but decided against it. Making someone else's life miserable wouldn't improve her own.

Inhaling deeply, she tried her best to ignore the fact that the reason her life had become a living nightmare was hanging around her neck. Every now and then the arrowhead twitched, and she had to bite back a scream.

Finally she reached the hospital. After taking the corner tight, she drove into the lot on squealing tires, bypassing the parking-lot maze in favor of emergency. Several attendants in hospital whites rushed outside when she killed the engine, but as soon as they spotted her truck, they left her alone.

Maria jogged down the antiseptic-smelling hallway, pushing past nurses in candy-colored smocks. Her partner wasn't hard to find. With that sixth sense he'd always had when it came to her, he was already waiting in triage as she burst into the room.

"What's wrong? What is it?"

His expression was so grave that for a panicked moment, she feared for the safety of her own family. But Jorge would never have been that cruel. If something were wrong with Heidi or Ben, he would have told her.

"It's really bad, Maria." His tone carried more gravity than his words, sending her a warning, but it was a warning she didn't have the time or patience for.

"So you told me. Spit it out, Jorge. What is going—"

It was then she heard the cries.

The hospital staff flinched as one, but she could tell the outburst wasn't unexpected. Maria saw matching expressions of sympathy and concern as the staff communicated with each other in that wordless way of nurses everywhere.

Jorge led the way and she followed, silently urging him to move faster. Another heartrending shriek made her jump. This time she was close enough to make out words

"Mommy, it hurts. It hurts, it hurts, it *hurts*!"

A young man in a lab coat raced out of the room, colliding with her partner. Jorge put out an arm to steady him, but it didn't do much good. The doctor seemed dazed, and no wonder. Running into Jorge would be like running full-tilt into an oak tree.

"My partner is here," Jorge said, motioning to Maria. "Detective Greyeyes will need to see the boys and take their statements."

The doctor's eyes flicked over her in a dismissive manner she didn't much care for. "This isn't a good time, Detective. They have to be treated for their pain, and, as you've no doubt heard, they're in a bit of a panic. I doubt they'll be much good to you."

Underneath the screaming, Maria could hear a second voice. It sounded very young. "It huuurts. Mommy, it *huurts*."

"I know it does, honey. The doctor's going to bring you something to make you better. Just hold on." The reply was calm, but did Maria detect a note of revulsion underneath? What on earth had Jorge gotten her into?

"We'd like to pop our heads in all the same, if it's okay with you. I need her to see what we're dealing with," Jorge said.

The doctor shrugged. "Suit yourself." He was already rushing down the corridor away from them.

"He's a charmer," Maria said. "And what is he, twelve?"

"They're not getting younger. We're getting older." Jorge waited a beat to make sure his next words sunk in. "Brace yourself."

She'd seen some atrocious things in her career, but what she witnessed in those hospital beds would trouble her for years. Before she could stop herself, she winced.

The first boy was scarcely recognizable as human. His body was covered in vicious-looking blisters. They were on his lips, in his ears, even on his eyelids. Some of the sores were oozing, while others had burst, leaving raw, red wounds. He writhed in pain, and the woman who sat beside his bed reached out a hand to comfort him, but let it hang awkwardly in the air. It was impossible to know where to touch him; Maria didn't see an inch of unblemished skin.

The woman, presumably his mother, was dressed in operating-room garb: blue smock, shower-type cap, and latex gloves. Before Maria could wonder why, Jorge caught hold of her wrist.

"Don't touch him. The doctors think this could be contagious."

She felt weak at the thought of bringing this plague home to her daughter.

"Where is the other boy?"

Her partner bit his lip, looking miserable. "They've got him in another room. He's even worse."

"Worse? How is that possible?"

"He keeps passing out from the pain. Probably a blessing."

She was growing more and more confused. What was Jorge doing here? And why had he insisted she meet him? As appalling as the two boys' condition was, this was a job for medical professionals, not cops. There was little they could do, and if the doctors were right, having more people in this room increased the likelihood of spreading the contagion.

"You're wondering why I called you." Jorge always could read her mind.

"Yes. This is dreadful, and I feel for the families, but I don't see how we can help."

"These boys were fine a few hours ago. Then they decided it would be fun to sneak into the Strong Lake campground."

The arrowhead pulsed underneath her shirt like a heartbeat. In horror, she stared at the boy on the bed, who rolled his blistered, oozing eyes at her and screamed.

*   *   *

"Mrs. Haverstock?"

Fresh tears cascaded down the woman's cheeks. "Please help me, Officer. I—I feel so helpless. I don't know what to do to help him. He's in so much pain."

Standing this close, Maria could hear the boy's blisters popping every time he moved. Yellow pus ran down his skin to stain the white sheets, and her stomach clenched. Swallowing hard, she forced herself to focus on his mother, who looked to be on the verge of a panic attack.

"Have they given him anything for the pain?" Maria brought over a chair to sit beside her.

"They tried to get an IV in him so they could give him morphine, but…." Her voice broke, catching on a sob.

Maria patted the woman's arm, trying to imagine how she'd feel if it were Heidi in that bed. She'd be inconsolable. "I understand."

There wasn't an inch of skin free of sores to insert a morphine drip, and puncturing the blisters would have caused unbearable agony.

"They gave him some pills, but they haven't seemed to help much. He could barely swallow them. The sores are inside his mouth too, his throat. I just don't know what to do."

She smoothed her boy's light brown hair back from his bubbling forehead with a gloved hand. He moaned.

"Mom, make it stop."

"I wish I could, sweetheart. Don't worry, the doctor is going to make it all better."

Her eyes pleaded with Maria, begging her to fix this, to make her life return to the way it had been that morning, when everything had been right in her world. "He's only ten years old," she whispered.

"Mrs. Haverstock, do you feel strong enough to answer some questions? If you need more time, we can come back."

She nodded. "I want to do whatever I can to help Travis. Ask anything you like, but I don't know much."

"I heard Travis was fine this morning?" Maria took out her notebook, more to have something safe to look at than anything else.

"Yes, he was completely normal. He had such beautiful skin." She sobbed, and then pressed a tear-soaked Kleenex to her mouth. "I'm sorry."

"Don't apologize. Maybe we should speak in the waiting room? Or the cafeteria? Would that be easier?"

Her gaze flicked to her son and then to Maria's notebook. She shook her head. "I can't leave him."

"Okay, I understand. I just need to ask you a few more questions. When did you notice something was wrong?"

"He asked if he could go play with Braden this morning. Braden's his friend from school," she said, her voice shaking. Jorge handed her fresh tissues, and she gave him a weak smile of thanks before using one to dab her face. "They often like to ride their bikes around the neighborhood, and I think it's good for children to get some exercise, don't you?" She seemed to catch herself, looking from Maria to Jorge and back again. "Sorry, I'm rambling."

On the bed, Travis writhed. His screams had died to defeated little whimpers, the kind you hear when an infant has cried himself out. "Jorge, can you find that doctor and ask him if there's anything more they can do? He shouldn't be in pain like this."

Jorge nodded, the gratitude obvious on his face. She was envious; she wished someone would send *her* out of the room.

"Thank you so much," Mrs. Haverstock said. "I've been asking, but I feel like they're not listening to me. What's your name?"

"I'm sorry, I should have introduced myself. I'm Maria Greyeyes, and I'm a detective with the Clear Springs Police."

"A detective? I don't understand. Why are two detectives here? Is Travis in trouble?" Her lower lip quivered.

"No, I don't think so. I just need you to tell me everything you know about what your son did today."

"Well, he left around eight this morning. I was putting away the breakfast things, so I admit I didn't see which direction he went. Then the door slammed open around noon, and I heard Travis shouting for me." Her voice shook, and she dabbed at her eyes again. "It scared the life out of me."

"I can imagine."

"When I asked what was wrong, he ripped off his shirt—" She sucked in a shuddering breath. "His torso was already covered in those... those *things*."

Maria resisted the urge to look at the boy's wounds again, but she could hear them. That was bad enough. Against her breastbone, the arrowhead thudded along in time with her heart. She hoped the poor woman wouldn't notice anything moving under her shirt.

"Even as I watched, the sores started to break open. He was in terrible pain, and I couldn't do anything to help him. I—I ended up calling 911. I didn't know what else to do."

"You did the right thing. Did Travis tell you what happened?"

"All he said was that he'd been to the campground. Sometimes they go up there and fool around, but he knows I don't like it. Especially since those poor young people died—" Her voice cracked, and she needed a moment before she could speak again.

"Do you want some water?"

She waved a hand. "No, just…give me a minute."

"Take all the time you want. This must be very difficult."

As Maria waited for the mother to regain control, she silently cursed the doctor. Where was he? There had to be more they could do for this kid. She felt someone watching her, and glanced up to meet Travis's tormented eyes. She gave him what she hoped was a reassuring smile. He didn't react – only continued to stare at her, and it was giving her the creeps.

"He admitted they went into your crime scene, but he swore he didn't touch anything." Mrs. Haverstock swallowed hard. "I guess that's why you're here."

"Yes and no. What your son did wasn't great, but we've finished with that part of the investigation. I'm sure there was no harm done. I still don't get the connection between the campground and what happened to Travis and Braden."

"I-I don't understand it either, but those boys must have gotten into something. M–Maybe poison oak? Or sumac?"

Maria didn't have to tell her this resembled no case of poison oak she'd ever seen. They both understood Mrs. Haverstock was clinging to any potential explanation. Every mother would do the same in her shoes.

A nurse bustled into the room, her eyes narrowing when she saw Maria sitting there. She wore a mask over her nose and mouth. "You're going to have to leave. You can ask your questions later. This child needs to be sedated."

The nurse said *child* in such a way as if to remind Maria she was nothing but an insensitive pig. Jorge waited in the doorway and nodded at her. It was time to go. There was nothing more they could learn, in any case. Not until Travis was able to tell her exactly what had happened at the campground.

"Thank you for your time," she told the boy's distraught mother. "I hope he feels better soon."

If Mrs. Haverstock heard them leave, she didn't acknowledge it. Her attention was riveted on her son, tears dripping down her chin as the nurse attempted to give him another pill.

Maria was more than happy to get the hell out of there.

"The good news is we've identified the contagion."

The doctor's tone left no doubt bad news would follow swiftly.

There was no way Maria would go near her daughter before learning what she'd been exposed to. She was furious with Jorge for bringing her into this situation without any warning of what they were dealing with.

"What is it?" Jorge asked.

"Smallpox."

"Smallpox?" They looked at each other in surprise before her partner asked the question that was on both their minds. "I didn't think you could get smallpox anymore? Maybe in third-world countries, but not here."

"It hasn't even occurred there since the seventies. We completely eradicated it from the planet, or so we'd believed. The fact that these two boys contracted it at a campground that's within a few hours of here is a concern."

"Is it like chicken pox?" Jorge asked. "Will it go away on its own?"

"Unfortunately not. There's no treatment for it, although we're giving them the vaccine now in the hopes it will ease their symptoms. We're going to need to keep them in quarantine for the next three to four weeks, until their scabs fall off."

Her partner winced. "Ouch."

"Did either of you touch the boys?" There was a challenge inherent in the doctor's voice, as if he expected them to lie.

Jorge shook his head.

"No," Maria said. "But I did touch Travis's mother." She cursed herself. She should have followed her instincts and stayed the hell away from all of them.

"You should be okay. She's wearing gloves, and I think we convinced her that her attempts to hold her son were hurting him. But if you start feeling like you're coming down with the flu, any severe headaches or fatigue, come see me right away."

"Headaches and fatigue? Sounds like my regular life. I might not be able to tell the difference."

She'd meant it as a joke, but the doctor didn't so much as crack a smile.

"You'll be able to tell the difference. Obviously, it's crucial we learn exactly where these boys went and what they did. If a public campground is a breeding ground for this virus, we need to confirm it as soon as possible.

"I've already been in touch with the Centers for Disease Control and Prevention, but in the meantime, I suggest you keep your distance from the site until it's safe. We don't want this to spread, and so we're going to vaccinate both of you before you leave."

Jorge shrugged, but she didn't like the idea of putting something foreign in her veins unless it was absolutely necessary. "Wait a minute. I thought you said we'd be fine as long as we didn't touch one of the boys. Well, we haven't."

"I said you *should* be okay, but I don't think we should leave it to chance, do you? You've seen Travis. Do you want to risk bringing that home to your own family?" The man's expression was grim, his lips compressed into a thin white line. He must have been worried about his own family as well.

"Come on, Maria. We'll get the shot. What's the big deal?" Jorge raised an eyebrow, surely wondering why she was fighting it, but she turned back to the doctor.

"What are the side effects?"

"Most of the side effects resulting from this vaccination are minor. Your arm may feel sore, and there may be a bit of redness at the injection site. Some people have experienced a mild fever. Very few have felt ill enough to miss work."

"I can't miss work. Not right now. Absolutely not."

"I think you'll miss a lot more work if you get smallpox," Jorge said. *What's wrong?* he mouthed, but she pretended not to notice.

"It's a very small percentage who are affected that way," the doctor agreed. "I'm getting the vaccination. My entire team will need it. I wouldn't do this if I wasn't sure it was safe."

"And what about the rare reactions, doctor?"

Jorge bumped her knee with his, a signal that he felt she needed to rein it in. But she was rewarded when the doctor had the good grace to look embarrassed, faint color blooming in his cheeks.

"In some very rare cases, it has been fatal, but we're talking about fifteen to fifty people out of a million."

"Which is it? Fifteen or fifty? Because that's a huge difference."

"Jesus, Maria. Get the damn shot," her partner said. "Think of your kid. You don't want Heidi to end up like that."

She didn't, and she couldn't figure out why she was being so prickly. But she was positive she didn't need the vaccine. She'd been careful not to touch Travis, and she was pretty sure patting the mother's arm through the hospital smock hadn't put her at risk. But she was hardly an expert on smallpox, so why would she take the chance?

It was the doctor's attitude more than anything. How dare he sit there, smug in his white privilege, talking down to the brown people as if they were too stupid to realize he wanted to inject them with something they didn't need, something that might make them sick?

What the – where the hell did that come from? It was like an alien had infiltrated her thoughts, substituting its own. She'd found the doctor to be high and mighty, yes, but more than anything, he was overly concerned. She didn't think he was racist.

"You okay?" Jorge touched her arm, giving it a little shake.

They both stared at her. She must have checked out for a bit. "Doctor, are hallucinations a symptom of smallpox?"

The man frowned. "Not usually, but I suppose if the fever were high enough, it could cause them. Why?"

"You seein' things, Maria?" Jorge asked.

Avoiding his eyes, which picked up on far too much, she concentrated on the doctor. "No. I think I – read that somewhere."

"Please tell me if you experience *anything* unusual. That goes for you too," the doctor told her partner. "I have to admit, I'm far from an authority on smallpox. I have some research to do. The Disease Control people will know a lot more, I expect."

"I haven't experienced anything unusual yet," she said, hoping she sounded reassuring. She wondered what the men would do if she took the arrowhead from under her shirt. It certainly qualified as unusual. It was still beating in rhythm with her heart, but she didn't want to guess what it looked like now. Bloody and bloated and glistening, most likely. If anything could make the men forget about smallpox, it would be that. "That's a good sign, isn't it?"

"Not necessarily." The doctor sighed, running his hand through his hair. "It can incubate anywhere from a week to seventeen days."

She nudged Jorge. "Then the campground had nothing to do with it. The boys only went to Strong Lake this morning. They wouldn't be showing symptoms this quickly."

Even as she said the words, she knew she was wrong. The campground had *everything* to do with the virus that had befallen the boys. She just wasn't sure how.

"There's a reason we think the boys came into contact with the virus at the campground, but I'd like to vaccinate you both before I take you to the morgue."

"The morgue?"

"I didn't have a chance to tell you, Maria," Jorge said, looking sheepish. "Once you arrived, things happened so fast. You think this case has been strange? It's about to get a lot stranger."

CHAPTER TWENTY-ONE

"Wake up. Hey man, wake up." A man's voice interrupted my sleep, but for a moment, I thought it was part of my dream.

"Oh, isn't that sweet. Would you look at that? Ol' Crazyhorse has made a friend."

"Have to be in pretty sad shape to make friends with that."

"You know what they say about the company you keep. I think they're perfect for each other."

The man's tone was kindly, but there was something underneath, like the stench of rot under cloying air freshener, that made me open my eyes.

"Your beauty sleep is over, Wallace. We have to talk to you."

"Yeah," another man said. "We need to tell you a few things."

Rubbing the sleep from my eyes, I blinked. Without windows, it was impossible to tell what time of day it was. I had no idea how long I'd been out, but I was exhausted. It was as if I'd gotten no sleep at all.

I looked across the cell at Crazyhorse, and my chest tightened. Something was wrong. The man huddled in the far corner of his cot, his knees clutched to his chest like he wanted to disappear.

"Hey, Wallace, I'm talking to you. You better start showing us some respect."

There was a loud metal clang. The man who had arrested me waited at the bars of our cell. He had a friend with him, and they both grinned.

I'd encountered his type many times before. I suspect every guy had. He was a bully, and you couldn't show fear in front of a bully. It only made them feel more powerful. I wanted to shake my cellmate, tell him to grow a pair, but of course it was too late. The men were already laughing at his reaction, having a great ol' time.

"Have you slept it off yet, you crazy Wagon Burner?" the guy's friend asked, leering at my cellmate through the bars. "You won't want a drink again by the time we're done with you."

"Yep, our program is a lot quicker than AA." The man who'd arrested me slapped a baton against his palm. "Instead of twelve steps, there are only two. Me hitting you, and you hitting the floor."

"Wow, that's original." I made a big show of rolling my eyes. "The eighties called. They want their joke back."

He swiveled his head toward me, baring his teeth. With his beady eyes and thin nostrils, he reminded me of a snake. Which was a huge insult to snakes everywhere. "Are you saying you want to go first, Wallace? Is that what you're saying? Because I reckon me and Dean here could beat the murder-loving rapist right out of you."

I heard a muffled cry and looked over to see Crazyhorse shaking his head at me. If he wanted to feed those assholes with his fear, that was his prerogative. I wasn't about to give them the pleasure. "In that case, your work here is done, because I'm not a murder and I'm not a rapist."

The asshole cop snorted at me. "Yeah, you seem real innocent, sitting in that cell."

"It's called 'wrongfully accused.' If you bring me a dictionary, I'll look it up for you."

The cocky grin vanished from the cop's face. He glanced at his colleague, who seemed uncertain what to do. The other guy fidgeted, eying his 'friend' warily. If I didn't know better, I'd think he was as bullied as we were. And that wasn't good. Men can do a lot of crazy things when they're under pressure from their buddies.

"You know what I hate, Dean?" the dominant cop asked, as casually as if he were ordering pizza. "Smart-asses. I hate smart-asses who think they know more than everybody else."

My apparent lack of fear had thrown the second cop. He obviously hadn't expected me to parry a few shots, but now that their agenda was back on track, he looked idiotically jubilant.

"Me too," he said.

"You know what I like to do? I like to scramble their brains a bit, let them see how it feels to be as stupid as the rest of us." He stepped back, giving his buddy a nod. "Open it."

The sharp, unmistakable odor of urine filled the cell. Wrinkling my nose, I regarded the old Indian, who was weeping, his head resting on his knees. He already had his arms folded over his head.

As the keys jangled in the lock, I leapt from the bed, searching for anything I could use as a weapon. The asshole cop laughed.

"What are you looking for, boy? There's nowhere to run."

And there was nothing to use as a weapon, either. Unless....

"Get up," I snapped at Crazyhorse, giving his shoulder a little shove. "Hurry."

The man looked confused, but he did what I told him, scurrying into a corner and covering his head again. What I had in mind wasn't much. It probably wouldn't even slow them down. But at least it would make beating us less pleasant.

The door swung open, and Asshole Cop strutted toward me. Our holding cell was so small there really wasn't room for all of us, so his friend had to wait outside.

When A.C. saw me tugging at Crazyhorse's bedding, he snorted. "I'm not here for a pillow fight, Wall—"

Whap. The pathetic excuse for a mattress came free, and I struck the cop full in the face with my cellmate's puddle of pee.

The cop stumbled backwards, colliding with his friend. He coughed and sputtered, shoving the sagging mattress away from him, but there was no place for it to go. It kept falling toward him. "You fucker. You little shit."

But his threats had lost their power as he kept swiping at his face and spitting. His features were twisted in revulsion, and no wonder – that was some powerful piss. The whole room stank of it, and Asshole Cop had gotten a face full.

From behind me, I heard the incongruous sound of someone giggling. I turned to see Crazyhorse smiling with the few teeth he had left, his eyes bright and sparkling. "Good one, Reese," he said, clapping when he saw he had my attention. "Good one."

If this had been a movie, or some other work of fiction, we would have bested the crooked cops and emerged triumphant from our cell. I'd buy Crazyhorse a suit and he'd magically lick his addiction to moonshine and become gainfully employed. Even when he was a successful businessman, he'd never forget the small kindness I'd shown him, and we would remain friends until he died. In his will he'd leave me a significant fortune.

But this wasn't fiction, and the sparkle in Crazyhorse's eyes quickly gave way to panic. I spun around in time to see the cop's baton coming full force at my head. It cracked against my skull, causing bright flashes of pain to explode in my vision.

The floor rushed to meet me, and I gratefully accepted its embrace.

★   ★   ★

The first thing I noticed was a long expanse of white. The second was that my surroundings no longer stank of piss.

I'd never been a religious person, but now I wondered if this was a near-death experience. At least, I hoped it was near death and not the real thing.

"I think he's waking up. Reese? Reese, buddy, can you hear us?"

Blinking to bring the room into focus, I lifted my hand, reaching toward my dad's voice, but all I touched was air. "I can hear you, but I can't see you."

A hand touched mine. It was much smaller and softer than my father's. I caught a whiff of my mother's iris perfume seconds before I heard her voice. "Thank God you're all right."

"He's not out of the woods yet," my dad said in his usual gruff, let's-cut-the-bullshit manner. "Don't give him false hope."

"What happened?" It felt like I was talking through a mouth full of marbles. I could only move one of my hands, and after shaking the other a couple of times, I realized why – that dreaded metal bracelet was around my wrist again, chaining my arm to the bed.

"Don't worry, son. We're going to get rid of that cuff soon. We're also going to slap that department with so many lawsuits they won't know what hit 'em."

It was the words 'hit 'em' that brought it back – the asshole cop's baton smashing against my skull. Now that I remembered, a dull ache thudded through my brain, almost begrudgingly, like it was tired of keeping up the signal.

It wasn't only my head that hurt. It felt like a truck had driven over me and then reversed. Maybe more than once.

What did that fucker do to me?

I thought of my cellmate, and how scared he'd been. I was willing to bet that hadn't been his only two-step with the asshole cop. "How's Crazyhorse?"

"Who?"

I sighed, frustrated. It was difficult enough to talk as it was. My head swam, like I was either going to vomit or pass out. "Crazyhorse. My cellmate."

"The old Indian?" my father asked, as if we were acquainted with many people of that name. Or cellmates, for that matter.

Nodding seemed like a bad idea, so I moved my hand away from my mother's clutching fingers long enough to give them a thumb's up.

"I think he's fine. He's not in the hospital, I know that much." The confusion in his voice was palpable. *Why is our son asking about that guy? He's a homeless, inebriated Indian.* It was easy enough to guess what he was thinking, because only a day or so ago, I would have thought the same myself.

I hoped I knew better now.

"He'll be a good witness for you, Reese. He can tell the judge those men hit you for no reason," my mom said.

Ah, my mother, forever the optimist. Whoever the judge was, he'd give Crazyhorse about as much credit as my father had. I was just grateful the older man was okay. If I felt this bad, I couldn't imagine what a beating would have done to him. He'd looked so frail.

"What did they do to me?" I managed to get the words out without groaning too much.

"You have a couple of cracked ribs. Those hurt like a bitch, but they'll heal fine. Bastards broke your nose and bruised your legs good, but Dr. McCormick has a surgeon who can fix your face. Shouldn't be much of a scar afterwards."

My father was hiding something, but I didn't have the strength or capacity to argue. Instead I waited for them to get around to giving me the really bad news.

"The only thing—" Dad cleared his throat, and although my eyes wouldn't focus, I could tell he was shuffling his feet and looking around the room, searching for something more pleasant than his battered son to fixate on. "The thing we're concerned about is – well, there's no nice way to say it, so I'm going to spit it out and be done with it. They fractured your skull, kid. The doctor thinks there might have been some damage to your optic nerve. That's why you can't see so good."

"But you're going to be *fine*." Mom's voice was so cheerful it was nauseating. I almost puked at the outpouring of positivity. Much more of that, and they'd have me convinced I was going to die. "It will take some time to heal, but in a few weeks, you'll be better than before."

"Cut the shit, Eloise," my dad said. "You're starting to give *me* a headache."

Metal rings complained against the rod as my privacy curtain was swept aside.

My new visitor gasped. "Those bastards. Those power-hungry bastards."

"Prosper," my dad said. "Thanks for coming."

"They're going to pay for this, you better believe it. The county is going to pay through the nose for what they did to your son." Only after this sweeping declaration did he direct his attention to me. "How are you feeling, Reese?"

"Okay, I guess. My head hurts, and I can't see too well."

"They will pay for that too. That MBA you hoped for? Consider it covered by the good people of Minnesota."

"Uh...." For the second time in recent history, I was at a loss for words. "That's not really my biggest concern right now."

Prosper patted my arm. "Of course not. Of course not. I only wanted you to be aware that a lot of options have opened up for you. You could go to Harvard if you wanted."

"Great. I'm sure glad those cops almost killed me. What a lucky break."

"Reese..." my mother warned.

"I think our son has a right to be upset, Eloise. I respect you have a job to do, Prosper, but this isn't the time or place. What we care about now is Reese's health. The rest can wait."

"How I wish that were true, Mr. Wallace. Unfortunately, even as we stand here chatting, the other side is preparing its defense. We have to be ready. There is no time to waste."

"Excuse me, but what defense could they possibly have?" My mother's anger rose to meet the level of my father's. "They cracked my son over the head with a baton. They kicked him while he was lying on the floor unconscious. He might never regain his sight. How on earth will they justify that kind of brutality?"

"I realize it doesn't seem possible, but I know the police, Mrs. Wallace. Those boys tend to stick together, and trust me — they'll concoct some kind of story to justify their actions. If we want to file an injunction against them and get your son released, I'm going to need to take a statement from Reese now."

The sound of them bickering made my head feel like it would split in two. I moaned, wishing they would get the hint. "Does it have to be now? I'm so tired. I want to sleep."

"I'm sorry, but it does. It won't take long, Reese," my lawyer said with his usual brisk efficiency. "I need to hear exactly what happened in your own words."

"This is ridiculous," my dad said. "We don't care about the money, for Christ's sake. Our son needs to rest. The other stuff can wait."

"How do you like the medical attention he's been receiving? How do you like this?" I felt a light tug as Prosper lifted the chain attached to my handcuff. "He can't take a piss without ringing for the nurse. Are you fine with Reese being treated this way, like a criminal? Because I'm not. And today is the best day to file for a dismissal of the charges against him. But it's your call. I work for you."

My parents were quiet for a minute, considering. I braced myself, knowing what was coming.

"Reese, buddy?" My dad leaned so close I could feel his breath against my cheek. "Do you think you could tell Mr. Prosper what happened?"

I had nothing to lose, and maybe if I gave him a statement, Prosper would crawl back under his rock and leave me alone.

I may have been blind, but at least I had a voice. And a lawyer. That was more than Crazyhorse had.

Someone had to speak for both of us.

CHAPTER TWENTY-TWO

Many people are afraid of morgues. Maybe it's because they've only seen them in horror movies, when a corpse unexpectedly sits up, scaring them half to death. Or maybe their trepidation stems from something more personal, the fear that some day they will find themselves there, staring into the ashen face of a loved one.

Cops get over this fear pretty damn fast. The morgue becomes a routine like any other, and though it isn't their favorite place by any means, that sense of dread anticipation is long gone.

That is, until it comes back.

Maria felt an almost irresistible urge to run as they took the elevator to the basement, and it increased steadily with every step down that well-lit corridor. By the time Dr. Wilder removed the sheet covering Jessica McCaffrey's remains, every nerve in Maria's body was in revolt, sounding alarms and waving red flags. Her skin was on fire; her eye twitched with the pain of a sudden migraine; and her stomach churned.

The girl's body was covered in oozing sores just like Travis's. But how? They hadn't been there before.

"Jorge…" she managed, unsure how she would tell him she was dying, but figuring she ought to say something. Her lips were dry and cracked. Just saying his name hurt like hell.

Her partner and the doctor turned at the same time, and when she saw their expressions, she knew she looked as bad as she felt, if not worse.

"What's wrong, Maria?" Jorge asked, but the doctor was quicker. He caught her a second before she hit the floor.

*　　*　　*

Grey Mother's prediction had come true. Little Dove was a natural healer, and it wasn't long before the community's women came to her in times of pregnancy and illness. She soothed their wounds and bound their cuts and guided their children into the world. If some of her sisters suspected Lone Wolf had superior skills, they didn't speak of it, and in truth, they were relieved not to have to deal with him any longer.

Four seasons passed, and then another four, and everything was peaceful in the camp. The men in need of medicine went to Lone Wolf, while the women came to Little Dove, and the shaman himself appeared fine with the arrangement. While he had made good on his threat not to come to a woman's aid, there didn't appear to be any residual bad blood between the healer and Grey Mother. Everything was calm.

Until the day the golden-haired woman returned.

They did not recognize her. The woman who had stumbled half-dead into their camp on the brink of a winter storm had been a pale shadow of the one who walked toward them now. A scowling man was with her, but he hung back by the trees, glaring at their people. He shoved the woman forward, making the warriors gasp, for females in their community were always treated with great respect. The woman glanced over her shoulder at the man as she stumbled, her eyes wide and fearful. But when she saw Little Dove, she smiled in recognition.

Placing a wrapped bundle upon the ground, she closed the distance between them, reaching for the medicine woman's hand. Little Dove, confused and a little embarrassed, for everyone was staring at her, offered her own. The white woman clasped it between both of hers.

"How can I ever repay you for saving my son?"

"Waste not your time, woman. She can't understand a bloody word yer sayin'." The man who had accompanied the woman did not bother to hide his disgust. "They're savages. They don't speak the Queen's English."

Little Dove could hear Grey Mother hiss as the matriarch raised herself to her formidable height. The older woman's nostrils flared, and in a moment, she would charge this disrespectful stranger, and there would be bloodshed. Before Grey Mother could react, Little Dove raised her hand.

"We are familiar with your language, stranger. But we prefer to speak our own." Then she said a few words in her tongue, thinking how it was so much prettier, even musical, with the words lilting and lifting over one another like a song.

The man sneered at her, and Little Dove knew she had proven her point. She and her sisters could understand him fine. *He* was the savage who understood only one language.

Beside her, she heard Grey Mother release her breath, but hostility still emanated from the Elder. Little Dove's protector would keep her eye on this rude man until he left their territory, and for that, the medicine woman was grateful.

Little Dove addressed the woman. "There is no debt between us. Our kindness is as free as the air we breathe and the water we drink. We are repaid by seeing how well you are now. How is the boy?"

The woman's smile trembled. "He is good. Growing big and strong, like his Pa."

Little Dove prayed the insulting man was not the infant's father. One creature like that in the world was certainly enough. "I am pleased to hear it. That is all the thanks we need."

Grey Mother harrumphed, and Little Dove suspected she knew what the Elder was thinking. The winter had treated their people harshly as well, although none of them had been as close to meeting their Creator as this poor woman. Perhaps the strangers would be willing to offer a gift in return for their good health. Lone Wolf had warned of sophisticated weapons and tools that could clear an entire forest in a whisper. While Little Dove had no desire to see her beloved trees disappear, or for her people to wield the killing machines Lone Wolf spoke of, the strangers might have something that would make hunting a little easier.

"Give them what you came to give them, and let's be gone," the man at the edge of the camp said, as if he had read her mind. "I'm running out of patience."

The woman flinched as if she'd been struck, and scurried to where she had left the cumbersome bundle in the grass. She seemed to have forgotten it was there.

She held out the package to Little Dove, but something made her hesitate. The healer had no problem reading the lines of confusion on the woman's face, or the tears that glazed her eyes. Something was obviously troubling her, but *what*?

"Give it to them, Beatrice," the man said. "Let us go."

Little Dove went to take the parcel from the woman's shaking hand, but the blonde woman seized her fingers. "You mustn't," she whispered. "You must burn them."

"*Beatrice.*"

The woman dropped the bundle on the ground at Little Dove's feet, and Grey Mother hissed once more at the sign of disrespect. However, the healer suspected nothing was as it seemed. Something was wrong with the gift, but what? And why? Her people had saved this woman's life, and that of her infant. Surely she would not agree to bring them anything that would do them harm?

Before she could question the woman, the angry man pushed his way into the camp, grabbing what Little Dove now strongly suspected was his wife by the upper arm. The sisters bristled, but none made a move to stop him. The woman was not their sister, and her fight was not theirs.

The man bent to speak into the woman's ear, chastising her as they left the camp. He kept his voice low, but Little Dove could hear him fine. He was angry with his wife for trying to warn them. Warn them of what?

As soon as the strangers were gone, Grey Mother hurried over to the wrapped bundle, which lay in the dirt at the medicine woman's feet.

"No, Grey Mother," Little Dove cried, but it was too late. Brightly colored cloth burst from the package, revealing itself under the Elder's tearing, clawing hands.

"They are blankets," the older woman said in wonder, holding one up to her cheek. "They're so soft. I've never felt anything like this. What animal made these?"

Her sisters quickly gathered round, pushing and jostling for their share. They reminded Little Dove of a flock of ravens fighting over a carcass. The image made her shiver.

She was deeply ashamed of the way her sisters clutched and pawed at the gifts. To her horror, the women tossed their own furs to the ground, dishonoring the brave and powerful animal spirits who had made the greatest of sacrifices so her people could survive the season of the long moon. The blankets *were* beautiful – how on earth did the strangers manage such glorious colors? The bright hues rivaled the turning of the leaves during the harvest season. But despite its beauty, the gift seemed false, weak, too thin to defeat sickness or provide true shelter against cold and ice.

"Why are you not celebrating?"

Little Dove startled before she could catch herself. She hated the way Lone Wolf appeared at the most unfortunate times. If she didn't know better, she'd suspect he could divine the future.

"You should claim your reward," he said. "You have earned it by selling out our people."

Forgetting her own misgivings, she turned on him with a fury that made him retreat a step. "Leave me be, hateful man! We are both medicine people now, worthy of respect. You will not speak to me this way."

Lone Wolf laughed, showing off the sharp canine teeth that had earned him his name. "You can study from morning until night and never be half the healer I am by the end of your long life. As for the way I speak, who is going to stop me? Your protector?" He indicated Grey Mother with a tilt of his head, the disappointment in his voice clear. "She is too occupied, wallowing in greed."

The embarrassment Little Dove had swallowed made her reaction stronger than either of them anticipated. With a cry, she lunged at him. In spite of his size, she soon had her hands around his throat.

She began to squeeze.

"When you speak of our Elder, you will do so with respect," she said, forcing each word from between clenched teeth. "Your sentiments are not welcome here."

Lone Wolf pushed his arms through hers, easily breaking her hold. "You will do well to control your temper, Medicine Woman." His tongue lingered on the title, instilling it with as much mocking as possible. "You are heading into dangerous territory from which you cannot turn back."

Little Dove lifted her chin. "Leave us."

"As you wish. When what I have foretold comes to pass, remember that when I offered my help, you cast me aside. Remember this day, little sister, for you will rue it."

In response, Little Dove did the most insulting thing she could think of. She turned her back on him, imagining he was not there. She heard his sharp intake of breath, as if something had struck him.

Then, as swiftly and silently as he had appeared, he was gone.

Before she could consider the repercussions of the widening rift between them, a shriek drew her attention to the women once more. When Little Dove saw what was happening, her entire body shook with rage. Without thinking, she rushed into the fray.

"What are you doing? Stop it at once."

A plump woman known as Quivering Birch continued to shriek, the short end of one of the blankets wound around her stubby fingers. At the other end was Red Sky Dancer, who appeared to be yanking on the cloth with all her strength. Each time the taller woman tugged, Quivering Birch stumbled forward – no mean feat, as Quivering Birch greatly outweighed Lone Wolf's sister. Little Dove saw she'd misjudged the cloth's strength. If it had been of doubtful quality, it would have been in two pieces by now.

"Did you hear me? Let go," Little Dove said.

Quivering Birch's forehead was beaded with sweat. "I cannot lessen my hold. If I do, this – this *weasel* will steal it."

"I can't steal something that was never yours," Red Sky Dancer replied. Either she hadn't heard the real insult, or she'd decided to ignore it. Before Little Dove could respond, the cunning woman leaned forward and spat at her opponent, hitting her in the face with foamy drool.

"Uck!" Quivering Birch dropped the blanket, swiping at her face, and Red Sky Dancer swirled the scarlet cloth around her like a cape.

"You see? It was made for me. You cannot pretend to think otherwise."

Even though Little Dove would never admit such a thing out loud, she had to agree the cloth suited Red Sky Dancer far more than it would the unfortunate Quivering Birch. Against Red Sky's golden skin and shining hair, the deep crimson was striking. It wasn't only her attitude that caused the other sisters to loathe Red Sky Dancer. Her stunning beauty enraged them. She was the only one who hadn't come to Little Dove for salves or poultices. Unless her brother had made an exception when it came to treating women, Red Sky Dancer was a natural beauty. Unfortunately, she was well aware of it.

"I am surprised your brother let you accept such a gift," Little Dove said, doing her best to coat every word with disdain. "Considering he wants us to have nothing to do with the settlers."

"My brother will tend to his own affairs while I attend to mine." Red Sky Dancer settled the blanket around her shoulders, her head held high. Unlike the others, she kept her fox fur as well, earning Little Dove's grudging respect.

As the woman left their circle, Quivering Birch collapsed to the ground, wailing into the dirt. Little Dove knelt beside her, alarmed. "What ails you, sister? Are you hurt?"

Quivering Birch shook her head, tears and mucus running down her cheeks. She struggled to speak, managing a few stuttered words before lapsing into sobs.

"She is upset there is nothing left, the poor child," Grey Mother advised, clutching a blanket the color of a harvest-season sky.

"Nothing?" Little Dove peered at the ground, but her Elder had been speaking true. Only a few shreds of cloth from the packaging itself fluttered in the wind. The children leapt and danced, trying their best to catch them.

"Red Sky Dancer took the last one. Of course she got the most beautiful."

Little Dove was not fooled by the outrage in Grey Mother's voice. She knew full well the Elder was hiding things from her. Without so many witnesses, both the crimson robe and the blue would have mysteriously found their way to the older woman's quarters.

Quivering Birch continued to sob into the grass. Pulling the furs from her own shoulders, Little Dove draped them over her sister. The woman sniffed, rubbing her eyes. She quit crying when she saw the quality of the furs that concealed her weather-beaten dress from view. It was Little Dove's best red fox, more lovely than the crimson rags that had been stolen in plain sight. "You honor me, Medicine Woman," Quivering Birch said, inclining her head. "It is with great sadness that I tell you I cannot accept it."

"You must accept it. I have many furs." The red fox was special, but Little Dove was determined Quivering Birch would have it. "If you feel a debt, use it to help others one day."

With a shy smile, the woman stroked the fur. Slowly, hesitantly, she drew it closer around her shoulders. "It's beautiful. And so soft."

"It will keep you warmer than the one you were fighting over. I think in time, you will be happy you lost the battle."

Little Dove had no idea just how true her words would be.

CHAPTER TWENTY-THREE

Even though I was blind, I knew I wasn't alone.

I waited, trying to be patient, and sure enough, a large, dark shape wavered into view. Whoever or whatever it was, it was sitting on my bed.

"Good morning, Reese. How are you feeling?"

The voice, a smooth, deep rumble, was somehow familiar. I was positive I'd heard it before, but couldn't place it.

"Better." My lower back ached something fierce from lying around for hours, but my busted ribs made stretching a risky proposition. I did my best anyway, feeling some relief as my vertebrae popped. It took me a beat to realize something was very different.

It was this difference that made me remember where I'd heard that voice before. "You're a cop, aren't you? You're Detective Greyeyes' partner."

"Detective Jorge Ruiz. I'd heard you'd regained some of your sight." Now I picked up on the slight lilt in his voice, the faint accent that told me his first language was Spanish. "But I didn't know it had returned that much. I'm glad for you."

"It hasn't. I just recognized your voice. And, well, there was this." I raised my right arm, rotating my newly free hand on its wrist. Damn, but it felt good. "I'm sure you were just feeling sorry for me, but please don't think I'm not grateful."

"My feelings had nothing to do with it. Free men don't wear handcuffs."

Did he say what I think he said? Maybe my ears were going as well, but I decided to chance it. "Too bad I needed to get the shit beaten out of me before I proved my innocence."

"Hey, the rest of us aren't like that. Maria is tore up about what happened to you, and so am I. We've sent Archer packing. He's not going to pull that shit again, at least not with a badge."

Rage churned in my gut. "And you think this makes me happy? That guy is a fucking psychopath, and instead of punishing him, you let him loose on the streets to hurt more people."

What if he ran into Crazyhorse? It was enough to give me chills.

"With luck, it won't be for long. He's being investigated, and once we have enough evidence, we'll nail him for attempted murder."

Prosper had told me Archer's ridiculous version of events. He and his fellow goon claimed the beating they'd given me was in self-defense. Supposedly Crazyhorse and I had charged them when they'd tried to serve dinner. As if the combined one hundred and seventy pounds of us would be a threat against the two of them. Good Christ.

"I've been hit on the head recently, officer, so maybe that's why I'm not following you. Shouldn't he be in a cell instead of wandering around free?" Rotating my wrist again, I marveled at the blood flowing through my veins with no restrictions.

"Everything in good time. This isn't the first time we've had a complaint against him, but he's always managed to weasel out of it, or the complainants were too scared to press charges. We have hope that this time, it'll stick," the cop said. And then he said something else that made my testicles shrink to the size of raisins. "We found another body."

"Anyone I know?" I tried my best to sound casual, but unless this cop had the observation powers of your average housefly, he'd hear how freaked out I was. Hell, he could probably see it.

Unlike his partner, Jorge didn't mince words. "It's Mrs. McGraw. Somebody tore her apart."

Mrs. McGraw. It was a sucker punch to the heart. Picturing the smiling woman with the gentle brown eyes, I wanted to scream. I hadn't known Dan's mother well, but I'd liked her. Everyone did.

"What happened?"

"That's what we'd like to know. We've got four people murdered – no, not just murdered – *massacred*, but I'm sure I don't have to tell you that. Then two kids are rushed to the hospital screaming bloody murder, covered with blisters, and it turns out they have a disease that hasn't existed for decades. And guess where they got it from? That blasted fucking campground."

My head was spinning. Resting against my pillows, I rubbed my forehead, hoping I'd be able to get the words out before I lost consciousness. "Sorry, Detective, you lost me. What's this about a disease?"

"The boys were fine this morning when they left the house, but they returned with a severe case of smallpox. The infectious disease guys are treating them, but we need to know if you experienced anything strange out there that night, anything at all."

In spite of my wooziness, I wanted to laugh. A couple of days ago, the police had charged me with murder. One of their compadres had done his best to split open my skull. And now they wanted my help?

"You mean, besides the fact my girlfriend and two of our friends were ripped to shreds?"

Jorge sighed. The bed creaked as he stood. "I feel like the world's biggest asshole asking you for help after what we did to you. But as of now, we have no other leads. Someone could be manufacturing biological weapons in the area, or God knows what else. Did you see or hear anything that seemed off? Was there anything that bothered you, anything strange?"

"There was one thing."

As I told him about hearing someone whisper *You're not welcome here* when no one was there, goose bumps puckered the skin on my arms and I shivered, pulling the flimsy sheet higher on my chest. Fucking hospitals and their cheap-ass blankets.

When I finished, Jorge was quiet, *too* quiet. It bothered me, especially since I couldn't see his face. Did he think I was crazy?

"Hey man, do you think you could ask the nurse for another blanket? I'm freezing."

"Sure, Reese, no problem. Are you absolutely sure you didn't see anyone other than your friends? Maybe whoever spoke to you took off before you turned around."

"There's no way anyone could have gotten away without me seeing them." *Those were the days.* "Or hearing them, for that matter. That place is covered with leaves and twigs and other crap. It's impossible to sneak up on anyone."

I waited a minute for reassurance that never came. "You think I'm crazy, don't you?"

"No, I don't, and I don't think this is a joke, either. Unless you're a sociopath, you're the last person who would fuck around with us.

I assume you want whoever tortured your girlfriend to pay for what he did."

Anger, guilt, despair, regret. So many emotions churned in me that for a moment I was afraid to speak. Clearing my throat, I said, "Of course I do." My voice had grown hoarse, the croak of a dying frog.

The cool plastic of my water glass pressed into my hand. Drinking gratefully, I drained it before giving it back. "Thanks. Biological weapons – is that really what you think is happening out there?"

I'd already gone over everything I could remember about that night. My memory had scoured every rock and tree and found nothing. No trace of any nefarious experiments, and no sign of life other than us. Obviously someone had been there, but who?

"To be honest, we don't know. But I can tell you one thing. I'm going to find out."

"I still don't understand what happened to Dan's mom. Who found her?"

The man swallowed hard. I could hear the rasp of his breathing. Either the stress of the case had put strain on Jorge's lungs, or the man was a couple of cheeseburgers away from a coronary. "We did. It was a nasty surprise for our team. For whatever reason, she decided to revisit the site of her son's death last night, and it cost her."

Remembering how Dan had begged me to come get him in that horrible nightmare, I wondered if his mother had experienced the same dream. What if my dad hadn't stopped me from leaving that night? Would I have been torn apart too? But no, that didn't make sense. Whoever the killer was, he'd had his chance to add me to the body count, and for some reason, he'd left me alive. Why spare my life one night, only to kill me a few days later?

"Where is Detective Greyeyes? I'd really like to talk to her."

Why had she sent Jorge? I'd always spoken to her. Was she ashamed of how she'd treated me after I was arrested? She hadn't struck me as a coward. I was disappointed she hadn't come to apologize personally.

"That should be easy to arrange. She's right down the hall. Once you're up to it, you can go visit her. I'm sure she wouldn't mind."

"Visit her? What are you talking about?"

"She's in a coma, and no one has a goddamn clue what's wrong with her. She was healthy as a horse one minute, and the next, she collapsed. Doctor caught her right before she hit the floor. Seems that whatever's infected that campground has gotten her too."

CHAPTER TWENTY-FOUR

Death was near. She could smell its foul stink on the old woman's breath, lingering over them.

Grey Mother's lips were cracked and blistered, but she struggled to speak. "It is the prophecy, dear one. I have failed you."

Little Dove's eyes filled as she dabbed the medicine-soaked cloth against the woman's forehead and cheeks. Though it was the most powerful poultice she knew how to make, it would have no effect. Still, she had to do something. Her days were long and contained nothing but tragedy.

"It is I who have failed you, Grey Mother. I was never meant to be a healer. If only I could take your affliction upon myself, you could save the others." Her voice was muffled through the barrier tied over her nose and mouth. Early on, Grey Mother had discerned the nature of the sickness that plagued them, and had made Little Dove wear the barrier for her own protection. It had worked, which caused the young healer more sorrow, as she had been forced to watch her beloved sisters die.

The old woman's hand, covered with both spots of wisdom and of the disease, trembled as it sought to find hers. "You are a wonderful healer. No one could save us from this. This is Lone Wolf's curse."

"You dare blame me for this?"

Both women gasped, Grey Mother's sounding like a death rattle in her throat. Little Dove knew the dear woman did not have long. She turned to see Lone Wolf darkening the doorway, the only time he had entered the women's camp since the terrible illness had struck.

The man was diminished, as if he had been starved. His features, always sharper than the others', now stood out in stark relief. Only his eyes were the same, burning with hate in his proud face.

"You have brought this plague upon yourself with your foolishness, as I warned you. And worse, your stupidity has not only placed yourselves in jeopardy, but my sister as well."

His sister? Little Dove realized she hadn't seen Red Sky Dancer in at least a moon. She'd been too preoccupied with attending to her own sisters to notice. It was pain that strained the shaman's features, then, not rage. Though his words were harsh, they must come from grief. She would respond to him in kindness. "I am sorry to hear your sister is not well. Is there anything I can do to ease her suffering?"

A troubling thought clawed at the edges of her mind. Perhaps Grey Mother was wrong about how the cursed disease traveled from one host to the other. Red Sky Dancer had avoided their camp in favor of her brother's since she was a child. She hadn't come near them since the settlers' visit. How could she have fallen ill as well?

"Save your sweet words for someone who will benefit. My sister is dead."

Dead. A flurry of images of the woman staggered Little Dove. The great beauty, vibrant and laughing, pulling the crimson blanket over her shoulders with a flourish. How could she be dead? Her brother's medicine was the most potent in the land. Grey Mother had pleaded with him for help many times since the terrible illness had cursed their camp, but Lone Wolf hadn't let her come near. All this time, Little Dove had fought to keep hatred from taking over her heart, sure that Lone Wolf could cure them if he'd wanted. Knowing that even their greatest shaman was powerless in the face of this new threat was more devastating than believing he'd let her sisters die.

Rising from Grey Mother's side, she went to him, intending to comfort, but he backed away. "Do not touch me. You're like the rest."

His rejection stung, but in the face of his sister's death, it was understandable. He had no reason to believe her touch wouldn't kill him. "I am truly sorry for your loss, Lone Wolf. We had hoped the other camps had been spared."

A sneer twisted his thin lips, exposing his teeth in a wolfish snarl. "No one is spared. I warned you this day would come. I told you they brought nothing but poison, but you refused to listen. My sister's death is on your hands."

"My hands?" In spite of her resolve to show empathy, to stay calm, anger flared in her chest. For over a moon, she hadn't had a moment's rest. She'd done everything possible to heal her sisters or, failing that, make their last moments comfortable. How dare he point the finger at her? "You have suffered a tremendous loss, but I don't see how you can lay the blame on my shoulders."

"You don't see? I should not be surprised, since you have been blind from the beginning, Little Dove. Your naivety is no fault of your own, which is why some have insisted on cossetting and coddling you." He glared at Grey Mother, whose rattling breaths had quieted. "Though I, too, was sympathetic in the beginning, I soon saw how your immense foolishness had the potential to doom us all. And then that one had to fill your already empty head with some silliness about you being a healer." He spat on the ground. "You are no healer."

Little Dove's skin burned with shame. His words sliced through her like spears, wounding her deeply. It was true; she was no healer. She could not dispute it, not in the wake of so many deaths. "Grey Mother has been too ill to help the sisters. You refused. I did the best I could with my limited knowledge."

"Your limited knowledge is the cause of this destruction. You still don't see it, do you? Even now, with the light shining in your face, you stumble along in the dark."

Closing her eyes, she summoned her patience. Continuing the fight with Lone Wolf would not help their people. It would be up to her to forge peace between them, even if that meant leaving her dignity behind. "I see that you are in great pain, so I forgive your harsh words. I even forgive you for abandoning us in our time of need. I understand your anger. I feel it as well. But directing it at me helps no one. We are in the same position, Lone Wolf. We must end this feud and work together for the good of our people."

His features contorted, turning him into a truly ugly man, a man who resembled a monster. She took a step toward Grey Mother, though the woman was no longer in a position to protect her. She was on her own.

"How dare you compare the two of us? I am a healer, and you are a destroyer. How can you not see the blood when it is raining from your hands? How can you persist in this miasma of ignorance?"

Lack of rest and nourishment had impaired her judgment. Little Dove's thoughts swirled, impotent and unhelpful. It crossed her mind that, in his grief and isolation, the shaman had gone mad. He needed someone to blame, and he had chosen her.

Raising his hand, he pointed a finger at her face. "*You* opened our home to the enemy. *You* welcomed them in, with their hatred and their evil intentions and their disease. *You* chose them over us, and in doing so, you have brought death and suffering to our people."

She could feel his fury like a physical force, and for a moment, she was grateful the illness formed a barrier between them. If the shaman forgot his fear of the disease and entered her camp, she was sure he would kill her in his madness. "You are not making sense, Lone Wolf. I have not welcomed anyone, let alone an enemy. I do not understand the source of our sickness any more than you do."

He continued raving as if she hadn't spoken. "You are the one who took their little worm of an infant to your breast when you should have dashed it to the ground. Worm is an appropriate word for it, because parasites are what they are, all of them. And you let them in, and told them they could feed."

"You – you are blaming the settlers for our misfortune?" The shaman was more ill than she'd thought. Though his skin was clear, the disease must have taken hold of his mind. No sane man could believe those poor, unfortunate people were responsible for this.

"Open your eyes, Little Dove. Open your eyes and *see*. See those parasites for who they are. The precious gifts they bestowed upon you were riddled with disease. As your greedy sisters leapt on them, biting and scratching for their share, they sealed their fate."

"The blankets?" The shame of that day resettled on her shoulders, bowing her. How her sisters had cast the cherished cloaks of their animal brothers and sisters on the ground, dishonoring the beasts' great sacrifice. How they'd fought each other, sister against sister, for those brightly colored scraps of cloth, cloth that quickly faded in the sun, revealing itself for what it truly was. Her sisters had sold their dignity for the lowest price – tattered rags that weren't worth the effort it had taken to weave them.

"Do you believe it is chance that has us both standing here, drawing breath, while those around us die?"

Her mind reeled. She was the only one from her camp who had not taken a blanket. She and Quivering Birch, but Quivering Birch had passed over a moon ago. The doomed woman had touched the tainted cloth – had fought over the crimson prize that had ultimately been taken by Red Sky Dancer.

Red Sky Dancer. The crimson blanket was how the dreadful plague had passed from their camp to Lone Wolf's.

The furrows on the shaman's face eased as he studied her. "You see it now," he said. "You *see*."

"The blanket – the red blanket," was all she could manage.

"I identified it instantly for what it was, but my sister would not hear reason. She clung to that foul thing, screaming it was hers, even when drawing her last breath." The man's eyes glittered in the waning light. "My sister, poisoned by her own greed. She would not believe me, would not listen. Not in the beginning, and not at the end."

Tears streamed over Little Dove's cheeks, falling onto Grey Mother's chest. When the older woman sighed, the new healer looked down and saw one of the hateful blankets clutched in the matriarch's hands. With a cry, she tore it off the woman's body and flung it into the fire, where it disintegrated rather than burned.

"I have been too harsh with you. You have lost your sisters, as I have lost mine. You have suffered greatly," Lone Wolf said. "Red Sky Dancer did not believe me. Perhaps it is enough that you do."

The shaman walked away, leaving her alone with death and despair.

CHAPTER TWENTY-FIVE

With her waning strength, Maria pulled away from the distraught woman. She'd glimpsed a light, shining through the darkness, beckoning her away from the crushing despair she'd found herself surrounded with. She hurried toward it, never looking back.

"Hey."

The man's face blurred in front of her, a kaleidoscope of color and shape. She rubbed her eyes and the image sharpened, revealing the extent of her colleagues' sadism.

"Oh, Reese," she tried to say, but it came out as a sigh. She struggled to lift her hand to his swollen, bruised cheek, but her limbs were stone.

"Don't move. I'll call the nurse." He moved out of view and she panicked.

"No. Wait." Her voice, raspy and coated with rust, gained strength. "I need to tell you something."

"You've been unconscious for a while, Detective. Your family — they'll want to see you. Detective Ruiz will want to see you. Whatever you need to say to me, it can wait. What happened to me, it wasn't your fault. There was no reason for you to believe me."

Gritting her teeth, she summoned the energy to lift one of her petrified limbs and grab his hand. "Something has happened to me."

"Yeah, you fainted, probably from the stress. You've been in some kind of weird coma for days, but the doctors couldn't find anything wrong. Don't worry, after they stick a few more needles in you, I'm sure they'll let you go home." Misreading the expression on her face, he patted her hand. She could barely feel it. "Sorry, too soon. Forget about the needles. It was a bad joke."

How would she ever find the energy to tell him it wasn't the thought of needles that frightened her?

Clinging to his hand, she urged him closer. "I've been having dreams, except I don't think they're dreams. I think I'm seeing something that really happened a long time ago."

"It's normal for people in a coma to have vivid dreams. The doctor said—"

"Fuck what the doctor said. This has nothing to do with that. It's the campground, Reese. Something happened to me at the campground."

His hand went limp in hers. He quit fighting her, stopped trying to pull away, but there must be a monitor somewhere that was broadcasting her change of status. She didn't have much time.

"Dan's mother died," he said, his voice brittle as breaking glass. "Did you know that? She went back there and she was torn apart, just like the others. Just like Jess."

"No, I didn't. I'm sorry." She waited a beat, not wanting to appear insensitive, but feeling new panic rising in her chest. Whatever was at Strong Lake didn't want her investigating, had done whatever it could to pin her here, trapping her like a caged bird. Reese was her only chance. "When will you get out of here?"

"The doctors are saying Wednesday. The day after tomorrow. I've recovered enough of my vision that they're ready to release me on the world, I guess."

"Listen to me. There's a chief up there, at the Strong Lake reserve. Chief Kinew. You have to go to him, let him know what happened to me. Tell him I've been having these memories about someone named Little Dove."

"Detective—"

She yanked hard on his arm, hearing footsteps in the hall now. Hurried footsteps. "Little Dove. Can you remember that?"

"Of course I can. But—"

"Go to him, Reese, please. Ask my husband to tell you about the arrowhead, and let the chief know about that too. Kinew will be able to help. He knows something, something he hasn't wanted to tell me."

"But I know about the arrowhead." His features still wavered out of focus, but she could hear the confusion in his voice. "I was the one who found it."

She clutched his hand with both of hers. "Not this. You don't know this. Ask my husband. Tell Kinew."

People burst into the room, a flurry of color and sound. It was too much, and she closed her eyes. She felt Reese being taken from her, and clung to him more fiercely. Someone pried her fingers off him.

"Good afternoon, Maria. Glad to see you're back with us. Your husband is going to be so pleased," said a voice oozing with fake compassion. Maria heard another voice, this one stern and unyielding, ordering Reese to leave.

"Don't go to the campground." Raising her voice, she fought to be heard, fought against the hands that held her down. "Promise me. Promise me you'll stay away from there."

There was the slightest pressure on her fingertips, an answering squeeze, before they ushered him out of the room.

"Reese," she called, but it was hardly a whimper. Her strength had left with him, leaving her weak.

"He's fine," the stern nurse said. "You'll be able to see him later. It's time to take care of yourself now. You've been through a terrible shock."

How to communicate that whatever shock she'd experienced, it was nothing compared to what was coming?

"Tell him he can't go back there. Tell him that if he does, he'll die."

★　　★　　★

The events of the last few weeks had regressed me, until I was nothing but a dumb kid again, waiting for my dad to fall asleep so I could sneak out. Only this time it wasn't to con someone into buying me beer. At least that had made sense.

Siri had helped me map the route. Getting there was easy enough, but my parents had shown predictable resistance at the idea of me driving again. Guess I couldn't blame them; they'd always been sticklers for little things like not breaking the law. While my vision was a lot better, my say-so wasn't enough. My eyes needed to be officially tested before I could legally get behind the wheel again, something Greyeyes hadn't considered when she'd commissioned me for this fool's errand. But screw it. I could still drive better than half the idiots out there, even with one eye shut.

"I'll take you anywhere you want to go," Dad said when he'd caught me with my truck keys. "It's no trouble."

Right. Picturing my father driving into a native reserve was almost enough to revive my sense of humor. I could imagine the color draining from his face as he learned where his son wanted to go. It was tempting.

But it would also never happen. I couldn't explain why I needed to see Kinew when I didn't understand it myself, and though my dad was a big believer in the great school of 'Do it because I say so,' such rules didn't apply to him. He'd want reasons, and reasons I didn't have. Besides, Dad held a special loathing for Detective Greyeyes. I told myself it was because he blamed her for having his son thrown in jail, not because of the color of her skin or the fact she had a uterus.

Reasons.

Thankfully, his beloved game did its job, working in tandem with the beer to knock him out cold. It had been more boring than usual, both teams hardly putting in an effort, even going into extra innings. Felt like fate to me. Dad's head tipped back, and his mouth fell open as he snored, giving him the appearance of a much older man. I got a glimpse of his future and it wasn't pretty. Shaking off my apprehension, I lifted myself from the floor. Dad had thought it odd when I'd stretched out there, but the armchair creaked. His faults notwithstanding, he hadn't raised any fools.

Creeping to the foyer like a thief, I held my breath as I stole my own keys, curling my fingers around the metal so they wouldn't jangle. Nothing but snoring from the living room. As long as I could make it out of here before Mom got home, I was free. The idea of escaping, of getting out of this house, sent a tingle of anticipation through me. My sneakers made no sound on the carpet. The front door, recently treated with WD-40 by yours truly, warned of my betrayal with a wheeze rather than a squeak.

The afternoon sun hit the hood of my truck just so, winking at me. The vehicle was my partner in this conspiracy, my ally in crime. Slipping behind the wheel, I put the Chevy in neutral and rolled out of the driveway, even though I wouldn't stop if Dad burst through the door. I hadn't yet left the property, but I'd already gone too far.

"All right, Siri. Do your thing. How do I get to Strong Lake reserve?"

"Drive three miles and turn right at the end of Oak Street," she chirped, her tone matching my mood. She sounded as happy to be out of there as I was. This enforced family time had been excruciating. Maybe I'd move away for grad school after all. Far away.

The iron bands around my chest didn't release until I left the hustle of the city behind. Only then did I quit checking my rearview mirror, positive my parents or that damn lawyer of theirs were on my tail. A disquieting feeling of déjà vu gnawed at my brain as I remembered the last time I'd hit the highway feeling this free. I'd been ready for a weekend of camping, and not even Jess's attitude could bring me down.

My eyes burned as I remembered Dan's cheerful banter from the backseat, as plainly as if he were still there. Squinting at the road, I forced myself to focus. The white line wavered ahead of me. I hadn't recovered as much as I'd thought. Visions of my parents viewing my truck as a twisted hunk of metal at the side of the highway shocked me back to the present.

"Keep on going straight," Siri said.

"Damn straight." Leaning forward, I clenched my jaw hard enough to hurt.

Thanks to my heavy foot, it took forty-five minutes to reach the reserve. Turning off the highway, I pulled onto a dirt road so badly graded my truck became a roller coaster, and I swore as my shocks took a beating. Several men stopped what they were doing to stare at me. Feeling like an idiot as I bounced around in the cab, smacking my head against the top, I smiled and waved.

They didn't smile back.

What the fuck am I doing here?

Knowing I liked to keep the truck in immaculate condition, Dad had washed it for me during my convalescence. I wished he hadn't. Sleek and gleaming, it marked me as an outsider. More stares. Gritting my teeth, I squinted at the road and kept going.

For white kids like me, reserves were places we knew existed but never saw, kind of like Antarctica, but a lot more bleak. As I guided my truck along the pockmarked excuse for a road, I began to feel like I'd driven off the highway straight into another dimension. Instead of Middle America, I was in the Developing World. Clapboard houses sagged to one side. Lawns, where they existed, were ailing and patchy. The people who stared at me had the same strained expression, as if the very act of living were painful.

I'd thought it would be easy to find this Chief Kinew fellow, but either I was going to lose an axle driving around like a fool, or give in and ask for directions. A woman sweeping the step of one of the better-kept houses looked like a safe bet. She squinted when I pulled into her driveway, shielding her face from the sun in order to get a better assessment. The prison guards had been more welcoming.

Pasting a grin on my face, I waved as I exited my truck, catching the tip of my sneaker on the running board and nearly tripping. The woman's scowl deepened. "Hey there!"

I was encouraged by her nod. "I'm looking for Chief Kinew. Can you tell me where to find him?"

Clutching the broom with her right hand, she pointed to the road to hell I'd just exited. "Keep going straight, about five miles. He's in the band office. Can't miss it."

Whew. "Thank you." Figured. The one time I'd asked for directions, I would have found the place myself if I'd kept on going.

"You here about the campground?"

Something cold trickled over my spine. The hairs on the back of my neck prickled. "What makes you say that?"

She shrugged, either already bored with my visit or a master at feigning indifference. "The campground is the only reason you people come here."

You people. It sounded like an indictment, and I felt like I should apologize, but for what, I wasn't sure. Driving a truck that cost more than her house? Dreaming of grad school, which my parents would pay for, when she probably worried about putting food on the table?

I gave myself a mental shake. I had no idea what this woman's life was like. For all I knew, she'd had caviar and crab cakes for breakfast, while I'd choked down a soggy bowl of Wheaties (which my parents had paid for). "Well, thanks for the directions."

She nodded again, already back to her sweeping. My hands shook as they grabbed hold of the steering wheel, pulling me into the cab. *Get a grip, Wallace. You're losing it.*

In my rearview mirror, I could see she paused to watch me as I drove away.

The nagging feeling that I'd done something wrong intensified in the band office. A rusty screen door shrieked of my arrival, making me wince, but the woman behind the reception desk only briefly glanced up from her smartphone.

I waited several minutes before daring to clear my throat, minutes in which she studiously ignored me.

"Yes?" she said, her voice heavy with resignation, as if I were the bane of her existence and she'd hoped I'd have gone away by now.

"Can I – I'm here to see Chief Kinew, please."

She raised an eyebrow. "Is he expecting you?"

"I'm here on behalf of Detective Greyeyes. She's a friend of his," I said, not knowing if it were true or not, and not caring. Nervous tension had made me jittery, like there were ants crawling up my leg, and all I wanted to do was fulfill my promise and then break every posted speed limit on the way home.

With a sigh and a shake of her head, the woman disappeared down a hallway, obviously disappointed I couldn't be dismissed with an admonishment to make an appointment next time. While Greyeyes' name had garnered a better response, I didn't sense the woman had any great love for the detective either.

She returned with a man so tall the top of his head brushed the ceiling. He was startlingly good looking with his dark, wavy hair and dimples deep enough to open a bottle with. Jess would have been most appreciative, even as she snickered over his floral-print western shirt and painted-on jeans. Hell, if I looked like that, I'd probably wear tight jeans too.

"Chief Kinew?"

If the man was surprised to see a dumb white kid waiting for him, he didn't show it. He extended his hand, the first person in his community to treat me like I wasn't some disgusting disease. "Welcome. You're a friend of Greyeyes?"

My impulse was to say no, but what was the better response? That I was her number-one suspect? Her former prisoner? Her guilty conscience? I thought of the way she'd clung to my hand in the hospital, how she'd trusted me to pass on her message, and nodded. "Yes. She asked me to speak with you."

"Glad to. Come on back. Would you like a coffee?"

Nerves had turned the inside of my mouth into the Sahara. "No, thank you, but a water would be great."

"Denise, will you get this young man a water, please?"

Denise's eye roll was nearly audible. Without waiting for a response, the chief led me to a room crammed with books. The towering stacks of volumes made the place look more like a used bookstore or an eccentric's library than a place of business.

"Wow. You must really like to read." The sight of that much literature was enough to give me hives.

A flash of perfect teeth. "I do." The chief cleared off a chair for me by moving what looked like an entire set of encyclopedias to the floor. "Please, take a seat. What should I call you?"

My cheeks burned as I realized I hadn't bothered to introduce myself. "Sorry. I'm Reese. Reese Wallace."

The chief paused in his sorting, his fingers resting on the cover of one of his many treasures. His eyes widened just the tiniest bit. "You're the survivor."

"Yes." The word surprised me. I hadn't thought of myself that way, as the fact I continued to suck air into my lungs seemed like dumb luck more than anything else.

"I'm sorry for your loss. If you need something stronger than water, I'm happy to get it for you."

"Thanks, I appreciate that, but water is fine. I'm driving," I said, as if I needed an excuse. "And I'm not a hundred percent yet."

"I can see that. Your face – is that from the campground?"

Sometimes I forgot that I still resembled a punching bag. "No, an overzealous cop."

Kinew's features hardened, and I could see he was a man you wouldn't want to fuck with. "Archer?"

"Unfortunately."

"There's no love for that man around here. I'm guessing now he'll finally pay for his savagery?"

Finally. One word that told me more than I'd ever wanted to know. I recalled how Crazyhorse had cringed at the sound of Archer's voice. How often had that asshole beaten the shit out of him? How many of Kinew's people had fallen victim to his nightstick?

"My parents are suing him, if that's what you mean."

The chief raised an eyebrow. "Got a good lawyer?"

I thought of Prosper, with his outlandish suits and air of importance. "He seems to think so."

Kinew's laugh filled the room, startling me. "As is the way of all lawyers. I hope he makes that bastard pay. It's been a long time coming."

"He's been suspended, and I doubt he'll be a cop again, if that's any consolation."

The laughter died. Kinew's eyes turned flat and dead, the mischievous sparkle vanishing as suddenly as if he'd snapped off a light. "Archer can do a lot more damage as a civilian, without the constraints of his job forcing him to keep on the straight and narrow. I won't be comfortable until I know he's behind bars, and if I were you, I'd watch my back until that reptile is in a cage."

Something heavy settled on my chest, making it difficult to breathe. "You think he might come after me?"

"That badge is the only thing that self-important prick had that was worth having. If he blames you for losing it…yeah, I do. He should have reserved his rage for my people. No one cared if he cracked one of our skulls in, but a college-educated white boy?" Kinew studied the ruin of my bruised and battered face. "I never thought he'd be stupid enough to make that kind of mistake. You must have really pissed him off."

"I was trying to help the other guy in my cell." It was a lie, but close enough to the truth that my conscience ached just a little. "He might be from around here. Think Archer had done a number on him before. The sound of the guy's voice was enough to terrify him."

The chief shrugged. "Wouldn't surprise me. We have a few fellows doing frequent rotation at that holding cell. Do you remember his name?"

How could I ever forget? "He said his name was Crazyhorse."

Once again Kinew threw back his head and laughed. "That would be George. He's from around here, all right. He's been telling this tall tale about a showdown with the police. Guess it's not as tall as we thought."

"George?" For some reason, discovering my cellmate had such an ordinary name disappointed me. "So Crazyhorse is a nickname?"

"Not exactly. Do you know the history of the real Crazy Horse, Reese?"

I shifted on my chair. We hadn't learned much Native American history in school, other than how some tribes had terrorized the poor, long-suffering pioneers until the government 'dealt with the problem'. I'd never taken any of it too seriously. History was written by the victor

– everyone knows that. "He was involved in the Battle of Little Big Horn. That's about it."

"*Involved* in the Battle of—" Kinew covered his eyes with a hand and sighed. "Never mind. A fellow by the name of George Crook ordered Crazy Horse's arrest. The fact that he was named George was always an affront to our Crazyhorse, so he took the name of the great warrior instead."

"Makes sense. Who wants to be named George, anyway?"

"My father's name is George." Kinew's eyes bored into mine, making me squirm, but as I fumbled for an apology, he grinned. "Just kidding." He leaned back in his chair, sending a haphazardly piled stack of books to the floor. "You said you had a message from Greyeyes. Should I take this to mean the great detective is employing college students as messenger boys now?"

The idea of being her lackey got my back up, even though it was obvious he was teasing me. "She would have come herself, but she's had some…health problems."

"I'm sorry to hear that. I hope she's on the mend?"

"She's out of the hospital now." That was all I was comfortable saying. It would feel strangely disloyal to discuss the detective's mental state with this stranger. "She wanted me to ask you about Little Dove."

"Little Dove?" His brow furrowed, adding another layer of ice around my heart. *Shit.* Whoever Little Dove was, she was driving the detective insane. If this guy didn't have answers, I wasn't sure where to go next. "I don't know anyone by that name."

"Detective Greyeyes has been having nightmares. *Bad* nightmares. But the thing is, she doesn't think they're dreams. She thinks she's remembering something that happened in the past. It started when I found this." Digging in my pocket, I carefully retrieved the arrowhead. Its edges were sharp as knives. Kinew reared back from it as if it were a viper.

"Last time I touched that thing, it nearly sent me through a wall."

I stared at the artifact, which was dull and dusty, both innocent and wicked looking at the same time. "What do you—?"

"I can't explain it. Somehow, it must harness static electricity, but that was some shock. It's a wonder my heart didn't stop. Are you sure this is the same arrowhead? When I saw it on Greyeyes, it looked new, like a replica."

"I'm pretty sure it's the one I found in our tent. I don't know anything about a replica."

"Damn thing was bleeding, do you know that? At first, I thought Greyeyes had been cut, but the blood was coming from *that*." The chief grimaced at the arrowhead. He'd inched backwards until he was right against the window now, as far away from the artifact as he could get.

I hadn't known, and though I didn't pretend to understand it, Kinew's reaction was a relief. I'd felt like a moron, coming here and telling him a bunch of stuff that made no sense to me. The arrowhead was just a plain ol' arrowhead whenever I'd seen it, but Greyeyes had experienced something very different. And now the chief's reaction was backing her up, at least in part.

As best I could, I reiterated everything she'd told me: how she'd woken up with the arrowhead hanging from her neck on a cord, how she'd doubled over with nausea whenever she'd tried to take it off, the strange dreams, how it had tangled in her hair so badly her husband had needed to cut it free. Kinew listened as I babbled on, his face expressionless. He waited for a moment after I finally stopped speaking, and then took a sip of his undoubtedly cold coffee.

"Strong Lake has always belonged to our people, but that doesn't mean its history has been peaceful. Some of the Elders speak of a lost tribe that settled the land. Perhaps this arrowhead belonged to them."

"Lost tribe?"

"These Elders believe there was another nation, a thriving community, long before we arrived, but something caused them to vanish. No sign of them was ever found, not even their bodies. Pioneers came later, but a smallpox epidemic wiped them out. The land stood empty for years. Even now, no one really wants it. It's a constant battle with the state, each of us longing to abdicate responsibility."

Smallpox. The little boys who'd visited the campground had been stricken with smallpox. I hadn't seen them, but Greyeyes and her partner had, and it sounded like an agonizing disease. Could their suffering be related to the lost tribe? Was it possible for a virus to live that long? And if so, why hadn't I been affected?

"But if you never found any sign of them, how do you know the lost tribe existed?"

"Same way Greyeyes knows about this Little Dove. Some of our Elders have had similar dreams, only we don't call them dreams or nightmares. We call them visions."

CHAPTER TWENTY-SIX

The woman's name was Rose. She had a shy, gentle smile and kind eyes. I had to duck to avoid smacking my head on the doorframe as I entered her home. Following behind me, Kinew nearly had to crawl.

Mom would be home by now. The thought of the fear she'd experienced, discovering I wasn't there, made my gut twist with guilt. I'd expected this to be a quick errand – get in, get out, get home before anyone noticed I was gone. But Kinew had insisted this Rose person hear Greyeyes' story from my own lips.

"Would you like tea?" Her voice was so quiet I had to strain to hear it. My initial impulse was to say no, to not put her to any trouble, but I glimpsed the chief nodding at me out of the corner of my eye. Maybe a refusal would be seen as impolite.

"Sure, that would be great. Please."

While she headed to the kitchen, Kinew beckoned me to a chair. Rose was a doll-sized woman, and her trailer was a doll-sized house. When I sat down, my knees nearly reached my chin. Just when I'd thought things couldn't get more awkward.

The arrowhead jabbed into my skin, making me curse. At the chief's insistence, I'd put it back in my pocket. It was obvious he didn't want anything to do with it.

"Problem?" Kinew asked, noticing my fleeting expression of pain. The guy was sharp. Nothing got past him, which didn't make him easy to be around. I preferred to blend into the background.

Since when, Jess taunted in my brain. When she was still alive, she'd mocked what she'd called my 'gigantic ego' countless times.

You know what I like about you, Reese? she used to say. *Your humility.*

Well, I had humility now, in spades. Getting thrown in jail in front of your family and having a cop play baseball with your face could do that to a guy, as it turned out. I wondered if Jess would like me any better now, if we'd argue less. To my surprise, my eyes twitched, stinging. "No," I said, finding my voice. "No problem."

We stared at each other in silence until Rose returned with a plastic tray. She handed me a mug from Yale University while I tried not to wonder where she got it. Old habits – and presumptions – died hard. "Thank you."

"Happy to give tea to the hero," she said, smiling so broadly dimples appeared on the top of her cheeks. "Thank you for what you did for my brother."

At my look of confusion, Kinew grinned. "Oh, didn't I tell you? Rose is Crazyhorse's sister."

I gaped at the woman in shock. Petite, pretty, and ageless, it was difficult to believe she came from the same planet as Crazyhorse, let alone the same womb.

Rose saw my expression and sighed. "We used to look alike, so much so that people thought we were twins. But my poor brother, he's let the bottle rot his mind and destroy his face, his teeth...his life."

Kinew reached for her hand, swallowing it in his. "It's a disease, Rose."

She nodded, closing her eyes for a moment. "I know. It's not his fault. It's just hard to watch." When she opened her eyes again, the sadness had disappeared. "In any case, my brother is now your biggest fan. You have made a friend for life."

"Then Crazyhorse is all right?" I never had been able to get any answers about what had happened to him since I left the hospital.

"He's fine. When that cop hit you, he started yelling, and those cowards took off. He told me how you stuck up for him, though, tried to protect him. No one has done anything like that for him in a long, long time. You're his hero, and mine."

Her words left me speechless. There was nothing I could say without making it worse. Any mention of Archer or what had happened in the cell would bring the dark cloud over our heads again. So I thanked her, even though being called a hero made me feel like a fraud. If I were really a hero, I would have found some way to save my friends. Jess would still be alive.

She leaned closer and squeezed my arm. "Now, what can I do for you boys? I'm getting the feeling this isn't a social visit."

"No, it's not. There's been more trouble up at the campground.

One of the detectives investigating the murder has been having some disturbing visions. Reese, can you show Rose the arrowhead?" Kinew asked.

"Are you sure?" After what it had apparently done to Greyeyes and Kinew, I didn't like the thought of exposing anyone else to whatever evil the artifact contained, but Kinew nodded.

"Rose has abilities the rest of us don't."

She held out her hand, waiting as I removed the arrowhead from my pocket, careful not to scratch my fingers. At some point, it had gotten a lot sharper than I'd remembered.

"Don't worry," she said. "It will not hurt me."

I wasn't so sure about that, but I handed it over. To do otherwise would have been patronizing.

Her fingers snapped closed around it like a hinge. She raised her chin to the ceiling, closing her eyes once more. In dismay, I watched as blood trickled from her closed fist and I moved to take the arrowhead back. Kinew put his hands on my shoulders, restraining me.

"Don't."

"But she's bleeding."

"She'll be fine. She's a strong woman. Let her do her job."

Her job? I couldn't fathom how her job had anything to do with the arrowhead, as she wasn't studying it like I imagined an archaeologist would. But there was no arguing with the chief. Resigned, I returned to my chair and waited.

After several anxious minutes, Rose lowered her head. Her eyes opened, as did her fist. She handed the arrowhead to me, and I was stunned to see no wounds of any kind on her palm. The blood had vanished. Had I imagined it? Was I going completely mental?

"Where did you find this?" she asked Kinew.

"It was in one of the murder victims' tents." The chief looked to me for confirmation, and I nodded. There didn't seem to be any point mentioning that it had been my tent too. "It's from the lost tribe, isn't it?"

Her jaw tightened. "You know I don't like calling them that. They were the people of Mescenaki Nation. They were real people, Kinew, not some fairy tale."

"What happened to them?" It was the first time I'd heard her sound anything but polite. My question was partly out of interest, partly in an effort to relieve the tension.

"They were destroyed, like many of our people. Wiped out by disease and murdered by those they tried to help."

"But why?"

She shook her head, her eyes dark with sadness. "Why does anyone kill anyone? Xenophobia. Racism. Greed."

"Reese, I should add there's no physical proof the lost...Mescenaki Nation existed. Rose has had some communication with them, and I believe her, but that aside, no one has been able to scientifically prove the nation existed."

The woman's eyes flashed with anger again. She indicated the arrowhead in my hand. "What do you call that?"

"If it can be proven that's where the arrowhead originated, then yes. But with no other artifacts, scientists will have nothing to compare it to. Any nation could have made that arrowhead," Kinew said.

"Wait, I don't understand something. If the people were destroyed, how can you communicate with them?" I asked.

"Sometimes I receive messages from the beyond. I also get visions, much like your detective is having. I've been communicating with the Mescenaki Nation since I was a little girl."

Before Jess died, I probably would have laughed in this woman's face. Messages from the beyond? What was this, an episode of *Paranormal Detectives*? But too many strange things had happened for me to shrug this off, pretend it was a joke. I guess if there were any silver linings to this mess, the fact that I'd grown up a bit was one of them.

"What do they say? I mean, what do they tell you?"

She smiled, but it was the saddest smile I'd ever seen. "Mostly, they tell me their story. They don't want to be forgotten or lost. They want people to remember what happened to them. They want to be seen."

The idea of a tribe of long-dead people wanting to be seen was enough to give *me* nightmares, though I was pretty sure Rose hadn't meant it literally. "Does the name Little Dove mean anything to you?"

If Rose was startled by the question, she hid it well. "Of course it does. Little Dove was a powerful woman, one of the most powerful people in the Mescenaki Nation. She was their medicine woman. Why do you ask? Have you dreamed of her?"

"Oh no, not me. But I think the detective has. She wanted me to ask Kinew about her."

As the woman's lips curled into a smile, the chief said, "You see why I brought him to you. I don't pretend to know anything about this."

"At least you admit your ignorance. Most men are not intelligent enough to do so." Rose reached for my hand, and I gave it to her, almost expecting to feel a shock as her skin touched mine. "It is just as I thought. You are of her. That's why you were spared."

"What do you mean, I'm 'of her'?"

Rose let go of me, and my hand hung awkwardly in the air until I brought it back to my lap. My mind raced. Everyone sounded like they were talking gibberish, and it was exhausting. More than anything, I just wanted to go home and crawl into bed, but given my luck, my parents wouldn't let me do that, either.

"You have her blood in you. That's why you survived the night. By birthright, part of that land belongs to you."

"There has to be some mistake. I'm English and Scottish. My last name is Wallace."

"Everyone's family tree has some surprises. Even mine. If you look hard enough, you might catch a glimpse of yours."

If I'd thought my mind was reeling before, now it was a maelstrom. So of course I blurted out the stupidest thing imaginable. "I've never heard anything about this. I don't even look native."

Kinew laughed. "Did you think you needed your hair in a braid? A drop of red blood won't necessarily turn your eyes brown."

I thought of the voice that had whispered to me that night. *You're not welcome here.* If the land belonged to me, why the warning? Had someone been trying to protect me, to get me out of there before my friends were murdered?

"Wait here," Rose said, getting up from her chair. "I have something for you."

"Rose is also our medicine woman," Kinew said. "If anyone can help you, she can."

I was about to say I didn't need any help when I thought better of it. Of course I did. Three of my friends were dead, Dan's mother had been murdered, Jess's parents blamed me for the whole thing, and my face looked like I'd lost a boxing match with a gorilla. It was a wonder I could put one foot in front of the other.

Rose returned with a small cloth pouch the size of an apricot. She tied it to a rawhide cord and handed it to me. "Wear this. It's for protection." I picked up the little bag and held it to my nose, inhaling deeply. It smelled clean and sweet. As I fastened the cord around my neck, she showed me a plastic baggie with what looked like tiny pieces of twigs and leaves inside. "Take this too. Brew it like you would a tea, in boiling water. Once it's cool enough to touch, soak a clean cloth in it and lay the cloth on your eyes. It will help restore your sight and ease your headaches."

How did she...? Then I realized her brother must have told her what the cops had done to me. Or perhaps it was obvious from looking at my face. "Thank you." Perhaps it was a placebo effect, but I felt better already. And hadn't I learned in college that a placebo could be just as effective as actual medicine?

"You're welcome. Don't take that off," she said, pointing at the charm around my neck.

"What is it?"

"It's called a medicine bag. Feel honored. Very few people in our community are special enough to have Rose make one for us," Kinew said.

Did he have one? The way he'd worded it made me wonder. "I am. Honored, that is. Thank you."

"Somehow you managed to release Little Dove's spirit. She is free now, and some day her spirit will return to you and tell you what it is she wants. The medicine bag will protect you from her," Rose explained.

"But if I'm her blood, why would I need protection from her?"

Rose's face creased with worry. "Little Dove is a vengeful spirit, Reese. Everyone needs protection from her. Until she is appeased, many more people will die."

CHAPTER TWENTY-SEVEN

The next few days were quiet ones, filled only with the rasp of Grey Mother's labored breathing. Little Dove watched the Elder with anxious eyes, praying that the Creator had seen her set fire to the hateful blanket and would take pity on her by sparing the woman she loved most. However, deep in her heart she understood it was too late for miracles. There were some things even the Creator could not fix.

On the third day since Lone Wolf's visit, Grey Mother's eyelids fluttered open.

"It is time. You need to let me go, little one." Her voice, once so lovely, had been ravaged by disease. It was the croak of a toad, the rustle of rodents in the grass.

Feeling the truth of the Elder's words, Little Dove clasped the woman's hand tighter, drawing it to her breast. "I cannot survive if you leave me, Mother."

A ghost of a smile briefly touched Grey Mother's cracked lips. "You have always been stronger than you believe."

They shared silence together for long minutes, Little Dove releasing Grey Mother's hand only to stoke the fire that kept them warm. Winter had the land in its teeth now, but the new healer would face its bite alone. If she had given any thought to her survival, she would have been afraid, for the hunters, preservers, and fire keepers of her community had passed. She had never spent a season without the care and companionship of her people. In this harsh land, solitude could be deadly.

"Lone Wolf spoke the truth," Grey Mother said, startling her. She'd believed the older woman had slipped into the endless sleep. "He saw what I couldn't."

Little Dove stroked the hair back from the woman's brow. Grey Mother's skin felt feverish under her hand. "No one is to blame, Mother."

"We gave in to our greed and must accept that, though we were tricked by the visitors, as the wily fox toys with his prey. You must be the spirit of our vengeance."

At the older woman's words, Little Dove's shoulders slumped in exhaustion. After taking care of Grey Mother and the others for a moon, she was a shadow of herself. Worn and weak, she had no energy for revenge. "I am tired, Mother."

With an effort, the Elder managed to apply pressure to Little Dove's hand. It was the kiss of a butterfly. "You are the only one remaining. You must make sure they suffer for their treachery."

How? She hadn't seen the settlers since they'd brought the diseased blankets to her camp, and she was in no condition to seek them out, not that she wanted to. The older woman would pass from this world soon, and there was no harm in saying whatever would give Grey Mother comfort, so Little Dove promised to avenge their people, as her eyelids grew heavy.

The healer flinched, startled awake. She shivered, appalled when she saw the cold, dead embers of the fire. Grey Mother's hand still clutched hers, but it was every bit as cold as the fire and stiff, her fingers forming into a claw around the healer's. Tears ran down Little Dove's cheeks, searing into her frozen flesh. The great mother of her nation was gone, slipping away while she'd been sleeping. Grey Mother had vanished into the Great Beyond without a kiss or last word of affection. The Elder's faded eyes, white with cataracts, were fixed on the sky. Understanding she'd forever feel guilty for leaving the woman to die alone, Little Dove gently slid the woman's eyelids closed.

"Rest easy, Grey Mother. Your journey is complete."

Her body shook with sobs. There was no point in reviving the fire now; its warmth had been for the dying Elder. Little Dove deserved to suffer in the cold. She deserved to die. She hadn't been able to protect or heal her people, and what good was a healer who couldn't heal? She couldn't bear to live without them. She wanted to join the Creator too.

There would come a moment when winter's teeth weren't so sharp, when its frozen embrace would comfort her, soothe her on her journey to the Great Creator. With her own teeth chattering, Little Dove settled in to wait, holding Grey Mother's frozen hand in hers. Her chin sunk to her chest, long hair drifting to cover her face like a raven's wings.

She slept.

"Well, well, well. Take a look for yourself, Beatrice. You can go right ahead and quit your blubbering. Your precious squaw still breathes. Jesus Lord in Heaven, these things are like cockroaches."

Tears had frozen to her lashes, sealing Little Dove's eyes shut, but the sound of the man's voice made her cold skin crawl. She pressed her palms to her eyelids to thaw them, but before her vision cleared, the man had grabbed her by the hair, yanking her to her feet.

Her cries were echoed by one from the woman – the golden-haired woman whose baby she'd saved from dying. "Stop it, John. You stop it! Don't you dare touch her. Why do you have to be so cruel?"

Little Dove heard the sound of slapping as the woman flung herself against her tormentor, striking out with her fists. The man laughed.

"I believe a mosquito landed on me." Then he shoved her aside. Little Dove's eyes opened in time to see the woman fall. She hit the ground hard, face reddened and miserable. In spite of herself, Little Dove felt sorry for her. She couldn't imagine living with that horrible man. In her heart, she knew the woman hadn't willingly given them the blankets, had in fact done everything in her power to warn them.

Seeing another woman in trouble brought new strength to her limbs. She gritted her teeth and straightened her spine, lessening the pressure on her scalp from the man's grip on her hair.

"Ah, you're awake now, huh? Good. I want you to be awake for every moment of this." As quick as a marten, the man wrapped her hair around his fist and yanked again. The pain was excruciating, but Little Dove wouldn't give him the pleasure of hearing her cry out. Her people were warriors, braves. She would make their spirits proud.

"Leave her alone, John! You just leave her alone," the golden-haired woman shrieked.

"Leave her alone," the man mimicked in a terrible, shrill mockery of her voice. "If you don't like what you see, woman, you don't have to watch."

He dragged Little Dove away from the dead fire, away from Grey Mother, away from anything that had once been warm and safe. Her buckskin boots slid across the packed snow, failing to offer any resistance. Even if she'd been strong enough, she could not have escaped from him. The other woman leapt on his back, her arms flailing and legs kicking. Her teeth snapped at his neck as she tried to bite him, and Little Dove gasped to see a human woman behave like an animal. Though the woman appeared to have recovered from whatever weakness she had suffered from her illness, her efforts had no effect. The man brushed her away or, if she got to be too much of an annoyance, threw her into the snow.

"I am the healer of the Mescenaki Nation. I demand you unhand me this instant."

"Sure thing, lady. Your wish will be my command." He dropped her under a tree, the back of her skull bashing against the gnarled bark. A wave of dizziness swept over her, and she shook her head. All the while, she could hear him laughing.

Then the laughing stopped. He was on her, pinning her to the ground, tearing at her hides like a rabid creature. She struck him with her elbows, bloodying his nose.

"Wench!" His hand lashed out, exploding against her jaw. Little Dove's face was forced to the side with such speed her neck made an alarming cracking sound. Bright specks of light danced in front of the pain. She had never been struck before. Her people had always treated her with kindness.

Little Dove tried to kick away the greasy fingers that tore at her clothes, but her legs were trapped beneath his weight. He panted, sending clouds of fetid breath into her face. She'd never known a man to stink this way before. He smelled rancid, like something inside him had spoiled.

Shoving aside her chin, he rested his forearm against her neck, pushing hard enough to cut off her air. The pressure on her windpipe was excruciating, and she coughed and struggled to breathe, tearing at his arm. She could no longer hear the other woman's cries, and wondered what had happened to her.

An intense, fiery pain burned between her legs, reaching into her insides and setting them aflame. Little Dove tried to scream, but his arm strangled her vocal cords. Inches above hers, the man's face twisted into something demonic as he grinned. He thrust his body forward, and the pain intensified until she thought she would die. This wasn't lovemaking as she had known it. It was wrong. She knew it was the worst kind of hate.

It didn't make sense. Why would he hold hatred for her, when all she'd done was save his woman and child?

"That's right, wench. Enjoy it. Feels good, don't it?" As he spoke, his spittle struck her face. She squeezed her eyes shut, wrinkling her nose against the stink of him, and moaned. She couldn't get air into her lungs, and the sky above them had gone black.

The Creator. He had taken mercy on her at last. He was freeing her.

The pressure on her chest and throat eased, and the sharp pain throughout her lower body was gone, leaving behind a throbbing ache. Little Dove rolled on her side, coughing and choking as she fought for air.

"Little Dove, Little Dove. Are you all right?"

Lone Wolf bent over her, helping her to her feet. He rearranged her torn hides so they would cover her again. Her face burned with shame, but she didn't have the strength to walk on her own. She needed his support to stand.

As she leaned against him, she saw the evil man lying in the snow, his blood pooling around his head. An arrow protruded from his neck.

"John!" The golden-haired woman rushed toward them from the trees, sobbing. She fell to her knees in front of the man, getting his blood on her skirts. Gently propping Little Dove against the tree, Lone Wolf reached for his bow. With her remaining strength, the healer touched his arm.

"No," she whispered. "She's not to blame."

The shaman shook his head, but tucked away the weapon without a word. Lifting Little Dove in his arms, he left their camp and the crying woman behind. The ground was slick with ice, but his step never faltered.

"I should not have left you alone. I knew they would return one day to claim the land. I am sorry."

She wanted to reply, to tell him he had nothing to be ashamed of, that there was no way he could have predicted such evil, but the effort to speak was too much. With her head jostling against his chest, she fell asleep in his arms, wanting only to forget.

★   ★   ★

"You should have let me die."

Lone Wolf handed her a cup of tea, remaining expressionless at her words. His silence infuriated her more.

"Did you hear me? I said, you should have let me die."

"I have always thought it better to ignore nonsense. Grey Mother would not want to hear you speaking this way."

She threw the cup into the fire, where it shattered. "Grey Mother is dead. Everyone is dead. There is no place for me anymore, no purpose."

"You are still alive. Grey Mother was a warrior, fighting for every breath until the end. You disrespect her by saying these things."

He was right. It was what had always made Lone Wolf infuriating – how often he *was* right. He'd been right about the pale people, right about their tainted gifts, and right about her unsuitability as a healer.

"You are not to blame," he said, in a voice so low she almost didn't hear it. "You believe I have pinned the reason for our misfortune on you, but I have not. You were the only other one who tried to stop it, Little Dove. What happened to our people had been foretold. You are not at fault."

Rage turned to shame and hot tears burned her eyes, blurring her vision. "It *is* my fault. Grey Mother would be alive if not for me." She had been the only sister capable of nursing the golden-haired woman's baby back to health, the only one whose milk had still flowed when the creature stumbled into their camp, a breath away from death herself. With her errant act of kindness, Little Dove had sealed her sisters' fate.

"I know you did your best to discourage our sisters from taking the diseased offerings. Red Sky Dancer told me. At the time, she sneered at you, but bear that no mind, as she also sneered at me. When she lay dying, she recognized your wisdom. She saw that you had attempted to save them, and told me so. I hope that brings you some peace."

The idea of that lovely being, so free and beautiful like her name, dying from the same terrible disease that had taken Grey Mother and Quivering Birch, brought her no joy. "If I'd refused that hateful woman and her child, as you'd told me to do, none of this would have occurred. My mother would still live. Your sister would as well."

"Little Dove, look at me." Reluctantly, she raised her eyes to his and finally noticed how exhausted Lone Wolf looked, his face set in tired lines. For once, the man was showing his age. How far had he carried her? How much had he sacrificed to save such a worthless life? "Do I appear a happy man?"

Startled by the question, she could only shake her head. Lone Wolf was many things, but joy had always been an emotion that eluded him.

"You are correct. Anger and a desire for vengeance turned my sister and me against our people long ago. There was no one to mourn her, save for me, and now that she is gone, no one left to mourn me. Do not make the same mistake we did. Do not let bitterness twist your heart into something unrecognizable."

"There will be no tears shed at my passing into the next world. Everyone I've loved is gone."

The shaman tipped his head at her abdomen. "The pale man has planted a seed in you. It is tiny now, so tiny you could not see it, even if I were to show it to you. But it will grow into a child, a child who will have the best qualities of both their people and ours."

Little Dove's entire body shook with such violence she felt the earth under her tremble. Spying Lone Wolf's spear, she seized the blade, intent on plunging it into her womb. He leapt on her, using his strength to pry the weapon from her fingers. "No, Little Dove. No! You must listen to me. This is your destiny, to live. To love this child. That is why you have been spared."

She cared nothing for destiny, or for the shaman's visions. She would have nothing of that hateful man's legacy growing within her. Her hand went limp as she recognized Lone Wolf's superior power. While she may not be able to best him now, he could not watch her night and day. Eventually his guard would be down, and then she would do what must be done.

"You gave everything you had to save your sisters, to the point of nearly dying yourself. You made sure they knew comfort, and warmth, and dignity, at the moment of meeting our Creator. Do you see what a gift that is? Do you see you have nothing to be ashamed of?"

At the mention of her sisters' deaths, each one more painful than the last, new tears flowed. How could he so easily forgive her for allowing the monster into their camp? She would never forgive herself, never. How could she explain that a woman whose heart had been ripped to pieces by her sisters' suffering could not love?

"I see nothing," she said.

"You are in mourning, Little Dove. In time, the skies will clear, and your vision with them. You will see, and you will regain your capacity to love. You will love this child – it is your destiny."

CHAPTER TWENTY-EIGHT

A knock on her door startled Rose out of sleep. For a moment, she was tempted to ignore it. It was bitterly cold in her trailer, but cozy in her feather bed. As the pounding on her door grew more insistent, she sighed and pulled on her robe. She had pledged to use her gifts to help her people, no matter how inconvenient or ill timed their need for her might be.

The knocking continued without pause as she made her way through her darkened home. Whoever her visitor was, he or she must be in crisis to act so boldly. Her people tended to treat her with consideration and respect – almost too much, as if she were a queen. It made her uncomfortable, but she understood. She represented hope, a quality often in sparse supply in their community.

Rose touched the latch, hissing at the coldness of the metal. It was freezing, the warmth of her fingers leaving faint circles in the frost that coated it. Something was wrong. She had survived the worst of many winters in this home, and the latch had never frozen.

The knocking ceased. She fancied she could hear breathing on the other side of the door, but that was impossible. No one breathed loudly enough to be heard through wood and metal.

Her heart thudded in her chest, pulse pounding in her throat. She was surprised at her own fear. Rose had never had anything to fear from her people. Even when her visions of their futures had been less than auspicious, they had never been anything but kind to her. Her little home was full of their offerings, proof of their affection.

Still, every instinct she had warned her not to open the door. Each exhalation drifted in the air as vapor. Her furnace must have died in the night as the temperatures plunged. She rested her head against the door, straining to hear more, but the night was silent again. Perhaps she had dreamed the strange knocking, or her visitor had decided to return at a reasonable hour. Perhaps she was dreaming now.

"Rose?"

At the familiar voice, a powerful sensation of relief rushed over her. Hands clammy and knees shaking, she hurried to unfasten the latch, pulling the door wide. "I didn't expect to see you back here so soon. Are you—"

Her words died as she beheld the spectacle on her doorstep. Rose's keen mind slowed to a crawl, belatedly informing her she had been tricked. Her eyes landed on an emaciated chest, protruding bones…and the pulsating arrowhead, swollen and grotesque like a gluttonous tick overfed on the blood of its host.

She didn't have the chance to scream before her head was ripped from her body.

★   ★   ★

Miles away, another woman awoke in the middle of the night. She felt unclean, disgusted with herself. She longed to shed her skin like a snake and become someone else.

The problem did not reside with her, though, and so it could never end with her. She had to take other measures. Lone Wolf may have forced her to bear the pale man's hateful offspring, but he could not make her raise it. For the good of her people, it must be destroyed.

She followed the sounds of the creature's snoring. As if it knew of her intentions, it moaned in its sleep. Had there ever been so evil a sound in the world? Padding on thick carpet, her feet made no noise as she crept toward the monster's lair. Her fingers tightened on the butcher knife she'd lifted from the kitchen after dinner. No one had noticed. One of woman's greatest gifts is the ability to blend into the walls and disappear. Sometimes being ignored had its advantages.

Tiptoeing to the place the creature slept, she raised the knife overhead, its blade wicked in the moonlight. One strong thrust would send the weapon through the foul thing's body, and it would all be over. The world would be safe once more. She was responsible for this wickedness – she couldn't fail.

The room flared with light, blinding her. She heard a cry from behind, a man's voice. *Shit. The guardian.* That man had sharper senses than a crow's. His body connected with hers, knocking her to the ground. The knife skittered across the floor, just out of reach of her grasping fingers.

"What are you doing? Jesus Christ, have you gone crazy?"

The woman struggled against him, managing to turn so she could face her tormenter. He squeezed her wrists, grinding the fine bones against each other, holding her to the ground. Above her, the creature wakened and wailed.

"Let me go." The woman spat in his face. He didn't flinch.

"Fuck! There's that *thing* again."

One of his hands went for her neck. She seized the opportunity and punched him with every bit of strength she had. Blood spurted from his nose as she heard a loud *crack*.

The guardian cried out in pain, but didn't falter. She felt a sharp tug against her throat as he went for the amulet and jerked it free. Before she could take it back, he flung it across the room. The power left her body; her vision clouded.

The woman blinked. "Ben? What are you doing? Oh my God, what happened to your face? You're bleeding!"

Maria's husband gathered her in his arms and sobbed, his body shaking against hers. In all their years of marriage, she had seen him cry maybe twice. His tears scared her more than the blood pouring from his nose.

"What's wrong? Talk to me, Ben. What happened? How did I get in Heidi's room? Was I sleepwalking?"

He cried harder, and she saw her questions would have to wait. His arms crushed her to his chest so tightly she found it difficult to breathe, but she stifled her own discomfort, stroking his hair and murmuring what she hoped were soothing words, that it was going to be all right – even though she suspected that wasn't the truth.

"Mommy?" Heidi leaned over her bed, her eyes wide when she saw her mother rocking her father on the bedroom floor. "What's wrong with Daddy?"

"Nothing, sweetheart. He had a bad dream. Grownups have them sometimes too, you know, just like little girls. Try to go back to sleep." But as she said it, Maria recognized it was futile. What child could drift back to sleep after witnessing something so dramatic?

Two small feet dangled over the mattress, soon followed by the rest of their daughter. Heidi threw her arms around her father's back, making Maria's attempt to comfort Ben a group effort. Her heart swelled with love for her little girl, who was already showing signs of the compassionate woman she would one day become.

"Mommy, what is that doing on my floor?" Once Ben's sobs had quieted, Heidi pointed at something on her rug. Lately, she'd grown quite possessive of *her* belongings: *her* room, *her* blankie, *her* teddy bear. It worried Maria, but Ben had assured her it was a normal stage of development, as children tried to exert some form of control over their world. While that was a relief – Maria couldn't bear the thought of raising a selfish brat – Heidi's new insistence on everything being in its proper place was tiring, to say the least. She wouldn't have bothered to pay the question any attention if not for her daughter's repeated insistence.

Maria felt cold when she saw the large butcher knife winking at her from the carpet. "I don't know, sweetie, but let's get it out of here."

She cupped her coffee in her freezing hands, but the hot liquid refused to warm her. "It's not what either of us want. It's not what *I* want. But obviously I can't stay."

"There's got to be another way." Ben cradled their daughter to his chest, his eyes bloodshot and so pained it broke her heart to look at him. She'd wanted to take Heidi back to bed, but he'd refused, and she couldn't blame him. If the situation had been reversed, she wouldn't have wanted to let the girl go, either. As a cop, she'd seen how a split second could turn tragic too many times. "We've been through so much, and we'll get through this too. Splitting up isn't going to solve anything," he said.

"Ben, you caught me about to *stab* our daughter." She was careful to keep her voice low, and studied Heidi's features for any reaction. Thankfully, the girl was exhausted enough to sleep through the most horrible conversation of her young life. "What would have happened if you hadn't woken up? I can't risk it. It's not safe for me to be around her right now."

"It's that damn arrowhead. Whenever something's happened, I've found it around your neck. Why do you keep wearing it?"

Maria tugged the afghan closer around her body. She'd been vaguely aware of her husband yanking the arrowhead from her neck as they'd struggled in Heidi's room, but afterwards, they hadn't been able to find it. "You honestly think I'd touch that thing willingly? I must have put it on in my sleep."

His face darkened. "I want it out of here. It never should have been in our home in the first place. It belongs in an evidence locker, or whatever you want to call it. As soon as it's light out, I'm going to find it and take it to the station."

"Okay." How could she tell him about the insane thoughts that ran through her mind? About how he could put that evil thing on the bottom of the ocean, and it wouldn't matter. It would always find its way back to her. Until she figured out what was happening at Strong Lake, she would never be free of the arrowhead. And neither would her family.

"Why don't you talk to Doctor Wilder? I'm sure there's something he could give you, something that would help you sleep."

Frustration and fear had worn her nerves until they were thin as piano wire, but she couldn't snap at him, not now. Not when he was pleading with her to stay, looking like his best friend had died. Ben knew as well as she did that this had nothing to do with insomnia or sleepwalking. She'd almost killed their child. "It's too risky," she said as gently as she could, as if that would soften the blow of her leaving.

"Talking to Doctor Wilder is too risky, but going back to that bloody campground isn't? Christ, Maria, three – no, *four* – people have died out there in a matter of days. Two little boys are in the hospital in serious condition. That campground is the last place you should be going."

"It's still an active crime scene, Ben. It's my job to go."

His eyes flared with rage. She had never seen him look so angry. "So let Jorge handle it."

"Jorge is my partner. *Partner* means that neither of us handles things on our own. This investigation is a joint effort, and the sooner we resolve it, the sooner it'll be safe for me to come home."

"Are you sure that's what you want?" He spit the words at her like acid, and they burned as he'd intended. She reached for his hand, and forced herself to swallow her hurt and anger when he pulled away.

"I'm not leaving because I want to. I'm leaving for our daughter's safety. For *your* safety."

His lips tightened. "I can take care of myself, thank you."

Maria barely stopped herself from rolling her eyes. Though her husband was less Neanderthal than most, the suggestion that a mere woman could cause him damage still caused that ol' machismo to surface. She refused to get into a pissing contest. "Why are you so angry? I'm not happy about this either, but I'm going to do everything I can to make things right as soon as humanly possible."

"Why am I angry? Why am I *angry*?" Ben's voice rose, but as their daughter whimpered in her sleep, he dropped it to a whisper. "Because it's always about what you want, Maria. For once, just once, it would be nice if you listened to me."

She felt like he'd slapped her. "How does this have anything to do with what I want? You know what I want? I want our life back. I want us to be happy again. I want to stop having nightmares and fainting spells and feeling like I can't trust my own mind. I want to look in the mirror without worrying that that goddamn arrowhead is going to be around my neck again. Nothing about this situation has anything to do with what *I* want."

"Okay, okay." He raised a hand in the air, cradling their daughter with the other. "Calm down. You've made your point."

"Don't you *dare* fucking tell me to calm down. You pretty much insinuated I'm leaping at the chance to get out of our marriage."

Ben pushed away from the table. "Fine. I'd thought we could discuss this like rational adults, but obviously you're not capable of it. I don't want our daughter to hear this."

"Then maybe you should have put her to bed, like I suggested."

She seethed, breathing hard as her husband left the room with Heidi. It was just like him to throw these unfair accusations at her and then get pissy when she reacted poorly. What a big man, fleeing the uncomfortable conversation. Gripping her mug, Maria closed her eyes and tried to calm down. She loved the guy, but sometimes she wanted to throttle him with her bare hands.

Her cell vibrated, making her jump. *Who would be calling at five in the morning?* It had to be Jorge. Or dispatch.

But it wasn't.

It was Kinew. *What the hell does* he *want?*

"Greyeyes," she said, hoping he wouldn't detect the strain in her voice.

"Maria." Mr. Laidback sounded panicked. Her hackles rose. "There's been another death. I think you better get down here."

"I'll call for backup," she said, already rising from the table, mentally going through her checklist.

"Don't. I need you to come alone for this one. There's something—" She was surprised to realize he was crying. "There's something you need to see."

CHAPTER TWENTY-NINE

As Maria sped down the highway, guilt over the truth of her husband's ugly accusations nagged at the edges of her brain. She might be able to lie, however unconvincingly, to him, but she couldn't fool herself. It *had* been a relief to get the hell out of there.

When had her marriage become a battleground? She wasn't sure, but she suspected whatever was broken between them had been breaking long before the murders at Strong Lake. Was it the strain of raising a precocious child? The stress of her job? Or something more, a persistent incompatibility that had made itself more and more apparent as the years went on?

"You're sick, Maria. You are mentally ill, and do you know what mentally ill people do? They go to the doctor. They don't run off to a homicide in the middle of the night."

She'd resented his attack on her sanity, but now that she was alone, miles of highway unwinding in front of her like a ribbon, she was able to sympathize with his point of view. What was he supposed to think? He'd found her standing over their sleeping daughter with a butcher knife.

But she wasn't crazy, and the only way to prove it to him was to finish her investigation and find whoever was responsible for the killings at Strong Lake. Once she did, this other madness would stop. It had to.

"I could call the captain. One word about what happened here tonight and you'd be suspended. They'd force you to get help, force you to take this seriously."

Her fingers clenched as she recalled Ben's threat. Didn't he understand the work was holding her together right now? That without it, she would give up, become the madwoman he so obviously thought she was? Of course not. When had he ever understood what this job meant to her? It wasn't a *job* at all; it was a calling.

Her own response had been every bit as harsh. *"You do that, and this will be a permanent situation. I mean it, Ben. If you involve the captain, our marriage is over."*

They'd survived some tough times in the past. There had been many heated arguments, objects thrown, even some pushing-and-shoving matches she wasn't proud of. But never before had she threatened divorce.

The door she'd slammed behind her had punctuated the point. Now she had to wait and see if her husband did the right thing, if he still believed in her.

She had to focus on the subject at hand. Whatever mess her marriage had become hadn't happened overnight, and it wouldn't be fixed overnight, either. The turnoff for the campground loomed ahead, ominous in the dark. Maria sighed in relief as she drove past the sign, pressing harder on the gas on her way to the reservation.

Traversing the dirt road in her Suburban felt like surviving the spin cycle in a washing machine. Maria gritted her teeth, clutching the wheel and fighting for control as she was jostled and bounced all over the place. Simply keeping the vehicle on the road required so much concentration that she almost missed Kinew waving at her.

A house light illuminated the chief, casting a ghostly glow. She wished for the hundredth time that Jorge were there with her. Why had Kinew been so insistent she come alone? She couldn't bear to contemplate how many rules she'd shattered just by being there. Any murder on the reservation was the responsibility of the state and tribal police. She was so far out of her jurisdiction she might as well have been on the moon.

It's a trick, her well-trained cop's brain whispered, but she knew it wasn't. Kinew had asked for her, and that could only mean one thing. Somehow, this homicide was related to the others.

He moved to meet her and opened her door. "Detective." Whatever emotion she'd heard on the phone was gone. Kinew was back to his tightly reined, impassive self. Good. That would make her job easier.

"Chief. Where's the body?"

Even in the meager light, she could see pools of blood on the trailer's step, spilling over to soak the ground beneath. Whoever the victim had been, they hadn't gone peacefully. Her stomach lurched at the telltale stench of death.

"She's inside, but that's not what I wanted you to see. Not yet." He studied her, appearing to have aged several years since she'd last seen him. "It's not pretty. Damned thing tore Rose apart."

Damned thing? "I can handle it." What in the hell did he think she'd seen at the campground, for Christ's sake? A Disney movie?

Giving the front walk a wide berth, Kinew beckoned for her to follow him. Maria's pulse quickened. Maybe Ben was right – maybe she *was* insane. Why else would she be on a reservation in the early morning hours with a man she didn't know?

Her indecision vanished the moment Kinew crouched in the dry grass next to the step. He pointed at something, gesturing for her to bring the light closer. This was it – this was why he'd called her. She kneeled beside him, shining her Maglite over his shoulder.

She tightened her grip on the flashlight when she saw it. There it was, every cop's dream. Clear prints in the blood on the step. A killer's calling card.

Only these weren't shoe prints. They were *hoof* prints.

"This is what you wanted to show me?" She bit her lip to keep from groaning. "So a deer walked through your crime scene, so what? There are probably plenty of deer around here."

"Open your eyes, Detective. Clear your mind. These aren't the prints of a deer."

Dumbfounded, she stared at the marks in the blood until her eyes crossed. Her frustration increased as her knees began to ache from kneeling so long. Not a deer, so what else had hooves? An antelope? What was he trying to tell her?

Kinew appeared to understand she needed to figure it out for herself, for he kept silent. The man's patience was infinite, as always.

And then she got it. There were *two* hoof prints in the blood. Two, not four. The pool of blood was large enough that there should have been four.

"What the – is this a joke?" Maria had the ludicrous image of a killer using a deer's foot to make the prints.

"You see it, don't you." It wasn't a question.

"I see that there are two prints instead of four, as if the deer was walking upright."

"It's not a deer."

"If it isn't a deer, what is it?"

He stared at her in silence for a moment, like the passage of time would help impart the proper seriousness to what he said next. In the shadows, his eyes were impossible to read, just endless darkness. It was unnerving.

When she was about to seize him by the shoulders and shake him, he spoke.

"Wendigo," he said.

Rose's once cozy home had become an abattoir, with streaks of blood and gore coating the walls and furniture. Maria took a quick look inside and then backed out again, but not before she saw the poor woman's head. Rose's eyes were anguished, her mouth frozen in a silent scream. For the first time in her career, Maria had to turn away.

"We shouldn't be here. You need forensics. The more people who go in there, the harder it will be to find out who did this to her."

"I know what did this to her. Now it's a matter of finding out who in our community has been infected."

While many in her department would find this talk of wendigos ridiculous, they were no laughing matter to those who believed. Her own grandmother had told her frightening stories of these creatures with ferocious appetites, who possessed people and turned them into monsters. She needed to tread carefully. Brushing off Kinew's theory would be seen as disrespectful.

Then there was the matter of that nervous flutter in her gut as she studied the strange prints with the echo of that word *wendigo* in her mind. As much as she hated to admit it, her cop's instinct agreed with Kinew. Did that make her insane, or unusually open minded?

Rose's body looked like it had been torn apart by an animal. Maria couldn't reconcile the crime with anything human. Perhaps forensics would be able to tell them more.

"I need to call this in," she said, hoping he wouldn't be offended. It was one thing to believe in wendigos, but another altogether not to properly process a crime scene.

He nodded, moving away while she phoned, and as he faded into the darkness, panic took hold, squeezing the air from her lungs. The feeling of vulnerability, of being watched by something with evil intentions, was strong here. She found it difficult to breathe until she stood next to him again.

"I have some questions for you, but I'd rather we went somewhere else."

"Don't you need to wait for them?" he asked.

"I've told dispatch I'm questioning a potential witness. They'll be able to start without me. Your tribal police will need to be involved."

"They won't want any part of this as soon as they see those prints."

"Still, this is their jurisdiction. Legally, we can only get involved if they ask for our help."

"I'll make sure they do. They'll be more than happy to hand this one over."

Maria waited as he made the necessary calls before suggesting she follow him to Happy's, the same diner they'd been to before. Once she was in her truck, she realized how much her hands were shaking. She couldn't get the image of Rose's horrified face out of her mind. For some reason, the gruesome scene at the woman's trailer had bothered her even more than seeing what had become of Reese's friends at the campground. Perhaps because his friends had been barely recognizable as human, while she knew she'd be seeing the terror in Rose's eyes for the rest of her life.

"She was a good woman. She didn't deserve to die like that."

No one deserves to die like that. But Maria stayed silent. She understood what he meant, and he was upset enough as it was. Kinew sat across from her, not saying a word until he had a full cup of coffee in him.

"Tell me about her."

He stared at the table for so long she thought he wasn't going to answer. She couldn't help but wonder what his relationship to Rose had been. He was too upset for them to have been casual acquaintances.

"Everyone loved Rose. She had no enemies." He shifted his focus to Maria, voice hardly above a whisper. "The community is never going to recover from this."

Everyone turned into a saint once they died, but Maria suspected it was different with Rose. Kinew had told her about the woman's work as a healer and seer on the reservation, work she often hadn't had the heart to charge for.

She decided to risk saying what was on her mind. "You must have cared for her a great deal."

"Everyone did. She was special."

"Forgive me for asking, but was she—"

"Were we lovers?" A wisp of a smile touched his lips before vanishing. "No, Rose had more sense than that. Not that I didn't try to convince her otherwise in my impetuous youth. But that was a long time ago."

Maria found it hard to imagine this cautious, guarded man ever being impetuous, but she understood better than most how age and experience could change a person. "Can I ask what you were doing at her trailer in the wee hours of the morning?"

He looked down at his hands. "I had a dream—what our people call a vision—that Rose needed me. So I went to check on her, figuring that if everything seemed all right, I'd leave her be. But it was obvious from the second I arrived that *nothing* was all right."

"I'm really sorry. She sounds like a wonderful person."

"She was. I know you've had training in observing witnesses, and I realize you're seeing the depth of my grief and wondering what it stems from, but it's not what you think. Rose was a dear friend, but there was nothing the slightest bit untoward about our relationship."

"It doesn't have to be untoward if you loved her and she loved you. That's nothing to be ashamed of."

"And if that were the case, the woman would have had a ring on her finger so fast it would have made her head spin, believe me. I'm no fool. But, like I told you, my feelings for Rose were very much unrequited, and she was better off for it."

Unrequited love was often a motive for murder, but Maria had no doubts that the man sitting across from her was telling the truth. Kinew wasn't the most forthcoming person in the world, but he also wasn't a liar. And he'd loved the victim too much to have ever hurt her – she'd stake her own life on that.

She felt an unfamiliar twinge and was startled to realize it was jealousy. Had Ben ever loved her this way? She doubted it. Kinew had met his ideal woman, and when she'd refused him, he'd remained single. Maria couldn't picture Ben pining for her. If she'd rebuffed his attentions, he would have simply married someone else. Probably a pretty young music teacher who was far less complicated, and who never would have tried to murder their daughter.

"Are you all right?"

She jumped at Kinew's touch on her hand. "Yes, I'm fine." And then she heard how ridiculous that sounded. "Considering."

"I'm sorry. It was wrong for me to drag you into this. You've been ill, you're under enough stress. I shouldn't have let you go inside. It was selfish of me."

"No, you were right to call. I'm not sure how Rose's death is related to the campground murders, but they were both so brutal. Somehow, there has to be a connection."

He hadn't mentioned the wendigo theory since they'd left Rose's trailer, and she certainly wasn't going to be the one to bring it up.

"There is. What you're picking up on with me isn't my love for Rose, though there was plenty of that and always will be. It's my guilt."

"Guilt?" Survivors often felt guilty after the death of a loved one, particularly a person as saintly as Rose, but something in his voice gave her pause. "What reason would you have to feel guilty?"

Reaching into the inside pocket of his jacket, Kinew retrieved a small, cloth bag, which he laid on the table before her.

"Because," he said, "I'm the reason she's dead."

CHAPTER THIRTY

He never left her alone, not even while he slept. Whatever uncanny abilities the man had always demonstrated remained, and he read her mind with ease. His primary task had been removing every weapon from her reach, but a sharpened branch would do what was needed, should she manage to get her hands on one.

That was impossible as long as he had access to her every thought. As soon as she moved toward the forest, he was on her, pulling her back. Being the subject of his constant surveillance drove her mad. She yelled at him, and hit him, pummeling her fists against his chest, but he didn't react, which infuriated her more. Causing him discomfort would have brought some small measure of satisfaction.

Each and every night, as she glared at him across the fire while he cooked their dinner, he simply smiled.

"You are very angry with me now, but one day you will be grateful."

"I will *never* be grateful to you, ever."

He did not argue, but she could *feel* his smugness, his sureness that he was in the right and that if he waited her out, she couldn't help but come around to his way of thinking. Maddening.

"You cannot force me to have this child, Lone Wolf. Someday, you will not be watching, and when that moment comes, I will rip it from my womb if it kills me. I will use my bare hands if that's all that's available."

"You are a born mother, Little Dove. You will see. There will come a time before too long when your natural instincts take over. Whether the child you carry follows your path or his father's is your choice." He handed her the best of the rabbit he had cooked, and even that enraged her, as it was a time-honored sign of respect their people gave to the mothers of the community. And she was not a mother, not anymore. She would never be again. She imagined her womb as a cold, dead place full of despair, very much like the rest of her.

But as always, Lone Wolf was right. Once her belly rounded and she felt the flutter of life inside, her anger deserted her. She thought of Grey Mother and the others less, and more of the new life to come. The shaman began leaving her alone again, but she didn't notice. She was too busy preparing for the birth of her second child, a child that would be born and raised without the benefit of many mothers. How could she do it on her own? Lone Wolf was hardly a substitute for the lullabies of Quivering Birch or the expert swaddling of Rushing Waters. Still, they would have to find a way.

The child came in the spring, which promised good things, as it followed the cycle of their animal brothers and sisters.

He was a stocky little boy, born with a thatch of thick, brown hair and tiny hands that grabbed at everything. From the time he was a newborn, he would seize an offered finger and hold on with surprising strength. In the beginning Little Dove fretted over how pale her son was, but as the days turned warmer, his skin tanned to a golden nut-brown and wild poppies bloomed in his cheeks.

When he began to walk, his exaggerated swagger made them both laugh. Lone Wolf had spoken true – a new life was a blessing, no matter how it had come about, but she tried her best not to think about the boy's father. Her son already appeared to be taking measure of her, tilting his head and gazing at her with his huge eyes, as if he could see through her. She didn't want him to glimpse her sadness and wonder where it came from.

The moons passed quickly, and soon it was time to name him. Since neither the son nor the mother would exist without the patient care of the man who lived with them, she decided her child's name would be a tribute.

"I would like to name him Little Wolf," she said, feeling almost shy.

The shaman shook his head. "He is your son, Little Dove."

"He wouldn't have drawn breath if not for you. It would be an honor if you'd lend my boy your name."

Her son chose that moment to stagger toward them on his chubby, dimpled legs, waving his tiny hands in the air and making a strange, guttural noise as he struggled to speak. Lone Wolf burst out laughing as he held out his arms in time to catch the boy. "This one is a Little Bear. He has chosen his own name."

She smiled, for he did resemble a brown bear cub, comical and clumsy, and trying so hard to be ferocious. "Little Bear it is, and Little Bear you shall be," she said, kissing her son's nose as he struggled to escape Lone Wolf's embrace. Sometimes it troubled her that the boy didn't like to be cuddled or coddled. He was always waddling off on his own, with her forever running after.

Lone Wolf's wisdom held true. As her son aged, he became more and more like a bear, strong and steadfast and quick to anger. It was like the anguish and anger of his conception had infected him, a disease that festered in long silences and countless skirmishes.

It soon became clear Little Bear had no interest in being a healer like his mother and uncle, so Lone Wolf taught him to be a warrior. Her son's arms and legs grew lean with muscle, and though she had to admit he threw a spear and shot an arrow with astounding accuracy, she took no joy from it. She had seen too much killing, too much death.

Some nights she dreamt of Grey Mother, and woke with tears cascading down her face. She wondered what the great Elder would think of her child. Would she have taken pride in his fierceness and skill, or would his nature have troubled the woman, as it worried Little Dove? Lone Wolf occasionally dreamt of his sister as well. There were mornings when he was especially quiet and refused to speak for hours, his face set in deep lines, and she suspected Red Sky Dancer had visited him, dancing in a field with a crimson blanket over her shoulders.

Little Bear grew stronger as she became frail, threads of silver replacing the ebony in her hair, which had always been black as a raven's wing. She could feel her influence over her son, forever faint, waning further, until it was a challenge to get him to listen to her at all.

"Respect your mother," Lone Wolf said again and again. "She gave you life. You would be nothing without her."

Though her son worshipped the shaman, even the man's words had little effect on the boy. He carried some deep resentment toward her, and she was certain it came from the dark time, the time she hadn't wanted him in her womb.

She accepted this resentment as part of his nature, as unchangeable as his strength or stubbornness. There was much to admire about her son, but his lack of a loving heart made her weep. It lined her forehead with worry too, for the time of a confrontation with the pale people was drawing near.

For all of Little Bear's life, they'd been able to avoid the new arrivals, living off the land and keeping to the forest. They refrained from setting up elaborate camps so they could move quickly as it suited them, following the animals that gave them sustenance or avoiding the pale man's path. But every moon seemed to bring more and more visitors to the land, and Little Dove saw they would not be able to avoid them forever.

"You must have a firm hand with him. Teach him respect, to honor the pale ones," she told Lone Wolf. "It is the only way he will be able to survive among them."

Her son was truly one of their people now. It was difficult to remember she'd once fretted over his pallid skin. The only sign of his paternity were his eyes, which had matured into a deep and startling blue. The visitors would never embrace Little Bear, who was part fire and part earth. He would be seen as a monster, an abomination. If he didn't instantly win their favor, Little Dove feared they would kill him.

Even after everything that had happened to her, she hadn't lost her faith in the goodness of people. She had forgotten the shaman's true nature, the rage that boiled beneath the surface.

She had forgotten his need for revenge.

Little Dove was in the winter of her life when she once again heard the voice she'd long been dreading.

"Well, well, well, what do we have here?"

Her entire body trembled, her aged fingers opening, depositing the basket of the berries she'd been gathering at her feet. The fruit scattered on the ground, drops of blood on the earth.

"Looks like a squaw to me, Thomas."

"I think you're right. It *is* a squaw. Whatever shall we do with her?"

The men snickered, and in her fright, her bladder released, the warm fluid running down her legs under her deer-hide dress. Her face burned with shame, but the men didn't appear to notice.

"Seems we need to teach her some manners. Squaw, look at me when I'm talking to you."

Knees weak, shoulders quaking, Little Dove shuffled in the grass until she faced her tormentors. She tried to plead with them not to hurt her, to leave her be, but she'd forgotten the strange sounds of their language. She could only remember her own.

The men laughed. "She's an old one, isn't she? What are you saying, squaw? Speak up, will you? We can't make any sense out of your muttering."

She saw then that this was not the visitor she'd been dreading. These men were too young. They were of him, though, of that she was positive. She recognized the eyes, the same eyes she saw every day. Had one of them been the child she'd once suckled? It was impossible to tell.

"She may be old, but that doesn't mean we can't have some fun with her. You remember what Father said." The man seized her by the elbow. She cried out in pain, feeling her elderly bones grind against each other, but he ignored her distress as he yanked her close. The smell of him was foul, and she was taken back to that day when everything had changed, when the stink of his father's breath had made her gag.

"Remove your filthy hands from her."

Little Dove stiffened, hearing the danger in that voice, though the men holding her did not. They craned their necks, searching for the source and not finding it.

"What will you do if we don't?" The one called Thomas said, pressing thick, wet lips against her cheek.

"Then it will be my pleasure to kill you."

For so long she'd begged Lone Wolf to teach her son the pale man's language, hoping it would help him assimilate, but the shaman had claimed Little Bear had shown no interest. Was this one of the medicine man's tricks, or had her son fooled them both?

The men guffawed, but she detected fear behind their merriment, and felt the grip Thomas had on her ease as Little Bear revealed himself. Tall and thick with muscle, he looked as powerful as the trees surrounding him. He'd painted his face as Lone Wolf had shown him. His eyes burned with hate.

Raising his arm, he pointed his spear at Thomas's face. "Release my mother."

She closed her eyes, praying that these men would show more intelligence than their father had, that they would recognize the threat standing in front of them.

"Ah, feck off, you crazy savage," Thomas muttered, and before he could speak another word, Little Dove heard a whistling sound and then a *thump* as her son's spear struck the man in the forehead. She screamed as Thomas fell backwards, nearly taking her with him.

The other man turned to run, but he was peppered with arrows before he could take a step. He collapsed beside his brother, their blood running together on the grass.

Little Bear was silent as he moved forward to retrieve his weapons, his face impassive as he yanked his spear from Thomas's forehead and cleaned it with a leaf. He paid her no attention, not even when she clutched his arm.

"Why did you do that? Why did you kill them? Now you have brought war upon us."

Her son would die at the hands of his father's people, never recognizing their connection, the tainted blood that flowed through them both.

"Let the war come." He returned the arrows to the quiver he always wore, and she finally recognized he'd prepared for this moment for a long time. *Lone Wolf has used my son as his instrument of vengeance.* "They would have hurt you, Mother. Like they did before."

"What do you know of that?" Her tone was harsher than she'd intended, but his conception had been her secret to keep or reveal, no one else's. "What did Lone Wolf tell you?"

In his war paint, Little Bear was unrecognizable as her son. "Nothing more. What else is there to tell?"

She bent to gather the berries she'd lost, the ones that hadn't been trampled, as an excuse to hide her face. Her son could still look through her as he always had. She couldn't risk him learning the truth. What if he hated her, or even worse, hated himself?

"You shouldn't have done this. Killing is not our way."

"Lone Wolf taught me otherwise."

Why must he always be so unrelentingly stubborn? "Lone Wolf is wrong. He still grieves the loss of his sister. His mind is not clear."

"These men destroyed our people. They deserved to die. They are fortunate I showed them as much mercy as I did. Look at them – they did not suffer. They got a better death than they deserved."

"These men were not yet born when our people passed on. They shouldn't have paid for the crimes of their forefathers."

"You would prefer I'd let them disrespect you, Mother? Is that your wish, to have had their disgusting, grubby hands on you?"

Disrespect. Such a gentle word for the searing pain that had cleaved her sex in two, had humiliated and shamed her and robbed her of any joy in living.

"You should not speak to me this way. It is not how a son should speak to his mother. I gave you life."

He curled his lip, and she was dismayed to see how capable he was of ugliness. Could this be the same little boy who had staggered over to her on dimpled legs, laughing and smiling? What had blackened his heart so?

Lone Wolf.

She cursed the shaman under her breath. He had no right to tell her child such horrible things, to damage him in this way.

"Only through duress. If Lone Wolf hadn't watched over you, you would have extracted me like a disease. Isn't that right, Mother?"

The blood rushed to her face, roaring so loudly she couldn't collect her thoughts. Still, she had to try. "The event of your conception was... difficult. It is impossible to explain, as you are not female and will never in your life be used as I was." She swallowed hard, but her throat remained dry. "My indifference ended when I felt the flutters of life inside me, when I felt *you*. I have loved you from that moment with all my being, exactly as I loved my daughter."

She'd hoped her words would soothe him, erase some of the painful ugliness Lone Wolf had used to poison her son's mind. His eyes hardened.

"No, it is not true. You don't love me. Even now, you fear me. I felt your rejection in the womb, and I feel it now."

A cry escaped from her broken heart as she dropped to her knees at his feet. She reached for his hide boots, wanting to pull him to her, but he stepped away. When had he grown so hardened? How had she missed the hatred in his face?

"You need not cry for me, *Mother.* Lone Wolf has accepted me as his son, and together, we will take back the land for our people. We will no longer hide in the shadows as if we have something to be ashamed of. You can stay here and pick your berries and serve as their instrument as they require. I won't trouble you any longer with my misguided loyalty."

He slipped into the forest and vanished as silently as he'd arrived, and she collapsed into the leaves and wept, feeling more broken than she had after the pale man had used her, after Grey Mother had died in her arms, for she had lost her only remaining child.

Her child, who had become a monster through Lone Wolf's diligent tutelage. What fresh horrors would he unleash on the pale man's people? How far would his lust for revenge carry him? How long before his vengeance resulted in his own death?

One thing she was certain of.

Blood would be shed.

CHAPTER THIRTY-ONE

My eyes snapped open. A sickening stench filled the room, like rotting meat mixed with something metal, industrial.

Ugh. What is that?

Stomach churning, my gorge rose, and I choked back bile to keep from vomiting on my bed. The stink was overwhelming, unbearable. I had to get away from it.

"Reese!" My mother's voice – shrill, impatient. Like she'd been calling me for some time without a response. Maybe she had. She was probably the reason I was awake now. "*Reese.*"

"What?" I yelled, sounding every bit as irritated as I felt. In that moment, I hated my mother, hated the way she fussed and nagged and tried to control my father and me. Why couldn't she just fuck off? Why couldn't she just fuck off and die?

"Detective Greyeyes is here to see you. And there's someone with her." Her voice was softer now. No need to holler, as she was right outside the door. The idea of my mother separated from me by only a piece of flimsy particleboard made me panic. She couldn't come in, couldn't smell this foulness – she'd freak. I needed to open a window.

"She isn't here to arrest me again, is she?" *Stupid bitch.*

"No...." Mom paused, as if the thought hadn't occurred to her. "I don't think so. Why would she be? You haven't done anything wrong."

Maybe I hadn't before, but I had the sneaking suspicion that had changed some time in the night. The awful smell was terribly familiar. My heart thumped harder in my chest, until I fantasized I could hear it, pounding away beneath my T-shirt. The room was flooded with sunlight, too much light for it to be early morning.

"Reese, are you all right? Do you need help?" The knob turned, and I bounded from the bed, slamming the door shut with my weight. Mom let out a little squeak of surprise and I didn't want to kill her any longer. Why would I want her dead? She was my mother, and pretty decent, as far as mothers went.

"Don't come in. I'm not dressed."

"Okay. Well, please hurry. I don't know what's going on, but they look upset."

"What time is it?"

"Three o'clock. We figured you must have been tired after your big adventure yesterday, so we decided to let you sleep."

Big adventure. The sarcastic edge to her voice.

My illicit trip to the reservation. It was coming back to me now. I wasn't supposed to drive because of the problems with my vision.

Except those problems appeared to be over. My vision was as strong as it had ever been, if not better. Everything in the room looked sharper and brighter. I watched the dust motes and lint dancing in the air like lovers. I'd never noticed how much junk was floating around in the atmosphere before. Why hadn't I seen it? It had to be some trick of the light.

Three o'clock. I hadn't slept that late since my worst college bender, and I wasn't drunk. Still, something was off, different.

I could no longer smell whatever it was that had nauseated me when I'd woken up. Either I'd gotten used to it, or it had never existed. It had probably been a dream.

When I heard my mother go back upstairs, I reached for the doorknob. If Greyeyes was here, it was important. Better hurry. I'd splash some water on my face and brush my teeth for a minute and then—

Then I saw my hand. It was crusted with blood, brownish-red flakes falling from it, drifting to speckle the carpet as I watched. My other hand was the same, gore embedded into the nails.

From the knees down, my legs and feet were coated in crap – dried mud and leaves and who knew what else. The nausea surfaced again, and I yanked the door open and ran for the toilet.

I vomited until my stomach was empty and aching, tears and sweat mingling on my face.

The sickening stench had been real after all.

The sickening stench was me.

★　　★　　★

"I'm really sorry. I don't know what's taking him so long. He said he would be right up, but he's been having so much trouble, you see, with his eyes...."

"I'm here, Mom. You can stop apologizing now."

Detective Greyeyes waited on the loveseat, looking like she hadn't slept in days. Kinew stood to greet me, offering his hand. I was scared to take it. What if I'd missed something? What if he could smell the blood on me? But it would raise more suspicion if I didn't shake. I had no choice.

His eyes searched my face as his strong fingers grasped mine. "Doing all right, Reese?"

"As good as can be expected, considering."

"We were hoping you wouldn't mind going for a little drive with us. We need to talk to you."

I glanced at the doorway where my mother fretted, twisting her hands. "What about?"

"We'd rather this stay between us for now." Kinew's eyes flicked to Detective Greyeyes, who nodded. They both looked like they'd come from a funeral. I didn't like this, didn't like it at all. *What had I done?* I suspected they were going to tell me, and the truth was, I didn't want to know. "If that's all right. We won't keep you long."

"Reese has a lawyer. He shouldn't be talking to the police without his counsel present."

Way to go, Mom. Watching those cop shows had obviously paid off. She'd crossed her arms, probably in an attempt to appear forbidding, or at least stern.

"This isn't about the case," Greyeyes said, her voice as hoarse as if she'd been talking for hours. "It's unofficial. Even if your son did say something incriminating, which he won't, it wouldn't be allowed in court."

"I don't understand. If this isn't about the case, why do you need to speak to him?"

Good question, Ma. Of course it was about the case. They wouldn't be here otherwise. Couldn't she tell that something else had happened? It was in their matching grave expressions, the somber mood they'd brought into the house like a shroud over their shoulders.

Kinew cleared his throat. "A member of our community passed on last night, Mrs. Wallace. Someone who thought highly of your son. We thought Reese might want to pay his respects."

Crazyhorse? Oh fucking hell. I'd ended up liking the old guy, or at least having respect for him.

Hopefully he'd died peacefully in his sleep, rather than having his skull cracked open by some cop with a grudge.

Mother's face flushed. "I'm – I'm very sorry to hear that. Well, if Reese feels up to it, of course he can."

Three pairs of eyes bored into me. The silence weighed heavy as everyone waited for my answer. Crazyhorse had been pretty cool for an old drunk, but so what? What was I supposed to do? I'd met him once, and it wasn't like we'd had a ton of time to chat.

"Is this a funeral or something? Do I need to change?"

"No, it's nothing like that. What you're wearing is fine. This is informal," Kinew said.

"Okay, just let me get my coat." I headed for the closet, releasing the breath I hadn't realized I'd been holding. Something else was going on, something beyond Crazyhorse's death. They wouldn't tell me in front of my mother, though – that was obvious. As much as I didn't want to go with them, I had no choice. Not if I wanted to figure out what was happening to me.

Mom held me tighter than usual when I said goodbye, and I felt guilty for the horrible thoughts I'd had earlier. What was wrong with me? We'd never been especially close, but we'd always gotten along. "Don't worry," I told her. "I won't be long. Will I?" I directed my question to Chief Kinew, as he seemed to be the one most capable of speech.

"No. Maybe an hour or two, and most of that will be driving time."

"Call Dad if it'll make you feel better. Call Prosper too," I said in her ear. It couldn't hurt. Prosper at least had been paid to look out for my best interests.

"Be careful."

"Don't worry," Greyeyes said, touching my mother's shoulder as she left. "We'll take care of your boy."

Somehow, I didn't find that comforting.

"So, what happened to the old guy?" I asked when we were on the road. We were in Detective Greyeyes' Suburban, but Kinew was driving, which I found curious. I hadn't realized the two of them were so close.

"What old guy?" The chief squinted against the late-afternoon sun, never taking his eyes from the highway.

"Crazyhorse. Isn't he the one who died?"

"Crazyhorse will probably outlive us all. Sadly, the same can't be said for his sister."

Rose? Recalling the woman's kind face, the gentle way she'd spoken to me, something behind my eyes ached. "But she was so young. What happened?"

Detective Greyeyes turned to face me, holding on to the back of her seat. "She was murdered, Reese."

"Murdered? But who would want to hurt her? She was so nice."

Kinew said nothing, but I could see something twitch in his jaw. I'd noticed their chemistry, wondered if maybe they'd had a thing going… if not now, then in the past.

"That's kind of what we hoped you could help us with," Greyeyes said.

Whaaa? "I wish I could, but I really didn't know her. I only met her the one time, yesterday, and Kinew was there. He can tell you as much as I could about it. She told me I was related to a tribe that used to live around here, and she gave me something to help with my headaches. Oh, and that little charm thing."

"You mean this?" Greyeyes held up the cloth bag in the same moment I discovered it was no longer hanging from my neck. "We found it on Rose's doorstep. After she was murdered."

I'd watched enough reruns of *CSI: Miami* to know exactly what they were getting at. "Pull over."

"What's that?" Kinew's tone was casual, as if his companion hadn't just accused me of murder in her charming, roundabout way.

"I said, *pull over.* Now. Turn around and take me home. I've had it with this bullshit." My stomach churned again, but this time with rage instead of nausea. How dare they? I wasn't some dumb kid anymore, and I was through taking their shit.

"Reese, you're overreacting," Greyeyes said.

"Fuck you." As her mouth dropped open almost comically, it only made me angrier. "Seriously, fuck you. You lied to me and my mother to get me out of the house under false pretenses, and then you have the nerve to go and accuse me of murder."

"No one's accusing you of anything." Greyeyes pushed a strand of hair out of her eyes, which were wide and hurt. Kinew cut his speed, moving the Suburban over to the side with a flick of his indicator lights and the crunching of gravel. "If anything, you're a witness."

"But that's not what you said at the house, is it? You said you were taking me to pay my respects. So where were we actually going?"

"We were hoping you'd have a cup of coffee with us and talk, that's all."

"I'm not saying anything to you without a lawyer present. What you did counts as kidnapping, Detective, and don't think I won't sue your ass for it."

"What's going on, Reese? We've always gotten along."

"That was before you had your thugs barge into my home, arrest me in front of my family, and throw me in that disgusting cell. It was before Archer nearly killed me and made me fucking blind. But I guess you've forgotten about that."

Kinew and Greyeyes exchanged a glance that infuriated me even more. I gripped the leg of my jeans with so much force it pinched my skin. If Kinew didn't get moving soon, I'd jump out of the van and walk home.

"And don't fucking give each other that look, like I'm crazy. I'm right here – I can see you."

"No one thinks you're crazy, Reese." Kinew raised an eyebrow. "But you do seem extraordinarily angry."

"Maybe you can tell me what the proper reaction is after someone murders your girlfriend and her friends, you're falsely arrested, a cop beats the shit out of you and robs you of your sight, and then two assholes kidnap you with some bullshit story about paying my respects. How am I supposed to act? I'd love to know."

I'd hoped to provoke Kinew, to get the man to lash back at me, but the chief remained as expressionless as always. It only made me angrier.

Greyeyes held up a hand before I could unleash another barrage of insults. "It's true. We haven't been fair to you. You've gone through hell, and we had no right to expect you to help us with this, especially when we weren't forthcoming. I apologize. We'll take you home."

Momentarily defused, I leaned against the seat, arms crossed. "Jesus Christ, did you two ever stop to think that I probably dropped that damn bag when we left Rose's trailer?"

It sounded logical, and would have been, if not for the fact I remembered toying with it all evening, squishing the soft fabric and trying to guess at what was inside. So how had it ended up on Rose's doorstep? I recalled how the water in the sink had turned crimson when I'd scrubbed my hands that afternoon. I couldn't have done anything to Rose, though – I wasn't a killer. Besides, how could I have driven to the reservation without my folks hearing? They'd had a fit about me escaping yesterday afternoon. They would have been on high alert.

"There was blood underneath the bag," Greyeyes said. "Whoever left it there did so after Rose was killed."

"Then I left it in her house and the killer took it. Or kicked it outside by accident. Jesus, for someone you claim to have such a great rapport with, you certainly accuse me of murder a lot. I'd hate to see how you treat people you don't get along with."

"We don't think you murdered Rose, but we do think you could be the key to this whole thing. We need your help, Reese."

Greyeyes was pulling her doe-eyed act again, batting her lashes and acting innocent, like she hadn't convinced her stalwart friend that I was some kind of deranged serial killer. Well, fuck that shit. I was through cooperating. What good had come from my dealings with her? Less than zero.

"Then talk to my lawyer."

"We were hoping to keep this unofficial," Kinew said, and I threw back my head and laughed, not surprised when it sounded more like a snarl.

"No kidding. I wonder why."

"I thought you'd want to help get justice for Rose. You saw how kind she was, how generous. She tried to help you without asking anything in return."

"Yeah, and I saw you had a boner for her too. For fuck's sake, I don't even know the woman. I met her *once*. I don't owe her – or you – anything."

Greyeyes winced, looking over at her new partner, who stared straight ahead. "What about Jessica and Dan, Reese? What about Kira? Do you owe them something?"

I had no answer for her.

Without another word, Kinew shifted the van into drive and turned the vehicle around. A heavy silence settled over us as I tried my best to ignore the guilt plaguing me. I'd gone too far with my last comment. Kinew was a decent guy, and Rose *had* been nice. She had wanted to help me. She hadn't made a lot of sense, but she certainly hadn't deserved to be murdered. No one did.

Coming home was a lot faster than the abbreviated highway tour had been. Kinew parked alongside the curb without pulling into the driveway. If he could have gotten away with shoving me out of the vehicle while it was still running, he most likely would have.

"Hey." I dared to touch him on the arm. "I'm sorry for your loss. She was a nice lady."

The chief's jaw tightened. Under my hand, the man's flesh felt like iron. Best get out while the getting was good. I opened the door.

"Sorry to inconvenience you," Greyeyes said as I jumped out. "We won't bother you again."

I was about to snap some clever retort about lying cops and proper procedure, but it was too late. The Suburban sped off in a cloud of dust before I could get the door closed.

"Reese? Reese, what's wrong? Why are you back so soon?" Mom hurried to my side.

"Did you call Prosper?"

"Not yet. There hasn't been time. You were only gone a few minutes."

"Better call him. It looks like they're going to charge me with another murder."

CHAPTER THIRTY-TWO

"Well, that was a disaster." Maria buried her face in her hands. What the hell had she been thinking? Reese was right – she *had* kidnapped him under false pretenses. She'd probably lost her marriage, her family, and now she could lose her job too, and for what? One stupid mistake.

"What were you expecting?" Kinew added sugar to his coffee. She'd seen how much Reese's crude comment had upset him, but now that the chief had returned to his unflappable self, she wondered if she'd imagined it.

There was something about his calm demeanor that had the opposite effect on Maria. She wanted to scream at him, to shake him. Perhaps Reese had rubbed off on her.

"I don't know about you, but I've got a family at home. A little girl who depends on me to help put food on the table. If I lose my job over this—"

"You're not going to lose your job."

"How do you know? You heard what Reese said – he plans to sue me. And even if he doesn't have grounds, it will be an embarrassment to the department. We never should have lied to him."

"You'd prefer to have told his mother we suspect her son is possessed by a wendigo?" Kinew arched an eyebrow while he sipped his coffee.

Maria shook her head. "This is crazy. Are you listening to us? We sound insane."

"Yes, it is crazy. But that doesn't mean it isn't true. Anyway, you don't have to worry. Reese is not going to sue you."

"Would you mind explaining to me where you're gleaning all this special insight from?"

He shrugged. "He's a smart kid. Probably watched a cop show or two in his time. Get some luminol in that room of his, and the place is going to light up like a Christmas tree. And he knows it. I'm thinking that, while we chatted over tea with his mother, he was busting his ass to get Rose's blood off his hands."

"You really think he did this? He's never struck me as a killer."

"I'm sure you don't think of yourself that way, either, and yet, your husband found you brandishing a butcher knife over your child. Whatever did this to Rose wasn't Reese, just as the woman with the knife wasn't you. You're both puppets, as far as it's concerned."

"And what would be its motive for attacking Rose?"

"She knew too much. She told Reese he was related to the lost tribe. Reese the college student didn't believe it, but the thing inside him felt it was way too close to home."

The disbelief must have been clear on her face, for the chief leaned closer. "I get that this is difficult for you to process. For years, you've depended on reason and logic in order to do your job, but you're also Cree, Detective. Didn't anyone tell you about the wendigo?"

"Sure, in the same way white folks are told about the boogeyman. I never for a second believed it existed, even as a child."

"Well, it does. And it's got Reese. What we need to figure out is how to get him back — before anyone else dies."

★   ★   ★

That night I had a disturbing dream.

I was a warrior, lean and strong. Hiding in the trees, I watched my victims from afar, glorying in the power I had over them.

I was also starving. It had been a grueling winter, the cruelest of my life. The hunger was a constant gnawing at my gut, driving me half-mad with longing and *need*.

It fueled my rage.

When I took their women for my pleasure, I usually let them live. It delighted me to see their bellies swell while they wept, knowing the seeds they grew were mine. At the right time, I would rescue those children from their breeders and train them to fight, to kill. In this way, I would raise my army, and rejoice as the children, then grown, raped their own mothers.

I would destroy the pale people, as they had once destroyed everything that was mine.

The last woman had fought. She had sunk her teeth into my skin and screamed. I'd slit her throat before we were discovered, and some of her blood had splashed against my lips, salty and sweet.

Before I could stop myself, I buried my face in her neck and drank. For the first time in over a moon's passing, the pains clawing in my gut eased. The terrible hunger waned. I would not waste another opportunity to feast.

My enemy had become my sustenance.

Now the craving had grown strong again, and my insides growled as I surveyed my prey from above, watching them scurry like the vermin they were. This night, I would take a child – an infant that wasn't mine – reveling in the people's shrieks as they watched me tear it apart with my teeth. That tender, young flesh would taste so delicious.

Creeping from the trees, I moved among the shadows. The pale people were sleeping, but I heard their whimpers and cries as images of me invaded their nightmares.

A lone woman remained by the fire, cradling a child to her breast. Her yellow hair hung in curls to her waist, and it was all I could do to keep from crowing my victory to the moonlit sky. I had held a special preference for the yellow hairs ever since Lone Wolf had told me a female of their ilk was responsible for destroying our people. And now these fools had left one out for me like an offering.

As the moon painted my silhouette upon the ground, I bit back a cry. For it wasn't the shadow of a man, but a beast with the antlered head of a moose or deer and long arms that ended in wicked claws that dragged upon the dirt. My ribcage was prominent, my waist so miniscule as to be nearly nonexistent, and hooves punctuated my heavily muscled legs. What fiendish thing was this?

But the warrior appeared unconcerned as we continued stalking the village, comfortable in this hideous form. I wasn't a man any longer and not quite a beast, either, but some appalling hybrid of both.

Stepping over a thin wire someone had positioned around the camp, I smirked at their pathetic attempts to protect and warn themselves. Didn't they realize they could never hope to outsmart me? My nation's greatest warrior had trained me, and trained me well.

My intended victim stiffened as I approached, and I saw something flash – a glint of steel that attracted the moon's light. A blade or some other weapon. They had anticipated my arrival, then. Again, I stifled the urge to howl in delight. Did they truly believe a lone fighter to be a match for Little Bear? Circling to the woman's weak side, away from that hidden saber, I lunged, teeth bared to taste her blood.

She sprang to her feet and sidestepped, my fangs clipping a curl as she moved out of reach. Flinging off her cloak, she revealed her infant to be a child's toy, and her vibrant hair a fake that she cast upon the earth. 'She' wasn't female at all, but a man outfitted for battle. At his whistle, we were soon surrounded.

The pale people's torches illuminated the impending skirmish. Several women screeched among whispers of *"Monster!"* and *"Wendigo!"* but such terms meant nothing to me. These were the fiends who had repaid my mother's kindness with death, rape, and destruction. They were the monsters, not I.

My would-be victim advanced, thrusting his blade forward. I towered above him, much too tall for him to reach my heart, so he aimed for my midsection. With one swipe, I cleaved his arm from his body. The look of shock upon his face as he clutched the wound, life force spurting from between his fingers, was so amusing I almost let him live, but I preferred the screaming. Another swipe and his head rolled to a stop at my hooves, his torso collapsing into the ashes around the fire.

Their arrows pierced my hide, then, and I roared – more for effect than from pain, as I did love to impress. Yanking the missiles from my body, I sent them back into my enemy's midst at harrowing speed, striking at least two in the forehead. They would sully my land no more.

Resigned to fighting for my supper, I slashed and kicked, sending death in every direction. However, it did not matter. Whenever one man dropped, two more arrived to take his place. The pale people had called on their brethren for reinforcements. Their blades and pellets penetrated my flesh, burning and piercing, until a powerful strike brought me down to their level, my legs cut out from under me. They descended with every weapon they had at their disposal – rocks and sticks as well as swords and those ridiculous fire cannons. My vision dimmed and I realized I would not win this battle. My strength waned as I assumed my mortal form.

"Look, my fellows. The monster is not a beast at all, but a man."

I saw the grizzled face of an elderly man leaning over me. Mustering my remaining morsel of dignity, I spit in his face.

Wiping his eyes with his sleeve, the old man raised his blade above my neck.

"With my last breath, I curse your people. May you know only famine, disease, and despair. I curse this land for anyone but its true guardians – my people and their descendants. Until the end of all ends, your own descendants will pay for your cruel treatment of my mother and her kin. I curse you until and after death."

After the curse, I closed my eyes. My death was swift. I did not feel the cut that removed my head from my neck, ending my life. Power returned to my spirit as it soared into the woods, into the trees. As I merged my force with nature's, the bark twisted, becoming gnarled and blackened.

It had begun.

Nothing would grow or bloom here.

Until my people were avenged, no one would find peace.

CHAPTER THIRTY-THREE

James Archer headed for the kitchen, intent on getting another beer. He supposed he should make dinner to soak up some of the alcohol sloshing in his stomach, but on the other hand, why bother? Food was overrated, and beer was made from grain. Surely that had to count as nourishment, and if his logic were faulty, there was no one left to point it out. His girlfriend had left months ago, thank Christ. He'd had more than enough of her nagging.

Maybe he'd been having brews for supper a bit too often lately, but it wasn't like he had anything to stay sober for, not until he got his badge back. And he *would* get it back. There was no way he'd let that Indian cunt of a detective and a worthless, smug kid get the best of him. He was sorry he'd only blinded the bastard. Should have hit a little harder, cracked his skull beyond repair. Eliminated the witnesses. Had he learned nothing over the years? Not a single death on the reservation had been traced back to him. All those people he'd offered to drive home in the dead of winter – no one had kicked up a fuss when they'd gone missing. And no wonder. Human refuse, that was what they were. The world would have been much better off if his ancestors had wiped them out. Mercy was weakness, and now they were paying for it through their taxes as the vermin demanded handout after handout.

It was Darwin's Law. Those who couldn't survive on their own merits deserved to die. Wasn't worth feeling guilty about, so he didn't.

His German Shepherd stood at the picture window, looking out into the night, growling. Stupid dog had been a nuisance all evening. If he'd wanted a yappy barkbox, he would have gotten one of those little Spic dogs. Then he'd have the satisfaction of punting it through a wall.

"Shut up," he told the dog as he cracked open beer number…well, why keep count? He wasn't driving.

The Shepherd tore its attention from the window long enough to roll its eyes at him and whine, ears flattening. James took this as a sign of respect, or, at the very least, fear.

"I mean it, Dingo. I'm getting sick of your shit." He put his beer on the table long enough to smack his fist into his palm, showing the dog he meant business. Dingo cringed, his hackles rippling. With dogs like Shepherds, it was crucial to maintain dominance at all times. He'd been showing Dingo who was boss since the pooch was a pup, and he'd never had a single problem. If only he could have found work in a larger center, one with a canine unit. No one could train an animal like him. He was a born alpha, and dogs respected that. Hell, he could train a wolf if he had to, sure he could.

Retrieving his beer, James sauntered back to his recliner. He was about to sit down when Dingo went into a barking frenzy, startling him. Foam cascaded over his hand as he slammed the bottle down on the coffee table.

"That's it. I've had enough." He took off his belt as he returned to the kitchen, knowing the sight of the leather strap would make the dog pee itself. Which made a hell of a mess, but it would be worth it to teach Dingo some goddamn manners. Besides, he could always leave the piss for the cleaning lady. Make her earn her money for a change.

James froze. His dog showed his teeth, barking with a savagery the animal hadn't shown before. Outside his window, looking in, was the ugliest thing he'd ever seen.

"What the fuck—"

Antlers loomed above the thing's repulsive face. It had a long, pointed snout, fangs, and glowing red eyes. Flesh hung from its snout in ribbons, as if it was rotting from within.

Shaking his head, James rubbed his eyes. He'd been drinking too much, that's all. He was hallucinating things. After tonight, he'd cut down on the beer, join a gym, do a little running. Nothing like some good ol' physical activity to clear the mind.

The thing was still there. As James gaped at it, its eyes shone brighter, lighting the kitchen with a crimson glow. Yelping, Dingo backed away from the window, then scampered out of the room with his tail between his legs.

"Where you going, you stupid mutt? You're supposed to protect—" James's diatribe died in his throat as the thing outside punched the window, shattering the glass. "Hey, what did you do that for? You're going to have to pay for that, you know—"

The creature kicked through the glass, stepping into the house. It towered above him, had to be eight or nine feet tall. The stink of it was horrendous. Eyes bulging, James turned his head and gagged. Before he could face the thing again, he felt a powerful grip close around his throat.

"No, please," he gasped, his words coming out as a strangled gurgle. "What do you want? Money? I'll give you everything I have. Just please, let me go."

His feet left the floor as the thing lifted him by the neck. The resulting pressure on his windpipe cut off his air, sending black spots to flood his vision. Unable to speak, to plead for his life, James screamed with his mind.

WHAT DO YOU WANT?

The creature grinned, revealing blood-soaked teeth dripping with foulness. "Food," it said.

★　★　★

Maria stifled a yawn, hoping Kinew wouldn't notice.

"I'm sorry," he said. "Apparently I was wrong."

She patted his arm. "It was a good hunch. I would have told you if it weren't."

It had been a rocking Tuesday night at the McCaffrey house. No visitors, no wild parties, not even a hint of domestic discord to liven things up. Jessica's parents were obviously still in mourning. If so, she couldn't blame them. The thought of losing Heidi caused physical pain.

Kira's parents and brother had left to visit family in Florida following the girl's funeral, and Dan's father had also fled town after his wife's murder. The McCaffreys had been a safe bet, but now the night was almost over, and no wendigo.

"I have to admit, I feel a little silly."

Kinew's expression hardened. "You wouldn't if you'd ever gotten a look at one."

"You mean you've actually *seen* one?" This was new.

"Yes, a long time ago. I'd hoped to never see it again." His hands tightened on the wheel though he'd killed the engine hours before.

"Where was it? What happened?" The questions bubbled out of her before she could contain them, but to think he was a witness to this thing they were hunting! She'd never met anyone who'd experienced the supernatural before. Unless you counted the arrowhead, which thankfully had remained lost.

He gazed out the windshield, silent for several long minutes. In the past, she would have rushed him, or wondered if he'd forgotten she was there, but she'd become used to his deliberateness. It tried her patience, but it was nice that some people still thought before speaking.

"Can you believe I was an Eagle Scout once?"

Of course he hadn't sprung from his mother's womb in his current form, but she understood why he'd posed it as a question. It was difficult to imagine the serious chief as a young boy. "Sure." Maria pictured a severe-looking child with his hair tied in immaculate braids, his uniform pressed and spotless.

"Collecting those badges used to be *everything*. I lived for those darn things." A smile briefly touched his lips as he remembered. "Anyway, I can't recall which one I was after, but it necessitated a camping trip, something where I could demonstrate my survival skills."

A goose crept over her grave. "Strong Lake?"

He nodded. "I was fearless then. I had no idea how many things there were to be afraid of in this world."

Maria no longer wanted to hear the story. She was sorry she'd asked, but thought it would be rude to interrupt, so she let Kinew continue.

"Eagle Scouts is supposed to foster camaraderie, lifelong friendships, and things of that nature, but to be honest, most of the boys in my troop pissed me off. They were always goofing around, pulling juvenile pranks on each other, and half the time, our leaders were just as bad. Bunch of overgrown kids. None of them took any of it seriously. Not half as seriously as I did." He looked at her then. "I'm sure you're having trouble believing that."

She didn't need to see his eyes to know the glint of mischief had returned.

"Yes, it's a struggle."

"Indeed. In any case, the end result was that I often went off by myself, and that day was no different. I decided to leave the structured part of the campsite and venture deeper into the woods, searching for a certain mushroom or rock or whatever the hell I was supposed to collect.

"In the way of young men, I got so engrossed in what I was doing that I lost track of how long I'd been gone, and how far I'd traveled. All I know is, when I heard the growling and looked up, I couldn't see the campground anymore. Couldn't hear the others. It was like I was in another world."

Maria's chest tightened as she pictured that vulnerable child alone in the forest. Thank God girls weren't allowed to be Eagle Scouts when she was a kid.

"I thought it was a bear, which would have been bad enough. It had that throaty, snuffling sound to it, but usually you can hear a bear coming. They're not the most graceful creatures, except when they're swimming. I froze, and my initial thought was that bear better not attack me and mess up my uniform, because Mom would be pissed."

She smiled, more to acknowledge his attempt to lighten the mood than because it was funny. "You found your mother more frightening than a bear?"

"Hell, yes. Times a thousand. I crouched there in the dirt, wondering what the heck I should do. Every bear survival story I'd heard ran through my head, but it didn't do me a damn bit of good. They all sounded like suicide to me – playing dead, challenging it, curling into a fetal position. I'd about decided to take my chances with running like hell back to camp when it *whispered* at me."

Every hair on her arms stood at attention. The crawling sensation was so intense it was nearly painful. "What did it say?"

"This will sound familiar to you. It said, 'You're not welcome here – go home.' I've never forgotten it. It was like that thing spoke right into my ear, like I *felt* those words in my head rather than simply hearing them. Do you know what I mean?"

She nodded, unable to speak.

"I may have been a dumb kid, but I knew bears didn't whisper, so I looked up and saw it. It was standing a few feet away, staring at me."

"What did it look like?"

"Well, a wendigo is the most hideous thing I'll ever see. Death with antlers is the way I'd describe it. Take everything you're afraid of and multiply it by a million – that's a wendigo. And if that weren't enough, they reek something awful. I'll never forget that smell."

"What did you do?"

"What did I do? It told me I didn't belong there, and it didn't have to tell me twice. I ran my ass off back to camp, screaming and hollering like the Grim Reaper himself was after me."

"Wow." She tried to imagine Kinew small and scared, or the reaction of his troop leader and the other boys. "I hope they listened to you."

"Oh, I didn't tell them the truth. I was the only Indian kid in camp. None of the others would have understood what a wendigo was, and I was in no condition to explain. I kicked up enough fuss that one of the fathers gave in and drove me home. He tried to get me to talk, to tell him what had scared me so much, but I kept my mouth shut. If I'd told him, they wouldn't just have me for a sissy, but a crazy too."

They were quiet for a moment, watching the McCaffreys' deceptively peaceful house.

"It would make a good story, like one of those things you see in the *Weekly World News*," Kinew said. "*A wendigo ended my Eagle Scout career.*"

Before she could respond, her cell phone vibrated on her hip, startling her. She glanced at the number. *Jorge.*

"Excuse me. It's my partner."

Kinew nodded.

"What's up?"

"It's Archer. I'm at his place, and you better get over here too."

Oh no. What had that miscreant done now? "Why?"

"He's gone, Maria. Someone broke into his place and tore him apart."

★   ★   ★

Maria would revisit Archer's place in darker moments for the rest of her life. As much as she'd despised the man, he hadn't deserved this.

"You all right?" Jorge's eyes were kind, his voice soothing. She longed to lean against him, to let him comfort her. But of course she didn't. She had a job to do.

"As much as can be expected." Archer's killer had decided to decorate the place with the man's insides. Thick, glistening ropes of intestines dangled from a ceiling fan. His heart and brain had been splattered against the walls like a macabre Rorschach test. Blood was sprayed across the ceiling.

That wasn't the worst of it, though.

The worst of it was a lot of Archer was missing.

"Where's Dingo?" Maria knew the man had taken one of the K-9 rejects home. Though not suitable for police work, the pup would have made a fine pet. She shuddered to think of that sensitive animal witnessing this carnage.

"Markham took him home, said it looked like the dog had been abused. As soon as we opened the door, it ran for the hills. Required quite a bit of effort to coax him back."

"Jesus Christ." No matter how grisly Archer's death had been, Maria doubted he'd have many mourners.

"We've done everything we can. It's time to clear out." Jorge shifted his weight. You didn't badmouth other cops, especially *murdered* cops – that was the code they lived by. Archer's malevolence would remain the white elephant in the slaughterhouse.

"Did you find any unusual prints?"

He studied her, narrowing his eyes. "Unusual how?"

"I don't know." She avoided looking directly at her partner, but it was difficult to find a safe place to direct her attention. New horrors were everywhere. "Anything that looks like hoof prints, maybe?"

"What's going on, Maria?"

"How do you mean?" Even as she asked the question, she wondered why she bothered playing dumb with him. It wouldn't work. She mentally kicked herself for not searching the crime scene for the prints on her own.

"I think we both know a horse isn't responsible for this. So unless Archer was keeping another pet I'm not aware of, that's a very strange question."

"I guess it is, but I can't explain it right now."

The hurt in her partner's eyes was an accusation. "Are you cutting me out?"

"No! No, not at all. I'm working on a hunch, but I don't understand enough about it yet. If I tried to explain it to you now, it wouldn't make any sense."

"Try me. I've got the time. You know as well as I do that they're going to expect us to solve this."

"I know. As soon as I've figured it out, I'll tell you everything. I promise."

"Why don't we go for a coffee, try to shake this stink off us?"

"I'd like to, but I can't. Kinew is waiting for me."

Jorge wrinkled his nose. "That chief from the reservation? What are you still talking to him for?"

She decided to confide in her partner, if only the basics. Keeping anything from him, let alone something this big, was foreign territory. It was obvious Jorge had picked up on her deception, and it broke her heart to lie to him.

"There was a similar murder last night, on the reservation. A woman was decapitated in her trailer."

"That's the tribal police's business. Unless they officially requested our help, it's out of our jurisdiction." His frown deepened. "You could get in trouble, Maria."

"Don't worry, I'm not doing anything official. I went to help Kinew as a friend."

Jorge raised an eyebrow. "We're friends with this guy now?"

"*I* am, yes. I think so." She thought about the evolution of her relationship with Kinew. They *had* developed a camaraderie of sorts, unless it was in her head. "Yes."

"Okay."

"On the woman's step were two bloody hoof prints. It's only a hunch, like I said, but I wondered if you'd found anything like that here."

"I see."

She squeezed his arm. "I'll tell you everything soon, I promise. Not that there's much to tell. Why don't we reconvene early tomorrow morning? We'll get that coffee and we'll talk this out."

"Is something going on with him?" Jorge shuffled his feet and appeared to have great difficulty meeting her eyes.

"With who – Kinew?" The idea would have been laughable if they weren't currently surrounded by the innards of their former colleague. "Of course not."

"Ben came by the station tonight to drop off that arrowhead. He seemed pretty distraught. Said you've moved out."

She swallowed her impulse, which was to let loose with a string of invectives that would set her husband's ears ablaze. *How dare he dump our personal shit in my office?* "Not permanently. We're going through a rough patch, and I needed a little space."

Her partner's eyebrow appeared frozen in a perpetual expression of disbelief. Was she really that bad a liar? "Space from Heidi?"

Great. Now she was a terrible mother too. "It's only a couple of days. Heidi's too young to understand what's happening. Trust me, she'll be happy to get her dad all to herself for a change."

She saw the suspicion in Jorge's dark eyes, but she didn't care. She didn't have time to convince him. She had to get to Kinew and tell him his hunch had been right after all. They'd just been at the wrong house.

"I have to go. Call me tomorrow."

"What about talking to the neighbors, doing the grunt work?"

Her shoulders tensed. "We have plenty of people who can do that. I have another angle I'm working."

"Where are you staying, Maria?" At her look of disbelief, he went on. "If you're not with Ben, you must be staying somewhere."

The unspoken question hung in the air, poisoning the space between them. She decided to leave it there. "To tell you the truth, I haven't given it much thought. I'll probably get a hotel room."

"You're always welcome to stay with us."

"Thanks, I appreciate that, but like I said, this is temporary. It's really not a big deal."

But it *was* a big deal. She and Ben had never before spent a night apart by choice.

"Be careful," Jorge said. It took every bit of her resolve not to explode at him. Did he actually think she'd leave her husband and daughter for a man she'd just met? Did he really think so little of her?

She leaned in to kiss his cheek, pretending she'd misunderstood what he was getting at. "Thanks. You too. I'll call you tomorrow."

Maria headed for the door before he could cause any more damage, before she was forced to tell more lies.

"On the back step," he said.

She turned. "What?"

"On the back step. That's where we found the hoof prints."

CHAPTER THIRTY-FOUR

Eloise Wallace was unable to sleep.

She lay on her back, staring at the ceiling, listening to the sound of her husband's snoring. A sound that was usually irritating, but that she currently found comforting. His snoring made everything seem so *normal*, when, in truth, nothing was.

Their son wasn't in his bed. He was out there, somewhere, doing God knows what with God knows who. She'd discovered his nocturnal wanderings a few days ago, but hadn't been sure how to bring it up. She hadn't told her husband yet, because he would lose his temper, making everything worse.

Eloise turned onto her side, attempting to relax, but the niggling feeling of panic followed her. Before that dreadful camping trip, she could have asked Reese anything. He might not have answered, but her son had always been unfailingly good natured and cheerful. He'd loved to tease. Theirs had been a playful, light-hearted relationship, and she'd enjoyed their banter. She'd been proud that her son still spent time with her when the women she worked with complained about never hearing from theirs. Reese was different. Reese was special.

Reese had changed.

Of course, that was to be expected after going through something so traumatic. That's what Eloise kept telling herself. Anyone would change after losing his friends in such a violent manner.

She told herself this as she watched her son go from a wisecracking, prank-playing young man to a snarly, foul-tempered beast. Everything pissed him off these days, and good luck getting him to smile. It was like living with a bear.

She'd tried her best to be patient, to reassure herself these changes were only temporary. Eventually Reese would heal, and then she'd have her son – her *friend* – back.

But things got worse.

There was that disgusting smell in his room, for one. Whenever he could be coaxed to leave it for a bit, she opened the windows, but it never did any good. It smelled like an animal had been in there. A dead animal.

And her son, well, he did his best, but like most men, he wasn't much of a housekeeper. When he fell too far behind on his laundry, she'd help him out if she were feeling altruistic. No more. Not since discovering the pile of crusty, reeking sheets and towels in the back of his closet. Crusted with *what*, she didn't know, and didn't want to know. While she was sure it was something harmless, something like—

blood

—chocolate syrup or red wine, it was disgusting. Reese could take care of that mess on his own.

There was a part of her – a part she tried to ignore, but which spoke much louder late at night – that told her she should call the cops. But that was silly. Why would she contact the police? It was no crime to have sheets stained with—

blood

—chocolate syrup or whatever, and look what had happened the last time the police had gotten involved. Reese had nearly lost his sight. He appeared to have made a miraculous recovery recently, but still. Her son could have been blind or worse for the rest of his life. No, whatever was happening, she'd have to handle it on her own.

She steeled herself for the confrontation to come, and pretended she wasn't scared. Why should she be scared of her own son? Reese, who'd been rescuing spiders from the house and putting them in the garden since he was a boy? He was the kid who wouldn't hurt a proverbial fly. She had nothing to worry about.

Eloise tucked her trembling hands between her knees, praying the pressure would keep the bed from shaking. The last thing she needed was for her husband to wake up. This was her show, hers and Reese's. Ray had handled the sex talks; she would handle this. Whatever *this* was.

She watched the clock. Her son normally came home around five o'clock, before any of the neighbors left for work. He'd mastered the art of opening the front door and slipping inside without a sound, but she'd known he was there because she could hear him breathing.

4:58.

A light clicking noise on her front step, one she hadn't heard before. It almost sounded like high heels, stilettos. Oh God, was he cross-dressing now? Well, she supposed there were worse things.

Eloise eased out of bed, careful not to disturb the mattress any more than she had to. The key, she'd decided, was confronting Reese before he got to his room. She had to catch him in the act. Otherwise, he'd claim he was just up to use the bathroom or something like that.

She hadn't raised any fools.

The carpet was soft under her feet. She crept toward her bedroom door, the door she'd deliberately left open, and down the hall. The light coming in the windows that flanked her home's entryway was surprisingly bright, and it took a moment for her eyes to adjust. She blinked, waiting, her hand clutching the stair post to steady herself.

More clicking. Now that she was out here, it didn't sound like high heels at all. An image of a horse sprang to mind, but she pushed it away. What would a horse be doing on her doorstep?

The doorknob turned, slowly. Eloise was taken back to every horror movie she'd watched as a teenager, even though she told herself to be sensible. This was her son, for Christ's sake, not some Creature from the Black Lagoon. Still, her fingers tightened on the post.

The door whispered open. She bit her lip, pulse pounding. She had to wait until the right moment. If she confronted him too soon, he would leave. If she waited too long, he'd escape to that room of his and there was no way in hell she was going back down there.

For a second, Eloise thought her eyes were playing tricks on her. The silhouette in the doorway wore some kind of bizarre hat, a thing with huge antlers, like you'd see in the old *Flintstone* cartoons. Maybe this wasn't her son at all, but an intruder. As far as she knew, her son didn't own a hat like that. The thought made her stomach flip.

The accompanying stench drove her backwards. She lost her grip on the banister and retreated, clapping a hand over her mouth and nose to keep from retching. It was the same odor she'd noticed in her son's room, but far, far worse. There was no way anything that had come from her could smell like that, and yet she knew the truth, as a woman always recognizes her own child.

"Reese?" Shaking so violently she could barely control her fingers, she hit the light switch.

Her son stood in the foyer, wincing as he raised his arm to block the light. The strange hat, or whatever it had been, was gone. *Must have been a trick of the shadows.*

It took a moment for her vision to adjust, for her to get a good look at her boy, the young man who had watched television with her, picked her wildflowers on Mother's Day, made her tea when she was sick with the stomach flu.

"My God, Reese, what did you do?"

And Reese, his face and body streaked with blood and gore, positively covered in it, burst into tears.

"I don't know. Help me, Mom. Please help me."

★   ★   ★

The awkwardness in the room was so thick Eloise imagined it could be sliced like a cheesecake and divided among them. Everyone would have an equal piece.

Or perhaps she was in some bizarre alternate universe, with Rod Serling in the corner narrating the cause of her distress. It would make about as much sense.

For the first time in her life, she wished she were a smoker. It was a nasty habit, but it would have given her something to do with her hands. Faced with a distinct lack of cigarettes, she stirred her tea over and over again, spoon clinking against the side of the cup.

The silence was suffocating. *Why didn't anyone speak? Why did they keep staring at her like she was the unfortunate result of some science experiment?* Finally she couldn't stand it anymore. "How long have you known?"

"We didn't know, not for sure. We only suspected. As you can imagine, it's not the easiest thing to wrap one's head around," the chief said.

No. No, it wasn't. She hadn't liked this man when he'd visited her home before. He'd come across as aloof, as if he thought he were better than anyone else. Better than her, certainly. But he was different now, kinder. Almost sympathetic, not that she wanted anyone's sympathy. Reese was still her son, and she'd be damned if anyone pitied her for his existence. This was a temporary setback, that was all.

"So, if he is this...*wendigo*, what then?"

"We don't believe Reese is truly a wendigo, Mrs. Wallace, but we think he might have been possessed by one that night at Strong Lake."

"But why?" The question was as useless as asking why bad things happened to good people. They just did. Even so, she had to ask. Why her son? Why hadn't that filthy wendigo-whatever-it-was preyed on someone else? Her son hadn't done anything wrong.

"I don't claim to be an expert, but we think it might have something to do with Reese's heritage. Both your son and Detective Greyeyes have been experiencing vivid dreams, where they are living in another time and place. Before she died, our medicine woman told Reese he was a descendant of the so-called lost tribe, an indigenous community that used to live in the Strong Lake area before European contact."

Eloise inhaled sharply through her nose. "That's impossible. My people were British."

"My ancestor, Little Dove, was raped by a settler. She became pregnant as a result and we believe Reese is descended from her child," the detective explained. She'd introduced herself as Maria, but Eloise couldn't bear to call her that, could hardly stand to be in the same room with her. If it hadn't been for her, Reese would never have been arrested or beaten by that ghastly cop. Even learning that Archer was dead hadn't made her feel better.

"This is ludicrous. You're getting your information from *dreams*?"

"They're more than dreams, Mrs. Wallace." The detective shifted in her chair. "Let's just say they've begun to affect our reality. I've had to move out of my own home to protect my husband and daughter, and you've seen what's been happening to your son."

She couldn't argue with that. She'd never be able to erase the image of Reese covered in blood from her memory, no matter how hard she tried. Eloise put down her teacup and buried her face in her hands, seeking composure. "I don't understand what a wendigo *is*."

"Essentially, it's an evil spirit. Our people once believed that those who ate human flesh during times of famine would turn into wendigos. In that sense, it was most likely a cautionary tale designed to ensure peoples' civility. Some also believe extreme greed can make a person susceptible, but there's no reason to think that's the case with your son," the chief said. "My guess is he was in the wrong place at the wrong time.

Our community has long thought that campground is cursed. They won't go near it."

"Hey." Reese appeared, his hair wet from his shower. She was relieved to see none of the blood remained. He was her son again, same as before. "Thanks for coming." He shook the chief's hand and gave the detective a hug.

"Thanks for calling us," the detective said. "You did the right thing." She looked over at Eloise. "You're both doing the right thing. We know how difficult this must be."

"I'm sorry, but I don't think you do. We had a normal life, a good life. We're good people. I don't understand why this is happening to us. We didn't do anything wrong." Eloise heard her voice crack and knew she'd burst into tears if she said much else, but she couldn't help it. It wasn't *fair*. She'd been a good mother, done her best for both of her sons. Reese had been doing so well; he'd been planning to pursue his MBA. He wasn't some psychotic killer. He *couldn't* be.

"It's unfortunate, but you're paying for the sins of your ancestors. Reese happened to be in the wrong place at the wrong time, with the wrong DNA," the chief said.

"But what do my ancestors have to do with any of this? They came here with nothing, and worked themselves nearly to death so their kin would have a better life. I'm not sure what crime they're guilty of. Certainly nothing worthy of this."

Reese massaged her shoulders. "Easy, Mom. No one is attacking you."

"No, they're attacking my great grandparents, who aren't here to defend themselves."

"We don't mean to make it sound like an attack on anyone, but we can't ignore the fact that some of the settlers murdered an entire nation of our people. Women were raped, children were stolen from their parents. The spirits want vengeance, and one of them is using your son to get it," the detective said. "Another tried to use me."

"That is horrible, of course, absolutely horrible. And I don't mean to sound like I'm making light of anything your people suffered. But that was so long ago, ancient history. Why is this happening *now?*" Eloise asked.

The detective's face hardened as she turned to look out the window. The chief rested his hand over hers for a moment.

Did I say something wrong? Eloise wondered. It had seemed like a perfectly natural question to her, but the detective was clearly upset.

The chief gave her a wry smile. "Perhaps the spirits have no sense of time. Perhaps they don't know too much time has passed for them to be angry."

"It is very difficult to forgive someone who has never apologized, who doesn't realize forgiveness is required," the detective said without meeting Eloise's eyes, her voice low and soft. "It is difficult to forgive someone for a sin when the sin itself has never been acknowledged."

"I'm sorry, I still don't understand what any of this has to do with my son."

Before the detective could respond, Reese changed the subject. "If I am being used by this thing, this...wendigo, who killed Dan's mother? It couldn't have been me. I was locked up."

The chief glanced at the detective, and while Eloise struggled to figure out what the hell was going on, her son turned the color of spoiled milk.

"Oh no, *hell* no. You didn't kill her." He covered his mouth like he was about to vomit. "You couldn't have. You're a cop."

"I don't think I did. I *hope* I didn't, but the truth is, I really don't know what I did while I was under the influence of the arrowhead. I nearly killed my own daughter." The detective twisted her hands, lowering her eyes. "I didn't wake up covered in blood like you did, but I suppose anything is possible."

"So what do we do?" It hurt Eloise to hear the hopelessness in Reese's voice. He'd already been through so much. The possibility he might have a monster living inside him was unfathomable. "How do I get rid of this thing? I can't keep going around murdering people. Can you lock me up?" He directed his last question to the detective.

"There is a ceremony our people have, known as the wiindigookaanzhimowin, that is mostly performed as a satire these days, a warning of the dangers of greed," the chief said. "Still, many of these old traditions were created for a reason, and if done well, I believe it might be able to drive the wendigo's spirit back into the trees where it belongs."

"I'll try anything, but what if the ceremony doesn't work? Rose's medicine didn't help me, and you said her magic was powerful."

"If it doesn't work, the wendigo will continue to slaughter every one of the settlers' descendants until there isn't a white man, woman, or child left alive in this town." The chief shrugged. "In other words, we're all basically fucked."

CHAPTER THIRTY-FIVE

As the turnoff for the campground appeared in the distance, I found it difficult to breathe.

"I never thought I'd be back here."

Detective Greyeyes squeezed my hand. It felt nice, comforting. We were in this together. "Try not to worry. It'll be okay. It's different this time."

"How can you say that?" My voice rose, and I closed my eyes for a moment, attempting to maintain my cool. "I have a repulsive, supernatural creature lurking inside me that rips apart everything it sees. How can that possibly be okay?"

"Hang in there, Reese." Kinew raised his hand in greeting to a man wearing ceremonial dress who held open the campground gate to let us in. "Some of our Elders have done this before. You're going to be fine. Maria is going to be fine."

"But what if we're not? What if it doesn't work?" I sounded like a whiny little kid, but I couldn't help it. Anxiety was clawing the crap out of my insides.

"It will."

"But how do you *know*?"

A nerve in Kinew's jaw twitched. "Because it has to."

Sweat damped my back. I reeked of fear, but it was better than smelling like that other...*thing*. Detective Greyeyes had assured me I couldn't have killed Jessica, since I'd had none of her blood on me – or Kira's, for that matter – only Dan's, from being in the tent when he was murdered. Still, the notion that whatever had done those terrible things to her, to them, now resided in me, made me sick. Worse than that – it made me want to grab Kinew's knife from his pocket and slit my throat. That was guaranteed to be effective.

"You're not alone. I'm scared too," the detective said. She'd told me about the dreams she'd had, and what had happened with her daughter, how her husband had discovered her standing over Heidi with a knife. Kinew had spoken of the wendigo's need for vengeance, but it didn't make any sense to me. These were innocent people. What had Dan's mother done wrong? Or Jessica? Or those two little boys who got smallpox? Heidi was only a child, for Christ's sake. Why should she pay for anyone's sins?

That Archer guy, he'd been an asshole, sure. A sadistic fuck. But what about Rose? All she'd ever done was help people. Kinew had told me that once Little Bear became a wendigo, he'd lost perspective and reason. The only thing he cared about after that point was the hunt, the kill. But that didn't make it easier to understand.

Dan had been a great guy. He deserved to be here, not me. It had been my stupid idea to cut branches from that tree, my idea to break into the campground. Why hadn't I been the one to die? I deserved it. They didn't.

I pulled my hand away from the detective's to dry my eyes with my sleeve.

"You have to stop blaming yourself. It's not your fault," she said.

"Of course it's my fault. If I'd listened to Jess and camped somewhere else, none of this would have happened. She'd still be alive." The tears fell faster than I could wipe them away. "She told me not to cut the trees. Don't you get it? I killed my girlfriend and our friends. Maybe not with my hands, but it was still my fault."

I hadn't let myself think of her, *really* think of her, since it happened. Maybe I'd been afraid that thinking of her would lead to remembering how she'd looked when I'd found her that morning. And if let myself go there, I would lose my mind for sure.

That hadn't been fair, though. I got that now. Jess was so much more than her death. Somehow, her faults and quirks no longer struck me as annoying. Instead I remembered the way she'd laughed until she snorted, and then laughed some more. The fun we'd had. The way her body had responded to mine. She'd been a beautiful, funny, smart-as-hell woman, and she was gone. I'd lost her. Her family had lost her. The world would never know her name, or benefit from whatever she would have ended up doing with her life. And every bit of it was my fault.

Kinew's knife looked more and more tempting. It would be so easy, so fast. Over before either of them understood what was happening. I probably wouldn't feel much pain. Certainly less than I was feeling now.

Detective Greyeyes wrapped her arms around me and held me close. "Shh, shh, stop punishing yourself. That's not what she would want. She loved you."

My initial impulse was to push her away. I didn't want comfort, didn't *deserve* comfort. Cruel words sprang to my lips, words that denied Jessica had cared for me. I'd just been a fling, a nice distraction from the stress of schoolwork and parental pressure and our looming futures, and all that crap.

But it wasn't true, and I knew it. I hadn't treated Jess the way I should have, hadn't always been kind. She'd put up with my shit and loved me anyway.

I pressed my face into the detective's shoulder and sobbed.

★   ★   ★

Twilight. The stillness shattered by drums. Shivering, I tugged my denim jacket closed, wishing I'd thought to bring something warmer. Winter would arrive soon.

"How are you feeling? Everything all right?" Detective Greyeyes studied my face like she expected to see fangs or something. Who knows, maybe she did.

"Okay, I guess. Cold." Was I supposed to turn into it? And if I did, would I be conscious of it? That wasn't how it had worked in the past, though. I'd fallen asleep and woken up the next day covered in blood. I wasn't a fricking werewolf.

She called to someone and asked for a blanket, and before I could tell them not to bother, one was placed around my shoulders like a cape. We sat with our backs pressed together in the center of a circle. I hated being so close to that damn tree. Fucking thing gave me the creeps.

The drummers walked toward us, moving in a long row through the growing dark. Their voices, raised in song, made the skin on the back of my neck prickle. There was something so eerie, so intense, about their voices, as if they weren't quite human. My mouth went dry. As if she could read my mind, Greyeyes took my hand in hers again.

We're in this together.

When the first drummer approached, I flinched, thinking he was the creature from my nightmares, but then I realized he wore a mask. They all wore masks, each one more monstrous than the last.

Their song grew louder as they called to the sky. They began to dance backwards around us. This was it, then – the ceremony. Kinew had explained that much. Greyeyes' fingers closed on mine, tightening and releasing, her non-verbal way of making sure I was fine. I tried to return the pressure with my nerveless hands. My body felt strange, like I had no control over it. It became lighter and lighter, as if it would float away from me.

Kinew shouted something in my direction, but I couldn't hear him over the singing. His mouth opened and closed like a fish's. It looked funny, and I would have laughed, but I couldn't stay awake any longer.

I closed my eyes, and that's the last thing I remembered.

★　　★　　★

The singing stopped. Screaming took its place.

"Maria! Maria, get over here *now*."

She blinked, feeling dazed. Where was she? And why was everyone yelling at her? It *hurt*. She pressed her hands against her ears, buried her face in her knees.

Someone yanked her to her feet, dragging her away. She'd been holding hands with someone – *Heidi?* – but felt the fingers let go of hers without a fight. "What's going on? Kinew? What's wrong? Where are you taking me?"

She'd never in her life seen anyone look so afraid.

"You need to get the hell out of here. Run. As fast as you can." The chief gave her a little shove and then stepped in front, taking up the song again, crying to the heavens. Drummers fell in behind him, pounding as if their lives depended on it.

Then she smelled it. It was the worst thing she'd ever smelled in her life, a combination of death, rot, and the gaminess of wild meat. Bile rose in her throat, and she covered her nose with both hands, choking at the stench. Even though every instinct she had warned her not to turn around, not to look, she did.

Reese was gone. In his place was the most hideous creature imaginable. Antlers sprouted from its shaggy gray head, each point dripping with blood and something darker. Its eyes glowed crimson, and when it opened its gnarled snout to reveal a maw of saber-sharp teeth, the resulting stink made her vomit down the front of her jacket.

She stood rooted to the spot, urine trickling down her legs as her bladder let go. She couldn't run, couldn't move. The heat of the creature's breath caused blisters to rise on her cheeks. As she gawked at it, it raised a powerful, ragged arm and struck her to the ground, slicing her jacket and sweatshirt through to the skin. Blood flowed from the wound, but she couldn't feel it, couldn't do anything to protect herself.

Maria waited to die, eyes bulging as the wendigo advanced on hoofed feet, steam rising from its repulsive form.

"Leave her alone." Kinew sheltered her with his body, stretching his arms to block her from the thing's view. "I'm the one you want — take me."

The creature's ferocity was nothing next to its glee, as it grinned with its disgusting, yellow-hued fangs. Before Maria could protest or yell or do anything to change Kinew's mind, he was gone, the living, breathing nightmare standing in his place.

Reese lay in the center of the circle again, gasping for air, his skin the shade of a dead man's.

It didn't work. This is the end.

If she'd hoped the wendigo would acquire some of Kinew's humanity, that optimism was shattered when the beast looked at her. If anything, the malevolent glint in its eyes had grown stronger, not weaker.

The thought of Heidi and Ben, waiting for her at home, helped her find her voice. "Kinew, it's me — Maria. You're stronger than this monster. Fight it."

The beast advanced, claws still dripping with her blood, its snarling snout twisted into a terrible smile. Its protruding chest heaved with each breath, exposing bone beneath the tattered flesh. Soon it was close enough to kill, but it paused, head tilted, as if undecided how best to do it. Stomp or slash? Or simply rip her to shreds like the others? Maria crawled backwards, trying her best to put space between them, until she struck something solid. A tree in her path. There was no time to turn, or to find a place to hide. The creature closed the distance with a single step. She could almost hear it gloating.

"Kinew! I know you're in there. You're better than this."

Still on the ground with his eyes closed, Reese moaned.

So this is it.

After all the near misses, her life would end here, torn from her by a mythological beast few believed existed.

Maria raised herself to her feet. If she were going to die, she'd be damned if she'd do it lying down. Standing, she came up to the creature's waist. She was close enough to see its wicked heart, bloody purple against the gray of its flesh, thrumming inside the exposed ribcage.

This close, the odor was overwhelming. It burned her throat and nasal passages, making it almost impossible to breathe. Her head swam. At this rate, she would be unconscious when the thing killed her. Perhaps it was a blessing.

"Kinew, please. You do not want to hurt me. I'm your friend."

Was that a flicker of consciousness in the creature's eyes? Could she get through to Kinew after all?

Gritting her teeth, her body paralyzed but her mind racing at warp speed, Maria dug deep for the words that would set the chief free of this evil, and hopefully send the spirit back into the trees where it belonged.

A memory flashed through her mind of the time she'd met Kinew in his office. His office full of books. This quiet, introspective man who'd read all the classics.

Not as well read herself, Maria drew on the only one she knew by heart.

"It was the best of times, it was the worst of times, it was the age of wisdom, it was the age of foolishness...."

The wendigo raised its arm – *foreleg?* So it had decided, then. It would be death by claw.

The words tumbled out of her as she spoke faster and faster. "It was the epoch of belief, it was the epoch of incredulity, it was the season of Light, it was the season of Darkness...."

With a jolt, Maria realized the creature had lowered its arm. Its head was tilted again, and she glimpsed something human behind its snarl. *Kinew?*

"It was the spring of hope, it was the winter of despair, we had everything before us, we had nothing before us...."

So focused was she on Dickens' famous opening lines that her brain didn't immediately register a familiar sound.

The click of a shotgun.

Maria whirled in that direction. "No, don't shoot! Hold your fire – it's Ki—"

In that moment, whatever trance the wendigo had been in vanished, and its roar echoed through the forest, scattering most of the drummers. It raised its claws.

The shotgun fired, deafening her. She fell to her knees as a shrieking whirlwind engulfed her in its funnel. It was black as pitch, and everything went dark until she saw the face of a confused, frightened man, his mouth twisted into a grimace.

My son, something within her cried, and she understood that she was looking at Little Bear – or who the man had been before losing his humanity. *Rest well, my son. The killing is over.*

And then he was gone.

Someone touched her shoulder and she looked into the eyes of Crazyhorse, who still clutched his shotgun, smoke curling from the barrel. "Are you all right, Maria?"

She spotted the body of Kinew, his eyes staring at a point in the sky she could not yet see, blood seeping out of the hole in his chest, and knew she'd never be all right again.

EPILOGUE

Crazyhorse never stood trial for the death of Chief Kinew. The incident hadn't been his fault. Everyone said he'd been suffering from alcohol-related hallucinations for some time, and they shrugged off his ramblings about wendigos and spirits as the result of a pickled brain. If he had killed a white man, he probably would have been dead before he glimpsed the inside of a hospital, but since his victim was 'just another Indian', no one made much of a fuss.

It was the kind of hypocrisy that ordinarily made her wild with rage, but for once, it had worked in their favor. The community would never forget the kind of man Kinew had been, or the sacrifice he'd made, and Crazyhorse would finally get the help he needed, the kind of help he couldn't afford until it was state ordered.

His sister would have approved of the serendipity. The man who'd given her his heart so many years ago had, in a strange way, helped her beloved brother by dying. Rose had never given up on Crazyhorse, and in her honor, the community would be there for him when he got out.

And so would Maria.

"Has your mother gotten used to the idea yet?"

Reese sipped his milkshake before shaking his head. "Are you kidding? She's hoping I'll wake up tomorrow and admit I've made a terrible mistake."

They'd gotten into the habit of meeting at Happy's, at the same table she'd once shared with Kinew. It made them both feel better to spend time with the only other person on the planet who understood.

Well, it made *her* feel better. When it came to Reese, she had to assume, for he didn't say. But she hoped he felt the same.

"She's going to miss you, but getting into Cornell is a huge honor. She'll come around. It'll just take some time."

Maria understood all too well what it was like to miss a child. Seeing Heidi a couple of times a week was torture. She longed for the days when her rambunctious little girl had driven her squirrelly, when getting her to settle down for bed had been a nightly battle.

"How are things with Ben?"

After a pause, she shrugged. "About the same. He wants me to give up the job, but police work isn't what I do. It's who I am."

"I get that. And if Ben really loves you, he will too. Like you said, it takes time to get over these things."

She recognized the pain in his eyes, the trauma that had aged him well beyond his years. He wasn't over losing Jessica and his friends yet, or the guilt from what he might have done when possessed by the wendigo.

Some wounds never heal.

"Any more nightmares?"

"Not a one," he said, signaling for the check. Their meetings had gotten shorter and shorter lately. "Otherwise, I'd turn myself in. Whatever Kinew did, it worked."

"I'm glad." She insisted on paying when the waitress came, grateful for the diversion. The next time Reese spoke, it would be to say goodbye.

The moment had passed, like it always did, without him asking her the same.

Have the nightmares stopped?

If he'd asked, would she have told the truth?

About why she didn't push Ben harder for a reconciliation?

About the butcher knife she kept finding in her bed?

About the arrowhead around her neck that she kept hidden under her shirt?

Thankfully, he never asked, so she didn't have to decide.

It would have been a tough call.

Because Detective Maria Greyeyes was still a cop.

And everyone knew cops didn't lie.

AUTHOR'S NOTE

While this is clearly a work of fiction, some of its most horrifying events are based on historical fact. Settlers murdered entire nations of indigenous people, and diseased blankets were given as gifts. Untold numbers of Native American children were taken from their families and forced into 'boarding' or residential schools, where they were beaten, verbally and sexually abused, separated from those who loved them, and forbidden to speak their own languages. That trauma from the past continues to affect indigenous people today – this is not ancient history. The last residential school closed in 1996.

Native Americans were denied all basic rights until 1924. In Canada, indigenous people weren't permitted to vote until 1960.

The plight of missing and murdered indigenous women in North America is a modern crisis, as thousands of young girls and women continue to vanish. Sometimes their bodies are found. Sometimes they disappear forever. It is estimated that eighty-four percent of Native American women experience violence in their lifetime.

The shameful legacy continues. It must end.

ACKNOWLEDGMENTS

Special thanks to my sensitivity reader, Blase Jenkins, for helping me tell this story with dignity and respect. Any errors are mine, not his.

Thank you to playwright Ian Ross, whose *An Illustrated History of the Anishinabe* had a huge impact on me years ago. It was through his brilliant play that I first heard the story of the diseased blankets, which I've never forgotten. I was horrified that people could be so intentionally cruel and murderous.

To all the indigenous families who welcomed me and shared their stories when I was a rookie reporter at *The First Perspective*, I have done my best to honor you.

To my editor, Don D'Auria, thank you for continuing to believe in and champion my work, from 2015's *The Bear Who Wouldn't Leave* until today. Mere words aren't enough to express my gratitude.

Thanks to the team at Flame Tree Publishing, and to all the readers and friends who continue to encourage my crazy writing dreams, especially Christine Brandt, Simon Fuller, Kay Deveroux, Nikki Burch, Lee Murray, R.J. Crowther Jr. from Mysterious Galaxy, John Toews and Dana Krawchuk from McNally Robinson Booksellers, Steve Stedulinsky, Erik Smith, Hunter Shea, JG Faherty, Russell R. James, Teel James Glenn, Henry Harner, Wai Chan, Catherine Cavendish, Somer Canon, Cedar Hollow Horror Reviews, Ladies of Horror Fiction, John R. Little, Lisa Saunders, and the amazing support system that is the Insecure Writers Support Group.

And thanks to all of my students – past, present, and future – who cheer me on and always give me a reason to smile. I have learned so much from you.

FLAME TREE PRESS
FICTION WITHOUT FRONTIERS
Award-Winning Authors & Original Voices

Flame Tree Press is the trade fiction imprint of Flame Tree Publishing, focusing on excellent writing in horror and the supernatural, crime and mystery, science fiction and fantasy. Our aim is to explore beyond the boundaries of the everyday, with tales from both award-winning authors and original voices.

•

Other horror titles available include:

Thirteen Days by Sunset Beach by Ramsey Campbell
Think Yourself Lucky by Ramsey Campbell
The Hungry Moon by Ramsey Campbell
The Influence by Ramsey Campbell
The Haunting of Henderson Close by Catherine Cavendish
The House by the Cemetery by John Everson
The Devil's Equinox by John Everson
The Toy Thief by D.W. Gillespie
One By One by D.W. Gillespie
Black Wings by Megan Hart
The Playing Card Killer by Russell James
The Siren and the Specter by Jonathan Janz
The Sorrows by Jonathan Janz
Castle of Sorrows by Jonathan Janz
The Dark Game by Jonathan Janz
House of Skin by Jonathan Janz
Dust Devils by Jonathan Janz
The Darkest Lullaby by Jonathan Janz
Will Haunt You by Brian Kirk
Hearthstone Cottage by Frazer Lee
Stoker's Wilde by Steven Hopstaken & Melissa Prusi
Creature by Hunter Shea
Ghost Mine by Hunter Shea
Slash by Hunter Shea
The Mouth of the Dark by Tim Waggoner
They Kill by Tim Waggoner

•

Join our mailing list for free short stories, new release details, news about our authors and special promotions:

flametreepress.com